Runaway Home

A NOVEL

ENDORSEMENTS

Amy Grochowski brings us another uplifting Amish story set against the beautiful backdrop of Prince Edward Island! I was swept up in this tale of family forgiveness, hard-won redemption, and a broken romance just begging to be mended. These true-to-life characters face difficult choices and soul-deep dilemmas, but as they follow their faith—and their hearts—old sorrows are washed away by new joy. The world needs more stories like *Runaway Home*!

—LAUREL BLOUNT
Carol Award Winner and Author of *Shelter in the Storm*

This book touched my heartstrings and reminded me that in order to find forgiveness and love, one must first find God. When Noah begins to put God first, everything else seems to fall into place. A beautiful reminder set in a lovely location and written by a gifted writer. I know you will love it!

—LENORA WORTH
NY Times, USA Today, and *PW* bestselling author

OTHER BOOKS BY AMY GROCHOWSKI

AMY GROCHOWSKI

AMISH DREAMS ON PRINCE EDWARD ISLAND | BOOK TWO

Runaway Home

A NOVEL

AMBASSADOR INTERNATIONAL
GREENVILLE, SOUTH CAROLINA & BELFAST, NORTHERN IRELAND

www.ambassador-international.com

Runaway Home

A Contemporary Amish Romance
Amish Dreams on Prince Edward Island, Book Two
© 2021 by Amy Grochowski
All rights reserved

ISBN: 978-1-64960-122-3
eISBN: 978-1-64960-172-8
Library of Congress Control Number: 2021940748

This is a work of fiction. Names, characters, and incidents are all products of the author's imagination or are used for fictional purposes. Any resemblance to actual events or persons, living or dead, is entirely coincidental. Any mentioned brand names, places, and trademarks remain the property of their respective owners, bear no association with the author or the publisher, and are used for fictional purposes only.

Cover Design by Hannah Linder Designs
Interior Typesetting by Dentelle Design

AMBASSADOR INTERNATIONAL
Emerald House
411 University Ridge, Suite B14
Greenville, SC 29601, USA
www.ambassador-international.com

AMBASSADOR BOOKS
The Mount
2 Woodstock Link
Belfast, BT6 8DD, Northern Ireland, UK
www.ambassadormedia.co.uk

The colophon is a trademark of Ambassador, a Christian publishing company.

To David

For sharing a love, a home, and a life—all worth the wait.

What gain has the worker from his toil? I have seen the business that God has given to the children of man to be busy with. He has made everything beautiful in its time.

I perceived that there is nothing better for them than to be joyful and to do good as long as they live; also that everyone should eat and drink and take pleasure in all his toil—this is God's gift to man.

Ecclesiastes 3:9-11a, 12-13

CHAPTER ONE

The air was brisk—even for early spring on Prince Edward Island. Rachel pulled her coat tighter with one hand to protect her chest and tugged her headscarf with the other to cover her ears. She despised wearing the scarf over her white prayer *kapp*, but her reasons were purely vain and not worth an earache.

The walk across the meadow between her home and the neighbor's farm was an easy hike. The hillside leveled for the length of the field before ascending once again on the far side of Saul Detweiler's house and barn, where she was headed to assist both Saul and Dr. Drake, the local vet and her boss.

On the far side of the barn, a wooded lot of pine trees stretched to the hilltop border between Saul's farm and Joel and Lydia Yoder's on the other side. All around her, the shades of new, green growth promised the coldness of this day would soon be replaced with the warmer days of spring.

As Rachel neared the barn, she didn't see Dr. Drake's truck but caught sight of movement in the pine woods. Seven-year-old Samy Yoder, no doubt, on her *datt's* horse, Amazon. Sure enough, the bay Morgan mare emerged into full view, along with her red-headed rider— bareback with leggings visible under her hiked-up dress. No matter how often she'd witnessed Samy on her rides to help the elderly Saul with his miniature horses, Rachel's heart felt lighter at the sight.

She waited for Samy to dismount and tether the horse to a post.

"How are you this morning, Samy?"

"*Mamm's* sick." Wind-blown curls framed Samy's face, which showed no sign of alarm. A mere statement describing her morning at home.

"Oh. I'll go check on Lydia after I'm done here."

"Yo-yo says not to worry." Samy shrugged. She'd called Joel *Yo-yo* since before her adoption, and the name had stuck. "He says this may happen for a while."

Could it be, after all this time, Lydia was expecting a child? Rachel would be checking on her best friend soon, for sure. She bent down to eye-level with Samy. "I'm sure your *datt* is right."

Samy skipped away to the barn, leaving Rachel behind. Of course, she'd be in a hurry on a school day. Although, Rachel knew Samy's love of the horses was more motivation than anything.

"*Goot mariye,* Rachel" came an unexpected greeting from behind her.

Rachel pivoted around to meet her white-haired, widowed neighbor. Saul had aged dramatically over the winter, appearing far older than his sixty years. Sometimes, Rachel hardly recognized him at first glance. His clothes hung loosely on his thin frame, and new, deep lines crossed his bearded face.

"*Ach,* good morning, Saul. I didn't know you were there. I see Dr. Drake hasn't arrived yet."

"*Nay,* he'll not be here for a little while. I asked him to come later." Saul stared down at his feet and shuffled them through the gravel. "I need to talk to you first."

Unsure how to fill the void as he paused, she was relieved when he finally looked back up at her. "That Tony is a fine man. He sure seems to think an awful lot of you. Course he's not too bad-looking either, as I suspect a young woman like you would've noticed."

"Saul!" Her conscience reproached her. She'd cut him off more abruptly than she should an elder. But really? "Dr. Drake is my boss and . . . and he's not Amish."

"I see." He didn't sound too remorseful for his insinuation. Instead, he appeared lost in thought again. "I only needed to know before I ask this thing of you." A sad determination tinged his voice.

Saul wasn't a timid man. His nervousness alarmed her somewhat. But then, she wasn't exactly surprised. His time in this world was coming to an end, and peace eluded him. The reason, though unspoken, was no secret.

"Would you like to go in the house?" A much more comfortable choice than the middle of the driveway for a difficult conversation— at least to her way of thinking. But Saul headed to the barn without comment, so she followed.

Samy had already begun her daily routine of feeding the animals and stopped to stroke her favorite miniature horse, Betsey. As he passed her, Saul rested a hand on Samy's shoulder. She looked up and smiled before they both went wordlessly about their chores. Perhaps the unlikely duo made such good friends because neither was required to say much. Or their bond forged by a love of horses was all the understanding required.

Rachel's thoughts drifted to a similar friendship she'd had long ago. She cut the memories short. Those emotions would only make talking with Saul harder.

Saul pulled up a small stool next to the one he was sitting on to milk the cow. Rachel took the offered seat. The warmth of the cow radiated through her chilled cheeks and nose. Saul's methodical squeeze of the cow's teats soon sent jets of milk into a foaming pool at the bottom of the bucket.

"Did you want to talk before Dr. Drake arrives?" Rachel hoped the nudge was gentle enough. "I will do whatever I can to help."

"*Ja.*" Saul turned his head enough to make eye contact without missing a single stroke of the milking, then looked away again.

The wait frayed her nerves. The longer Saul took, the more certain she became this talk was going to be about his son Noah.

Once he'd stripped the udder, he paused. Remaining on his stool, his voice only for her ears, he finally spoke his mind. "There's no need beating around the bush or getting into long explanations. We both know the story." He raised his weary, gray eyes—eyes so like another's—which begged for compassion. "I need you to find my son."

Rachel had hoped, ever so slightly, he was going to tell her Noah had contacted him. Over the past months, as Saul grew weaker and doctors diminished his hopes for recovery, she'd prayed—oh, she'd prayed hard—for *Gott* to move Noah's heart toward home before it was too late. Not for her sake, she'd promised, but for Saul and Noah to find peace. But to find him herself? *Nay,* she'd not seen this coming.

"How? Saul, I don't know the first thing about how to find him."

"Rachel, you have more schooling than anyone else among the people. You have a job where there is a computer and the internet. If anyone can figure it out, you can."

"You could hire someone . . . a private investigator. That's what they're called." No Amish person was going to use a private investigator. Her plea may as well have been for him to take her to the moon. Still, he was desperate after all. So was she. How was she supposed to find a thirty-year-old man who had run away at seventeen and never looked back?

"This kind of thing is a detective's job, Saul. They have been trained to find people."

Saul's mouth twisted as if he'd swallowed a mouthful of salt water. "Even if some detective found him, do you think he would listen to a stranger? Only you can do this, Rachel. You're the one Noah would . . . would come home for."

She would argue further, if the falter in Saul's voice hadn't caused her own throat to constrict with emotion. *Don't you think he would have returned by now if that were the case?* She couldn't say so to the broken-hearted man before her, anyway—not without injuring his old regrets.

"I'll do what I can, Saul." She dared not give him false hope for success from her efforts. "You know, I may not be able to find him, either. Do you have anything for me to go on?"

"The only thing he left was his journal." The one Saul had given to her five years ago, soon after her engagement to Joel Yoder. Had Saul known she'd call off the wedding plans after reading Noah's journal? *Nay,* of course not. Even she'd not fully understood her reasons.

As if she did even now. The heart was such a complicated puzzle to untangle sometimes.

No matter, the journal had been written thirteen years ago. She'd read the contents well enough. No secret messages hid on the pages to aid her in locating Noah. She'd have to find another way.

"I'll try, Saul."

"Very *goot,* then." He stood and reached for the pail.

"Let me." She grasped the bucket handle. "I'll take care of this. Dr. Drake will be here any minute, I'm sure."

"*Danki*, Rachel." Saul leaned against the stall wall for support and looked over to where Samy was now brushing Betsey. "I haven't told her yet."

About the sale, he meant. The vet was coming to confirm Betsey and her unborn foal were in perfect health for the buyer purchasing all of Saul's miniature horses. "She needs to know, *ja*, before the time comes."

His head bowed under the weight of his thoughts before he answered. "I'll tell her in a little bit, after you and Tony leave."

So many hard things for one morning. Rachel sniffed back at the sudden tears that threatened to release. No one should bear so many burdens alone. Saul's daughter would come later today to help him, but he needed his son—no matter what he'd done to cause the rift between them.

Why, Noah? Why have you stayed gone for so long?

She laid a hand on Saul's arm, and his eyes lifted in question.

"He will come," she vowed, somehow believing the impossible herself, then carried the milk to the house.

Gott help her. She'd do everything she could to keep her promise.

CHAPTER TWO

Noah Detweiler eased his young client's horse into a slow and steady gait. The cloudless day made for a pleasant therapy session. They were surrounded by the majesty of the Canadian Rockies, still covered with snow like a blanket for the frigid nights of early spring. The wide expanse of Second Chance Ranch stretched across the thawed valley in a patchwork of fresh green and early flowering color. But here, in the dirt-bare corral, Noah remained focused on horse and child.

He assessed their every movement and gauged their response to each other. Only the horse remained aware of Noah's presence. Ten-year-old Alex had tuned him out already—a great start. Noah watched as the boy's previous apprehension melded into quiet trust in Delilah's muscled strength beneath his legs.

Then came the smile—a moment Noah savored. He lived for these achievements with his kids. Trust, confidence, anxiety-free pleasure on the face of a child whose disability trapped him in social isolation because he had learned to communicate with his horse and now felt the powerful result of the bond between them.

"Easy now." He slowed Delilah to a smooth halt and didn't miss the disappointed frown on her rider's face. This could be tricky—avoiding a meltdown, which would ruin all the hard work the child had done. "All right now, Alex; this is your time to be her champion. Remember what to do?"

The boy's frown eased into a straight line of determination. Alex leaned forward and stroked Delilah's neck. His boy-sized hands disappeared under her mane, as he spoke with care. "Good girl. Good job."

Both boy and horse relaxed, as the boy tenderly lay his head where his hand remained buried in Delilah's mane. Noah felt the tension in his own body release. After a few moments, he positioned a box at Delilah's side for Alex to dismount.

Once they'd brushed Delilah and settled her in her stall, Noah and Alex walked outside to meet his waiting mother. Her eyes glistened with unshed tears as she wrapped Alex into a hug. "I'm so proud of you."

Alex squirmed out of her arms and climbed into the minivan behind her. She watched him go, then faced Noah with an apologetic smile for an action some would perceive as rude. Noah wasn't bothered in the least and hoped she never felt any judgment from him. He only wished more people would offer special needs children and their parents more grace.

"Thank you." A fragile note in her voice stalled her efforts to continue.

"All in a good day's work, ma'am." Noah was prepared to handle a child's tears to do his job. But a woman's? He dug the heel of his boots into the dirt to keep his feet planted when he really wanted to retreat. "Alex and Delilah do the work. We'll see you next week, then."

"I know you cowboys aren't much on emotion." She glanced back at her son in the van, then to Noah again. "But you can't minimize what you've done—what you're doing—for Alex. Giving him an escape from the small world where he remains trapped in his mind is no small thing, Mr. Detweiler. So, accept my gratitude and the fact that you deserve it."

She meant well, but she'd unknowingly reminded him of his own youth and feelings of entrapment of a different nature. He didn't much care for being called Mr. Detweiler either. The name belonged to a different man—one he'd do anything to never become.

He forced a smile. "Thank you. See you next week, then."

She gave him a nod and left him standing there feeling awkward as the van's bumper disappear around the bend in the gravel drive.

Horses and children were easy to understand, but he still had difficulty communicating with regular adults. All these years away from the Amish, and still he hadn't figured how to fit within the outside culture. Too often, his tongue failed him at finding the right words. English wasn't the issue. It was the unspoken expectations of how a conversation ought to proceed that tripped him up.

Communication was hard. But if his own frustrations were the reason he'd been able to identify with his clients with autism, then God had a purpose. And that made it all worthwhile.

Noah headed toward the big house to see Stedman before going home to his small cabin. The longstanding habit was as much a part of his life on the Albertan cattle ranch as breathing. As he gripped the door handle, the high-pitched beep of a car horn hit his ear. Pivoting back toward the drive, he recognized the front end of the mail truck coming around the bend toward him.

Sandy, the mail carrier, was ever efficient. Likely, she saw him and her opportunity to hand him a package or two and keep trucking down her route without slowing down. He walked to the edge of the drive to meet her where she surprised him by making a full stop.

"Can't throw this one to you." Sandy leaned out the window. Her salt-and-pepper hair spiked by the wind like a two-inch picket fence across her forehead. She leaned back to reveal a passenger in the truck. "Don't tell nobody I'm delivering humans now. But I couldn't just leave a soldier standing by the road. Turns out, we were both headed to Second Chance, anyhow. Maybe you or Stedman can help him go get his ride fixed. I'd really be in trouble if I got caught towing a motorcycle."

"Of course, we'll do what we can."

The door on the other side of the vehicle banged shut, and a young man in uniform slung a backpack over his shoulder and walked around to Noah.

"Here's your mail." Sandy thrust a handful of envelopes in his direction. "I gotta run." She had the car in gear before the mail was beyond her fingertips.

Noah gripped the stack a little harder and stepped back to save his toes.

"Thanks," the young man called but might as well have saved his breath. Sandy's lead foot had her out of earshot already. The stranded airman looked at Noah for the first time, and his expression sobered. "So, you're Noah."

Had Sandy mentioned his name?

The man wasn't much over twenty, if Noah had to guess. The insignia on his uniform denoted he served in the RCAF. His build was stout and muscular. If Noah had to guess, he'd say this fella cut his teeth on hard work, and the way he carried himself had a nagging familiarity.

The not-a-city-boy, motorcycling, RCAF private kicked a stone and shoved his hands in his pockets.

"I'm Noah. And you are?"

"*Ich bin der Mark Beller.*"

Noah shook his head to clear the fog from between his ears. The kid was Amish?

"I figured you'd still remember Pennsylvania German. Thought it would make explaining who I am a little easier."

"Can't say it does." Noah had a mind to report Sandy for this stunt. The last thing he wanted to deal with was an Amish runaway—as unchristian as he knew the thought to be. If Stedman had the same attitude, where would Noah be? "Mark Beller, right?"

The Amish-speaking airman nodded.

Noah tamped down his irritation. His issues weren't this kid's fault. "Well, Mark, what brings you to Second Chance Ranch?"

The backpack slipped off the airman's right shoulder and down to his elbow. "I have a letter. Rachel didn't know where to send it. That's where I came in. She figured I had the resources to find you—not that it was hard. Noah Detweilers aren't overabundant in Canada. There weren't even too many in the States. I could've just mailed her letter, but I had a weekend pass and nowhere to go. Since it was so important to Rachel, I decided a personal delivery was best to be sure I had the right man."

He went on about his motorcycle breaking down and some other details, but Noah stopped paying attention after he mentioned Rachel.

Long-buried emotions trampled across his heart at the sound of her name. He shook off the strange sensation of someone having to sort through his old things.

Mark was digging through his satchel, looking for the letter—important enough for Rachel to track him down.

Noah couldn't figure how this Amish-turned-military man was connected to Rachel Erb. But more than satisfying his curiosity, he needed to know she was all right. He should have followed his nagging conscience these past several months. What if God had convicted him about making things right back home because Rachel needed him? If he was too late . . .

"How is she . . . Rachel? Is she all right?"

Mark pulled a worse-for-wear envelope out of his bag. "Rachel's just fine. Here you go."

Relieved and perturbed at the same time, Noah took the extended letter. "That's all. I haven't seen her in a long time. Anything else?"

"I know how long. I was a boy when you left. A lot has changed, but I don't think I'm the one you need to be asking."

"Beller, eh?" Noah mulled the surname over in his memory. They were the dairy farmers. "You're one of Herschel's twins, then, all grown up." And decidedly not Amish anymore.

"That's right." He kicked another stone. Whether uncomfortable talking about himself or miserable being reminded of family, Noah couldn't be sure. Either way, he recognized a bit of himself after leaving the Amish.

"Is Rachel still Amish? You can manage to give me that much information, can't you?"

"As Amish as an unmarried, female, veterinary technician can still be."

"She did it, then."

A sudden surge of pride coursed through Noah. Even as children, he and Rachel shared a common love for animals. But she'd been gifted with a natural knowledge for caring for the sick and wounded. How had she managed to follow her dream of becoming a vet tech and still remained Amish? Ever the peacemaker, Rachel had managed a foot in two different worlds.

"Became a vet tech, I mean. She never believed it was more than a dream when . . . " The Beller kid didn't need to know the whole story. "When we were kids."

"Amazing, really," Mark interrupted his thoughts. "The bishop approved her training for the job. We—well, not *we* anymore—but *they* really needed someone like her to help with the livestock on the island."

"Yeah, it'll take a good, long time before you stop saying *we* to refer to the Amish." He warmed a bit to the young man, considering their shared experience. "I don't understand, though. What island?"

"Maybe you ought to read that letter."

Noah noted the postmark—*PEI*—Prince Edward Island, not Ontario? He had missed a lot.

"You can go in the house, Mark. The office is on the right. Stedman will be in there. Tell him I told you to make yourself at home. I'll be back."

"How about I just wait here?" Mark motioned to a wicker chair on the deck.

"Suit yourself." Noah shrugged before he headed toward his cabin. He had to be alone when he read Rachel's letter. Besides, he needed the walking time to get up the courage to open it.

He ran a thumb along the outside fold keeping the contents closed. If anyone else had sent this to him, he'd keep it shut. Maybe he still should. Toss it into the dark corner of a desk drawer to be forgotten and walk away.

He sure would've done so when he was Mark's age. But God had changed him. The same God Who had been urging his heart to rectify his past. He couldn't continue to ignore Him, and not knowing where to start wasn't a valid excuse anymore—not with Rachel's letter burning his conscience and his hand.

His strides toward the cabin grew swifter and longer.

How could Rachel still be unmarried? Apparently, her crush on Joel Yoder hadn't panned out for her. The thought gave him a jolt of satisfaction, as he pushed his cabin door wide open. Crossing the threshold to his desk, he rifled through leaning towers of papers and books to find the letter opener before he lost the nerve. What if Rachel needed him?

He'd still do just about anything she asked, that's what.

An ink pen clattered to the floor, soon covered by an old Second Chance brochure, that slipped over the edge of the desk to land on top. Noah bent down to pick up the mess, then pulled out a pocket knife instead.

The metal tip of the dull blade passed under the fold. The rip of paper broke the seal on his past, and the knife slipped out of his grasp to thud on a bare spot on the wooden desktop. Could he read it—even for her?

Maybe he ought to talk to Stedman first. The ranch owner was more father figure to him than the man who shared his DNA. The letter was important to Rachel, but Mark had assured him she was fine. After more than a decade, a little time to think and pray wasn't going to hurt anything. Was it?

Maybe he was stalling.

A rough laugh escaped with the thought. No maybe about it. Still, he ought to at least pray before he plunged headfirst into the murky waters of his past.

Noah opened a drawer, then took a long swipe across the top of the desk with his forearm. Everything fell in a heap, most of it in the open drawer. He lay the envelope dead-center on the table in front of him.

The rhythm of his drumming fingers on the desktop beat to the cadence of his indecision. Especially now that he knew she was unmarried, his desire to hear from Rachel warred with his fear of being pulled back into Amish life. Hadn't God been preparing him to face this, though, for months now? Noah's own heart, once hard and broken, had begun to yearn for peace with the man who drove him from home so long ago.

Still, he was terrified of it all. His dad wasn't the only one who'd made mistakes back then. Even now, Noah wasn't sure he was strong enough to face his own failures with both Rachel and his father.

He removed the contents of the envelope and unfolded three sheets of paper bearing the curves of a handwriting he still recognized.

Noah sucked in a deep breath like a drowning man. *God, I need Your help to do the right thing.* Unfolding the pages marked with Rachel's tidy cursive strokes, he released the breath and read.

The first disappointment met him from the very top. Even as children, Rachel's notes to him always began with a *Dear Noah*—noticeably absent from the page in front of him. The greeting on this letter rang cold and strange.

Noah,

Since you saw him last, Saul has aged beyond his years and is now very weak and ill. The doctors have given him no hope of a cure, and he is weary of the blood transfusions necessary to sustain him. I believe he has given up hope as well.

His one wish is for you to return before he leaves this world, and he has asked me to find you. I pray this letter reaches you before his time has come . . .

The words blurred as unexpected grief rose up from a well so deep, he'd believed it dry. Noah pinched his eyes shut and willed himself back to emotional calm.

Spring was about the worst possible time to leave the ranch. He ought to have made the trip a month ago, exactly when he'd known in his heart the Spirit was prompting him.

Turning his attention back to the letter, he scanned the pages—hungry for more about Rachel. Nothing. The letter may as well have been from a secretary sending a missive for his father. The one-two-punch hurt. First, an unexpected grief for a father for whom he thought he'd lost all feeling. Then the clincher—any spark of affection Rachel ever held for Noah had vanished.

He'd left behind a whole heaping mess of trouble and been running from it ever since. Time was up. Somehow, he'd manage to work out a trip back east—straight into more hurt, no doubt. But if he didn't deal with his mistakes and move toward forgiveness of his father, he'd be too late.

CHAPTER THREE

In the weeks since receiving Rachel's letter, Noah and Stedman had their work cut out for them to make a trip east possible during the busy spring season—especially since Stedman had insisted on coming along, at least for the first day. His offer to be there for Noah when he returned to the Amish community after so long meant more than Noah had found a way to express. Stedman, though, likely understood.

Almost a month should have been time to mentally prepare for seeing his family, starting this morning with his sister, Trudy. But Noah wasn't sure he'd ever be ready.

Behind him, Stedman paced the length of the small hotel room. He'd been itching to go for at least the past half-hour.

Noah reached for his cowboy hat and hesitated.

As hard as he'd tried over the years to quit thinking of himself as Amish, today he could think of nothing else. The black, felt Stetson was a statement of who he had become. But to his sister, Trudy, the look might seem more of an outright declaration that he wasn't part of the family anymore. Not a great first impression for a brother attempting to make amends.

Opening the suitcase, he grabbed his favorite, and less expensive, straw cowboy hat. He wasn't about to revert to an Amish man's hat. Still, he could compromise—a little.

Fretting over this meeting with his sister had worn him out. Trudy had offered to meet him at their father's house, but Noah wasn't much for jumping straight into a freezing cold pond. He'd rather wade into deep water and acclimate to the change in smaller steps. Noah had enough apologies to make for one day just to his sister. And Saul—he still struggled with even calling the man his dad—forgiving him face-to-face, well, that seemed best done alone.

As Noah settled the straw hat on his head, the reflection in the mirror was the image of his father years ago. Noah hadn't always resembled the man so much, but since he'd last been in Amish country at seventeen years old, he'd grown a few inches taller plus a good many broader across the shoulders. His hair had darkened from the pure blond of his youth and even showed some red in the winter.

The gray-blue eyes staring back at him had creases in the corners—more than usual for a man of thirty—except he'd lived year-round on the back of a horse in the harsh elements of the Canadian prairie from the age of nineteen to twenty-five. Of course, his appearance hadn't mattered. His social sphere had consisted of dogs, cows, horses, and the occasional buckaroo, whose looks fared no better than his own.

"You driving?" Ray Stedman's voice carried from the open door, soon followed by the reflection of a set of car keys flying toward the back of Noah's head. Leaning to the left, Noah snatched the rental keys out of the air with his right hand as they whizzed toward his ear. "Nice catch. We've come this far. No sense being late."

Noah turned to look the older man in the eye, an annoyed remark on the tip of his tongue. On further thought, he held back. If Stedman hadn't come along, Noah probably would have abandoned this idea before boarding Air Canada from Calgary to Charlottetown.

Noah crossed the room to the door. At least he didn't have to worry over making things right with Rachel, too. Without saying so exactly, her letter left no doubt she had no wish to see Noah again. He opened the exit to the hotel and held the heavy door as another patron entered before Stedman stepped out beside him.

Everything looked so different here compared to the ranch. And coming home held none of the familiar scenes he'd expected if he ever returned. Back home wasn't Ontario anymore. Everyone he'd been close to growing up had moved to an island province Noah had never even seen before.

Somehow, he didn't mind. Whether the cozy atmosphere of the island was the reason or the lack of familiar sights to stir bygones up to mind, only God knew. And Noah was right thankful to Him for the small benefit. Maybe the time had come to let loose of some of his fondest memories, too.

How he'd jumped to the conclusion Rachel's letter was some sort of call for his help was beyond him. Yet here he was. Her mission was accomplished. If Rachel had no desire to reconnect, then so be it. He couldn't blame her, no matter how it hurt. But grieving the loss of her all over again was about to push him to his limit.

Noah closed the vehicle's door harder than necessary and rammed the keys into the ignition. "Stedman, you know how to operate that GPS, don't ya? Which way am I supposed to go?"

"Listen, Son, I'm not pretending this meeting with your kinfolk is an easy task. I am proud of you for following through on your conviction to choose forgiveness and make things right where you can. After all these years of running and hiding from life, it's time to start fresh."

"I was working, Stedman." The excuse for ignoring his family over the years slipped off his tongue too easily.

"Right." Stedman's tone fell just short of a rebuke.

Noah took a deep breath and rested his head on the steering wheel. "I'm sorry, Stedman. I can't remember the last time I was this bent out of shape." Back at the ranch, he'd come to a sense of peace over this decision to visit his father, even been sure God wanted him to go. But now . . . "I don't know. Maybe I heard the Holy Spirit all wrong about reconciling with my dad. Or what's to say those thoughts weren't some lunatic idea of my own making?" Or worse, the devil. Right now, Noah's inner turmoil was definitely his enemy. And he wasn't feeling like a man who knew the first thing about anything holy.

Stedman's voice cut through Noah's thoughts. "I'm no preacher, Noah, but I do know God expects us to at least attempt to make things right with those we've wronged. Look, I know you were wronged greatly, too. Still, you gotta decide. This is family. Can you live with yourself if you let this opportunity pass and never get another chance?"

He'd already had this debate in his head a hundred times. The answer was always the same—no. He'd lived with himself for years on the prairie and hadn't enjoyed the company. Since agreeing to work for Stedman on his ranch as the cow boss five years ago, life with their family had changed him. And his new life in Christ had just begun. He was determined to do a better job with his second chance than he had with the first.

A visit with his sister and newborn nephew was a beginning. He cranked the ignition and pulled out of the hotel parking lot. Time flew so much faster in a car than on the back of a horse. In almost no time, they were navigating their way around the small community of Montague, then the outlying hills of farmland. A small pasture with a few horses caught his attention as he passed an animal hospital at a crossway in a little village. He didn't need a reminder that Rachel was somewhere nearby, but the veterinarian's sign on the corner brought thoughts of her back to the forefront of his mind.

"Which way?" He waited while Stedman pulled out the GPS on his phone again.

"Straight ahead to your sister's. The bed and breakfast she mentioned isn't far, either. You'd make a right turn here to get to it."

So, they were almost there.

According to Rachel, Trudy had married a Mennonite, who had also moved to Prince Edward Island along with some other members of his family. Even though Saul still belonged to the Amish church, Trudy had convinced him to move as well, joining other members of his own congregation, including the Erbs, Yoders, and Bellers.

Still, Saul asked Rachel to find him. Why not Trudy? Noah had at least one theory. If he was right, then Saul would be disappointed. Noah was returning for one reason alone—to see his father before God took him from this world. Any ideas Saul might have of Noah returning to the Amish—or to Rachel—were best laid to rest from the start.

Stedman was heading back to the ranch in the morning, and Noah would follow in a few days.

"Want me to stay in the car?" Stedman asked as they pulled up to Trudy's house, a traditional, two-story, white farmhouse with gables on a steep, black-shingled roof and surrounded by several acres of freshly plowed red dirt.

"Of course not." Noah edged into a spot beside a plain, black car in the driveway. Somehow, the image of Trudy driving a car struck him as odd. Which was stranger? His sister living outside the Old Order or his reaction? He certainly couldn't judge her. If anything, he was happy she hadn't abandoned her faith in God but had found a place in a more lenient church.

From the front porch, a young woman in a bright yellow dress waved to him. Her welcoming smile melted the years away. He'd know his little sister by her grin no matter their ages. A breeze blew her skirt, along with the loose Mennonite prayer veil covering her blonde hair.

Noah nearly tripped over his own feet climbing out of the car. How he had missed her. Regrets be hanged. He couldn't wrap his arms around his baby sister fast enough.

The intention carried him all the way to her at the bottom step of the landing. Only, when his feet stopped, he debated whether to actually hug his sister. She might not be as eager as he had suddenly become. His arms hung in midair. Maybe he ought to offer a handshake instead.

"Don't you dare give me some *Englisch* greeting, Brother." Trudy's hands landed on her hips. "You better hug me like you always did." Another smile teased the corners of her mouth. "Though, I doubt you can still swing me in a circle like the old days."

"Trudy, I can ride steer all day and still throw down a dozen bull calves."

"Oh, yeah?" She side-stepped, about to run from him. Noah caught her around the waist and spun her until both feet lifted off the ground, and her laughter thrilled his soul. "Put me down. I'm too old for this. I have children, for goodness' sake."

Noah gently removed his grip and looked down into the glistening eyes of the woman, wife, and mother who'd replaced the girl he remembered. "You'll always be my little sister, Trudy, no matter how old we get."

"*Ja*, and don't you be forgetting," she said gently. But Noah got the message loud and clear. She looked at Stedman standing off to the side.

Noah stepped back a few feet to allow Stedman into their circle. "Trudy, this is Ray Stedman. He's become like a father to me." A flicker of sadness crossed his sister's face at his words. Why had he added the last part?

However, she turned to face Stedman with a smile in place. "Welcome. We are so pleased you have come with Noah. Come in. The baby is napping, and the other *kinner* are at school. There's hot *kaffi* ready to drink."

Even as a child, Trudy never had lacked for conversation. Two cowboys seated in her simple living room didn't slow her down now either. Noah watched Stedman lean back and drape an arm across the back of the sofa. Yep, Trudy had him feeling at home already.

Just like *Mamm*.

A sharp pain stabbed Noah's heart. Trudy couldn't even remember their mother, who'd passed when she was only two.

Beside him, his sister and Stedman chatted about the ranch. She was curious, of course. Cattle and horses were relatively safe subjects.

Noah drained his coffee mug. He may as well get to the point. He cleared his throat. Stedman and Trudy both looked at him.

"I, um, Trudy . . . "

She reached across the armrest of her chair, touching her fingertips to his knee. "It's all right, Noah. Let's leave the past in the past, *ja*? It is enough you have come."

"I abandoned you, Trudy. Left you to handle . . . him. Alone."

"*Nay*. I was never alone and never will be. All is forgiven. Perhaps, you have to forgive yourself and *Datt*. But with me, all is well, Noah." With a delicate motion, she reached for his hand, squeezed, and then returned to her earlier chit-chat. All as if nothing had ever happened.

"Thank you, Trudy." Her forgiveness lightened the weight pressed hard against him for so long. The release shocked him into awareness of the enormity of the grief and guilt he'd carried so long. Speaking further might reduce him to tears.

Stedman jumped to Noah's rescue by engaging in small talk, as Noah's attention drifted far beyond the walls of his sister's home. Did she expect Noah to welcome their *datt* back into his life just as she had done for him? Well, there was no comparison.

Christian. Amish. Mennonite. Whatever a man called himself, some sins required more than a simple forgive-and-forget policy. But his father was the one he needed to be talking to about past grievances—not his sister, who chatted along with Stedman.

"I hear tidbits every now and again from the old community. So much has changed there. It's different from the church we knew growing up. Their new church on Prince Edward Island is called New Hope." Trudy spoke to Stedman but glanced at Noah to see if he was listening.

As much as he'd like to ignore news from his old community, Trudy had his attention. "The Amish don't change, Trudy; you know that."

"*Ja*, well, seems Bishop Nafziger gave a lot of thought to his stepson's ideas for a fresh start where farming could still be a profitable way of life."

"I remember Joel's talk about settling a new community, even way back before . . . " Noah hadn't thought Joel Yoder's ideas for a new beginning were outlandish like many others did. Still, he'd never believed anything real would come of the talk others easily dismissed.

"Well, the bishop's other son, Abe, married Sarah Erb, and they were the first couple to make the move."

"Abe and Sarah, huh? Seems like Joel would have been the first to go."

"At first, the bishop only allowed married couples to join the new church. Joel wasn't married. He was engaged to Rachel, but then . . . well, that's old gossip."

Noah hoped his face was a mask of indifference. Trudy was watching him closely. The fact he'd loved Rachel back then was no secret. He had to admit a part of him wondered what happened.

What had Stedman said earlier about missed opportunities and being too late? Had he dismissed a chance to see Rachel again too quickly?

Coming here today was part of a pledge he'd made to himself and to God to stop running. The problem with stopping was knowing which way to go next. Right now, if he followed his instinct, he'd be headed to the open prairie—with no company other than his horse and her complimentary silence. Facing Rachel might be harder than his upcoming confrontation with his father.

"Noah? Are you listening?" A faint cry from the upstairs reached his ears as his sister stood. "Don't run off, all right? I have to go feed the baby. Won't take long, and then you can meet your nephew."

His nephew. *Isaac.* Noah's heart squeezed. "I'll wait."

He gave Trudy a smile before she left the room. Stedman's gaze pinned him to his chair, daring him to even think about leaving.

Noah raised his hands in surrender. "Don't worry. I wouldn't miss meeting my own nephew."

Returning to a solitary cowboy life was a cop-out way of living, not the solution he wanted anymore. Working with Stedman at Second Chance Ranch was a blessed compromise. He was still working with horses but also helping people—the kind he understood, the forgotten ones in need of hope. He was finished with running from his life.

Seeing Rachel would mean dealing with the pain of a lost past all over again. Somehow, he'd muddle through. He owed her some explanation, at least. He'd do better at staying in touch with Trudy. And once he'd done his duty by Saul, he'd move on.

Soon enough, the sun would disappear into twilight. Rachel reached for her scooter by the backdoor of the veterinary office. If she didn't hurry, she'd be alone on the road after dark. What a busy day. Every animal in the district must have been through the clinic doors at one point or another.

"See you tomorrow, Rachel," Dr. Drake called as he locked the building behind her. He must've forgotten she'd asked for the day off. Probably because she never took a day off other than Sundays.

She turned to explain and looked up, way up. At such close range, her boss had to bend his head to look her in the eye. She sure could use a few inches of his height. He was as tall as she was short, as they'd both heard more than a few times.

"What? You look confused." His hazel eyes shone with sincerity.

"Only that I'd asked to take a holiday for my friend's wedding."

"Of course, of course. A wedding on a Tuesday—how could I forget that?" The vet's smile was contagious. He was a good-humored man, mostly. Rachel found herself amused alongside him on a daily basis and couldn't help but wonder how he'd never married. Gratefully, if he wondered the same about her, he never asked.

"The Amish way." He laughed good-naturedly. The words had become the only explanation necessary when her church's traditions conflicted with his ideas of how things ought to go. He accepted her as the expert in that area and compromised willingly for the sake of his Amish patrons. "I can't recall how I ever got along without your help. You'll be back Wednesday, then? Heaven knows, you deserve a day off, though. Do you need more time?"

"Just tomorrow. I don't know what I would do with more time." Fret and worry and wonder why she hadn't heard back from Noah, even though Mark had delivered her letter weeks ago. She hadn't asked for Noah's location or any other details, but Mark would be at his sister's wedding tomorrow. Maybe she ought to find out how to get a hold of Noah and give him one more chance. Or maybe a bigger push.

She'd done her best to convince Noah to do his duty toward his father without using whatever was left of their friendship to entice him. As if it would have mattered, Noah had abandoned anything between them long ago. Still, if there was any possibility she held some sway, maybe she ought to try.

Saul was going downhill fast. If she had to go drag her stubborn, runaway, former neighbor back home herself, then she would have to use more of her accumulated holiday time. She'd made a promise, and unlike another certain person, she'd keep it.

"Still thinking about it. All you have to do is ask if you need more time off."

"Sorry, I was thinking about . . . something else. I'll still see you on Wednesday, Dr. Drake." She knew her cheeks were flushed from embarrassment and hoped the half-dark covered the tell-tale sign.

"Rachel, please, call me Tony." He put his hand out toward hers, then dropped it. "I appreciate your professionalism. I do. And during work hours, you're right to call me Doctor. But I think we're friends now. Aren't we?"

"*Yo*, Tony. We are friends."

"*Yo*? More Amish vocabulary, I take it, but not what I expected."

"Sometimes, I just can't find the right English word." She kept a close watch on her speech at work. "*Ya* is the same as yes, but *yo* is more . . . emphatic, I guess."

"Indeed." With a glint of humor in his eyes, Tony motioned for her to walk ahead of him.

Indeed. "Oh, I get it. My *yo* is your indeed."

"That's right." He jangled his set of keys, then clicked the fob so that his truck unlocked with a beep. "How about a lift? I've got to go right by your place, anyway."

She'd ridden in his truck a million times to assist in house calls to Amish farms. A ride home in the vet's truck wouldn't even set a gossip tongue to wagging. Everyone was used to the sight.

Still, something within her hesitated. Tony was her boss. Now, he was even a friend. The bishop had bent nearly every rule in the book for her. But there was one she knew would never flex.

She was jumping to ridiculous conclusions and far-reaching what-ifs. But the hint was there. In his voice. In his eyes. And she couldn't ever cross beyond the realm of friendship with him. That was one fence she'd never be allowed to straddle.

Bishop Nafziger had never put anyone under the *Bann*. She wasn't going to be the first.

"Rachel?" His hand rested on the handlebars of her scooter, ready to lift it into her truck if she gave him her okay.

"I think I need the exercise this time." She choked on the words.

He'd think her a liar. Or by the way his eyes shifted from her as he let the scooter gently fall back into place, he knew. And that was the worst because of all people, Tony didn't deserve to be rejected.

"I'm sorry."

"Don't be sorry. I get it." Instead of turning around to get into his truck, he came closer to her. "Call me Dr. Drake if you need to. I'll be your friend no matter what. I know that's all we can ever be." His voice quieted, and the lump in her own throat grew as big as a softball. "Please look at me, Rachel."

She raised her chin upward to face him. His kind expression eased her embarrassment. She managed a weak smile.

He turned his head slightly and scanned the road. There was nothing to see, other than a car with a somewhat off-balance front end stopped at the intersection. His focus returned to her.

"I want to be the kind of friend you deserve. So, let me give you a ride. This island may be one of the safest places on earth, but it's still the twenty-first century, Rachel. I worry every time you take off on that thing at dark." He'd never so much as touched her or made any inappropriate remark. Truly, he might've stepped right out of a novel as the most chivalrous of gentlemen knights, except she knew he was by all means modern and islander through and through—for a half-dozen generations.

"Well, then." She stepped aside for him to reach her scooter. "It would be wrong to cause you unnecessary worry."

"Indeed." He placed the scooter in the truck bed. When he turned back around to open her door, she recognized her fun-loving friend and boss again. "Yo!" His eyebrows wiggled before he gave the door a firm push and jogged to the driver's side.

She couldn't help but grin as she slipped her seatbelt over her shoulder. Images ran through her mind of the facial expressions he'd make if she explained he'd used the Amish word all wrong. She laughed out loud. He was fun, and no wonder all the Amish loved him as their veterinarian.

"What's so funny?" Tony slid into the driver's seat.

"Nothing really. You could come to the wedding supper tomorrow. If we were still in Ontario, there'd be all kinds of friends and family showing up to congratulate Mattie and Winston throughout the day. The groom's family from the States filled up all the extra rooms our people could manage, plus Nancy's bed and breakfast. But for sure, the Bellers would take it as a compliment if you came as one of their friends."

"I'll do my best to make it, then. It's going to be a busy day without your help." He shifted the gear stick into reverse and checked the rearview mirror. "Just a minute." He threw the truck back into park. "Someone's turned into the lot with a flat."

After Tony got out, Rachel draped her arm across the back of the seat and craned her neck to see what was happening behind her. Tony approached a silver sedan, where an older man with hair to match the car stepped out. Another man exited from the driver's side. She barely got a glimpse of his face before he set a cowboy hat on his head but saw enough to gather he was younger. Maybe the other man's son? He nodded at Tony, then glanced toward the truck.

Her heart pounded.

He did a double-take return to her stare.

She couldn't take her eyes off of him. She swallowed, but the lump in her throat didn't budge.

Rachel. She couldn't hear him, but the movement of his lips was clear to her. She nodded. Didn't she? Her whole body felt frozen in place. Tony was anything but motionless. He'd stepped right in her line of vision, blocking the cowboy from her view. The men were talking, then walking back to the car, where the older man was kneeling by the front tire with a jack.

The leather seat creaked as she plopped into a forward-facing position.

He'd come. Noah had returned.

CHAPTER FOUR

Noah woke to the distant groan of timber and hinges of a barn door opening—a sound he'd recognize in the deepest of slumbers. The fresh bed of hay he'd spread in the empty horse stall itched through his jeans, and his dry morning-mouth longed for a drink.

Who knew he'd need a reservation for the bed and breakfast in such a tiny island village? The hostess had explained this week had been booked for months due to an Amish wedding, which also explained why the place was practically crawling with American Amish.

His eyes opened to the dim light of early dawn poking through the rafters above his head. He hadn't rested well enough to forget where he was. He and Stedman had napped at the airport until Stedman's midnight flight. Rather than stay a few hours in another hotel, Saul's barn seemed good enough.

Besides, seeing Rachel all cozied up in that vet's truck had flung every intention to avoid her to the wind. A reaction he couldn't understand. He needed some time to figure out what to do next. Quiet time. Uninterrupted by people and busy noise. And he hadn't come to any conclusions so far.

However, he had intended to exit the barn before his father found him there. Now, he had to figure how to make his presence known without startling a frail man to death.

"*Datt?* I don't mean to scare you. *Ich bin der Noah.*" Noah's own voice sounded foreign to him; the language of his childhood no longer slipped naturally from his tongue.

A slow, brightening glow filled the stall around him as a lantern and a girl's face appeared over the waist-high door.

"You're a funny-looking horse."

Didn't she know not to talk to strangers? Not that he wanted her to run, but she should without any way to know if he intended her harm or not. The fact she showed no sign of alarm at all triggered Noah's therapy instincts.

"I'm Saul's son. Who are you?"

The girl raised the lamp and shifted the light from one corner of the space to another. "Where's Betsey? Did you bring her back?"

"Who's Betsey?" Obviously, she was looking for a horse, or maybe a pony. She still hadn't answered his first question, but if she wanted to talk about Betsey, he'd go along.

"Didn't Saul teach you anything?"

"Well, we haven't talked much lately."

"But he's your *datt.* I talk to Yo-yo every day about everything. Maybe you can talk to Saul every day; then you would know stuff."

As much as he'd like to know who Yo-yo was, there didn't seem to be much point in asking her a direct question. She was looking him over from head to boot-tip while wisely remaining on the other side of the closed door. "Are you adopted, too?"

"No." Noah watched as her little mouth scrunched up in a question. "I don't look Amish like Saul, do I?"

She turned to face the front barn door, then trotted away, taking the light with her. "Where's Betsey?"

"Samy! What in the world are you doing here this time of morning? Your poor *mamm.*" The concern in the female voice was punctuated with a sigh. Trudy had said she wouldn't be over until later today. But then, the Amish likely took turns helping Saul with his chores. Or she was out searching for the child.

"*Mamm* is still sick. She vomits every morning. When I'm sick, I have to go to the doctor. You're a doctor. You could help."

Noah brushed what hay he could from his clothes before reaching to unlatch the stall door.

"I'm not a doctor, Samy. Besides, the midwife checks . . . " The woman caught sight of him and pulled the girl behind her. "Who are you?"

Noah stood still. He didn't want to frighten anyone. She probably couldn't see him well in the low light. His vision had acclimated to the low light, but the woman's face was shadowed. She was backing up slowly and keeping the girl behind her.

"I'm sorry to scare you." Noah remained still, hoping to show he meant no harm.

She stepped backward once more, and the outside light cascaded around her. How had he not recognized her voice? She hadn't changed as much as Noah over the years—still dark-haired and beautiful with the power to make his heart summersault. He hadn't gotten much of a look at her last night after the vet had stood in his path. Standing there now, she was as frozen as he was himself, softened as much by womanhood as he'd broadened from hard work.

His breath hitched.

Samy stepped from behind Rachel's skirt. "*Der Noah.* He's Saul's son. That's all right, *ja?* He doesn't look Amish, but maybe he's adopted like me."

"I see now." Rachel's voice was controlled, and he barely heard her. She reached for Samy's hand but made no move toward Noah.

"Hello, Rachel." She must wonder what he was doing in the barn in clear need of a hot shower. "The bed and breakfast didn't have any rooms. And by the time we fixed the car . . . and everything . . . well, it was too late to bother . . . him . . . Saul." The word *Datt* hung in his throat. The title still too intimate for a man he'd tried so hard to forget. Standing here explaining himself to Rachel wasn't much more pleasant.

Rachel bent down to the girl's height and spoke low into her ear.

The child's shoulders sagged. "But why?"

"Now, Samy."

Noah heard the final command plain enough and watched Samy trot out of sight.

"Rachel, I didn't mean to startle you."

"Obviously, you can do whatever you please." She brushed passed him. "I'm only here to do Saul's chores, since the boy who normally does so is busy with his sister's wedding today."

He followed her toward the milk cow. "So, this is how you want it to be, Rachel?"

She spun on him.

"Don't play like any of this is my choice, Noah Detweiler. You didn't bother to respond to my letter. Weeks it's been, Noah. No word you were coming, and then . . . then you ignored me, to my face, last night. The first time in thirteen years and what do you do? Fix a flat and drive off. Again. You've paid my feelings no mind since you . . . since you ran away. I'm only keeping this the way *you* like it."

Noah remained silent. He didn't have a ready answer, but he sure wasn't backing down before they'd hashed this out. He watched from a non-intrusive distance while she attacked the chore of milking a cow with more vigor than he'd reckoned possible. Warm streams of milk strummed a metallic tune against the pail at first, then changed to a slish-slosh rhythm as the creamy mixture deepened.

He'd loved her once as fiercely as she was draining that poor cow. How often had he vented his frustration with an axe on a pile of firewood after hearing her moon over Joel Yoder to her friends or being reminded by Saul that he wasn't good enough for her?

He was curious about the veterinarian. Without a doubt, the tower of a man was running interference between Rachel and Noah in the parking lot last night. And to be fair, Noah was a stranger showing up in a beater of a rental car. Still, to approach Rachel, he'd have had to go through the vet first. All things considered, Noah hadn't figured Rachel would appreciate that approach. Once he'd set eyes on her, though, he knew he couldn't leave again without talking to her.

He wouldn't have chosen this way, either, but here they were.

"I used to milk like that when I was angry. Trouble was, I was angry a lot."

"I'm not mad, Noah." She'd finished and turned on the stool to look sideway-ways at him. "I'm hurt."

The confession sliced like a sharp blade straight through his flesh. "Hurt and anger always go together for me. I usually can't tell them apart. And I never wished to cause either for you, Rachel. I know I have, and I'm sorry." His knees buckled, and he knelt right in front of her. "Truly sorry."

Her shoulders sagged. She looked away, first at the pail of milk, then at her fingers twisting together in her lap. Her voice, thin and fragile, was barely audible. "I don't know how to do this, Noah."

"Me either, Rachel. Me either."

She'd wanted Noah to come back, hadn't she? For years, she'd prayed and hoped for this day—wondered how it would be. And now, he was here, and all she felt was confused—and something else.

She was plain, old scared. Her feelings were wild and reeling beyond her control. Noah was kneeling in front of her, his bold, blue eyes searching down to her soul—if he could see beyond the veil of tears she held back. How long would he remain there waiting? She didn't know what else to say.

His attention moved to the milk bucket; then he pushed off one foot to stand again. "Right now, it looks like the thing for us to do is finish Saul's chores." He thrust out a hand to help her off the stool.

Uncertainty stopped her from accepting his simple gesture of goodwill right away.

He must have understood because he'd withdrawn the hand and rubbed it against his blue jeans instead. "What's next?" He surveyed the barn.

"Not too much since the miniature horses have been sold. Other than taking care of his cow, there's only the eggs to gather and chickens to feed."

Noah stared at the milk, which needed to be taken in the house, strained, and put in the icebox. He cleared his throat. "I, uh, haven't been in yet to see him."

So, she wasn't the only one who was battling her fears this morning. "Would you like me to go with you? I have to hurry. The wedding service starts at nine." And this errand was already taking twice as long as she'd planned. "Maybe just break the ice for you, so you don't scare the old man to death."

His eyes widened.

Ach, but that was a terrible choice of words. "What I mean is . . ." A low rumble of laughter interrupted her. "I didn't mean . . . Stop laughing, Noah. It's not funny."

Except, she was laughing, too. And heavens, the relief of it. She wiped at her eyes with her apron. "You're going to make me late for Mattie's wedding." She pierced him with as serious a stare as she could muster, which affected a small measure of solemnity on his sun-tanned face.

He'd aged—more than she realized in the brief glances she'd taken of him so far. Her hand flew to her cheek. She was suddenly aware how much she'd changed, too. His eyes dropped down. His face flushed, apparently with the same realization.

"We aren't seventeen anymore, are we?" He looked back at her with a bit of a cheeky grin. "But I'd say you've aged a good deal nicer than this old cowboy." He ran a hand through his thick waves of hair, redder than the strawberry blond she remembered. He'd aged well, to her thinking. "It's good to see you, Rachel. Real good."

Goodness, she'd made this harder than necessary.

Noah was still Noah. He'd visit a few days, maybe a week, and then life would resume a normal balance. He'd never be the knight in shining armor she'd hoped would rescue her from her loneliness. What a silly notion. He wasn't Amish anymore. Of course, she'd known that. But for some reason, she had to see so for herself to believe it. Now, she'd accept it as enough to know they were in harmony again, even if at a distance. What other choice did she have?

The same as she'd had the day she broke up with Joel. None—not so long as she was going to remain true to herself and who *Gott* had made her to be.

"Rachel, go get ready for the wedding. As much as I appreciate your offer to be a bridge between me and my *datt*, I should probably go it alone this time." He picked up the milk pail by the handle with one hand and motioned for her to go ahead of him with the other.

As their paths drifted apart—hers toward the pasture between Saul's and her *mamm's* house and Noah's toward the back door—a new fear emerged.

The unwanted emotion shivered up her spine.

"Raye?" She turned at the sound of Noah's old nickname for her. He was watching her from the bottom porch step. "I won't leave without saying goodbye this time. I promise."

There, he'd gone and put her worry to words. Would there ever be another who knew her so well?

CHAPTER FIVE

The screen door hinges creaked when Noah opened Saul's back door. Balancing the milk, he twisted the knob to the storm door, which opened easily. He should have asked for more information from Rachel before going inside the house unannounced, but from all his sister had shared, their *datt* remained in bed until Trudy or a home health nurse came to help him bathe and dress.

The back door led straight to the kitchen, which was remarkably similar to the kitchen in their home in Ontario. He set the milk on the counter next to the same old strainer he'd used as a kid. Sure enough, a clean jar was ready in the icebox. As he poured a steady white stream through the filter, Noah glanced around the wide-open room. The countertops were free of clutter, and nothing more than a simple table atop a dustless, wooden floor adorned the room. Then, he saw his mother's china hutch in the far corner.

The sight flipped a switch on the dark memories he'd forced silent over the past few days. He dumped the strainer and its contents into the sink. In a few long strides, he faced the cabinet doors and yanked the bottom doors open first.

Empty.

All of the drawers were empty, too. Behind the glass, his *mamm's* china collection appeared delicately arranged as if she'd placed them there herself. Of course, she hadn't. She'd died long before her husband's move to this island and before he'd adulterated her china hutch with his vile addiction.

Noah stormed toward the remaining kitchen cabinets and opened two doors on the top wall, then the next two and the next until he'd searched behind every cabinet door.

Not a drop of liquor or booze to be found.

Noah dropped his weight into a dining chair. His backside connected hard with the wood seat.

What was wrong with him? He was spying on a dying man. What did he plan to do if he'd found a stash? Bust up the bottles like he'd done years ago? Threaten to tattle on his own *datt* to the ministers? Swear his *mamm* was better off being dead than living with the man her husband had become?

Run. Run and never look back.

"Rachel? What's going on out here?" Noah barely recognized the disheveled, old man who shuffled through the entrance to the kitchen from a hallway. He stopped at the sight of Noah and leaned heavily on his cane.

"Hello, *Datt*." Noah stood but stayed in his spot at the table.

"*Sohn*." His hand shook as he transferred the cane to the opposite hand and shifted his weight to lean against the doorframe. "You won't find anything. Not a drop since the day you left."

One vice Saul Detweiler never indulged was a lying tongue. But somehow, Noah had trouble accepting the claim. If change had been so easy, why not before everything was ruined? Before Noah had finally given up hope?

A sinking sadness settled in his gut with one more thing to forgive before it was too late.

"*Kumm, Datt.*" The Amish words of his youth came more easily this time. "Let me help you *redd up* and get you something to eat."

"If you think I look bad, you should see yourself. You better clean up. There's a wedding today." Saul pushed off the wall and headed toward the table.

"I'm sure you're right." Noah ran a hand through his hair, then pulled out a chair for his father to sit. He'd no clue what the wedding had to do with it, but Noah knew he was in dire need of a rinse with soap and water.

"You gonna fix this mess you made?" Saul waved his cane at the open cabinets, then pointed to the spilled milk.

As the saying went, some things never changed.

"I'm going to do my best." But the kitchen wasn't all the fixing Noah had in mind.

Right now, God's grace was the only thing keeping Noah's feet grounded on his father's kitchen floor. Not to mention a pretty face he might not have the guts to leave again. But he was getting way ahead of himself with that kind of thinking.

If only shutting some cabinets and a little soapy water were enough to set all his mistakes back to right.

"You picked a good day to come home. Trudy told me you'd be in this week. Never did say which day, though. I reckon she didn't want me getting my hopes pinned on a specific hour. But now, you got here just in time."

"Time for what?"

"Mattie and Winston's wedding." He grunted as if the question were ludicrous. "We won't make it in time for the service. And I couldn't last that long, anyways." Saul grimaced, as if he'd not meant to speak so openly about his own weakness. Then he looked Noah over again. "By the time we both get *redd up,* I'll need a rest. Still, we can get there for the second meal at suppertime."

Showing up unannounced and uninvited didn't sound like a decent idea to Noah. Even if he wanted to go to this wedding—and he did not—Noah wouldn't ruin a happy couple's special day with the gossip he was sure to bring. But he hadn't forgotten the rules of being Saul Detweiler's son. Namely, never contradict the man. Arguing outright wouldn't do any good.

Saul's head bobbed, and his chin rested on his chest. If a short walk down the hall left the man exhausted, Noah doubted he had anything to worry about. Going by the picture Trudy had created in his mind of their *datt's* condition, Saul would never make it to a wedding party.

More worrisome than being roped into attending one simple wedding was the sensation this whole morning that his old life was tugging him back. He'd scarcely left Alberta forty-eight hours ago. Yet here in his father's kitchen, or while chatting with a little Amish girl and watching Rachel milk a cow, well, ranch-life had stretched a lifetime away.

Whatever God meant for him to do here, Noah prayed he finished quickly. He'd prefer to get back to Second Chance Ranch with his heart still intact.

Rachel watched the bride. Mattie wasn't one to enjoy the spotlight, yet she hadn't seemed to notice this morning. Her focus was solely on her groom. Winston returned her adoration, the love between them apparent to anyone who could see.

Weddings were always a big deal, but Mattie and Winston were the first New Hope Amish couple to marry on the island rather than the former church district in Ontario. No one was missing the party for Herschel's one and only daughter among his seven children.

First, though, the sacred union was to be sealed in a ceremony following a traditional worship service.

As the ministers led the congregation in the singing of hymns of blessing on the couple and their future, Rachel prayed in her heart for every word to come true. The prayers helped soothe her own longing for such a love. But as much as she rejoiced for her friend, still she couldn't completely deny her own hopes. Hopes which dangerously resurfaced over the past month while waiting for Noah. Then this morning—*ach*, she couldn't dwell on what any of it meant.

As the service ended in prayer, she sent her own heavenward plea for the strength to continue alone, if the Lord willed so for her.

As the barn began to empty, Rachel looped her right arm around her *mamm's* and navigated a path through the folks gathered all around the lawn. A stretch of the legs and some friendly chatter were always welcome after three long hours on church benches for the service and ceremony.

"You ought to be visiting, not playing nursemaid to an old woman. I can walk to the house alone, you know." Her *mamm's* soft, warm fingers patted Rachel's arm. "Winston must have an unmarried cousin or two from the States in this crowd."

"So, I've heard. We will be here the whole day long, *Mamm*. I'm sure there will be plenty of time for meeting Winston's kinfolk."

"I know you, Daughter, and I'm not talking about gabbing with the womenfolk while you bury yourself in serving others." Beulah Erb turned her head to survey the field adjoining the side lawn where a group of young people had gathered to play softball.

"*Mamm*, the men over there are barely more than boys. Let the youngies have their fun. I promise to mingle between the meals." Rachel didn't dare mention she'd be on the look-out in case Tony decided to drop in at some point between house calls or after the office closed. Spending time with an *Englischer* wasn't what her mother had in mind, for sure.

Rachel hadn't mentioned Noah's return either. Although she knew word was bound to travel fast with this many talkative tongues gathered in the same spot for a whole day. Unless Samy hadn't told anyone. Rachel sure hadn't.

"What you need is a *goot* Amish man, Rachel. And today, you have your pick all the way from Ontario and Pennsylvania, too. Don't you tell me all of this doesn't make you lonesome for a wedding of your own."

"How could I be lonely in this crowd?"

"Don't you sass me either, Daughter. My heart breaks over the thought of you alone when I die. The *goot* Man in Heaven hears my cries. You should listen, too."

"*Ach, Mamm*. Let's get you some dinner, *ja*? You'll feel better. And no more talk of dying. *Gott* will take care of me, no matter what. You know this. Let's be happy today. All right?" Rachel almost commiserated on how much she missed *Datt* today, too, but that would only make things worse. Ever since she'd been widowed, weddings put her *mamm* in a state of doldrums for a few days.

The flat line of her mother's mouth didn't move into any hint of a smile, but she quieted on the subject of matchmaking the rest of the way to the house. "I'm going to find Salome. I'll be fine. You go on now." Her *mamm* swatted her hand through the air.

Rachel stepped into the Bellers' house right behind her mother. The chatter of women at work raised in volume as she passed into the kitchen. She stretched onto her toes to look across to the next room.

"I see Salome over there." Rachel waved to the bishop's wife, her *mamm's* life-long friend. "If you get tired, *Mamm*, have someone find me. I'll take you home."

"I'm not going anywhere until after supper. I'm not so elderly as all that."

Rachel held back her own smile. Her *mamm* was able to worry over dying one minute and scold Rachel for implying she was old the next.

"If I leave early, I'll go with Sarah. She's not feeling so well." Her mother turned and headed in Salome's direction before Rachel could ask what was wrong with her sister, Sarah.

Come to think of it, she hadn't seen Sarah in the service, and she wasn't in the kitchen. But there were so many places she could be today. The barn was being rearranged for dining for the men. A giant gazebo tent had been erected for the ladies and children. The older women would likely eat inside the house, and picnic tables had been lined up in a field, along with a temporary softball diamond for the youth.

She'd have to wait to find Sarah. As one of the bride's attendants, Rachel was expected to help serve, and there were hungry folks a plenty ready to dig into the first wedding meal of the day. The bride's other attendant, a cousin from Ontario, didn't appear to have made it back to the house yet. Belinda Beller's simple kitchen was crawling with the groom's female kin, none of whom Rachel knew.

Feeling out of place at a church gathering in her own small, tight-knit community struck Rachel as odd as being unwelcome in assisting with a sick animal. It just didn't happen. Not here. Sure, she got an occasional wary look from a non-Amish customer, but no more than any Amish woman experienced on a regular basis.

Most of the community knew her now, and islanders were generally easy to get along with in any situation. At first, a few of her Amish brethren weren't thrilled about her occupation. Herschel Beller being one of the toughest to win over, now he or one of his boys called on her a couple times a week for one thing or another on the dairy farm. Now, here she stood in his house after his daughter's wedding feeling more out of place than she'd ever known as a female Amish vet tech.

A soft pressure landed on her shoulder. She turned toward the hand, which gave a gentle squeeze. Belinda, the bride's mother and a friendly face, leaned in close to her ear. "Thank goodness you are here. I can't think in my own house."

Rachel lay her own hand over Belinda's. "I believe we could disappear, and these Americans would run everything just fine without noticing we are gone."

"I suppose." Belinda's lips turned in an attempt at a smile. "I should be thankful, *ja*? They are accustomed to much bigger crowds and upwards of as many as three or four a week during their busy wedding months. I just didn't expect . . . you know?"

To be pushed aside at her own daughter's wedding.

"*Ja.*" Rachel took the woman's hand in her own. "Let's go find the bride and groom, eh?" Mattie was still outside with her new husband receiving congratulations from their guests.

"*Nay,* I don't think . . . "

Rachel nicked two sandwiches from a platter, gave a tug on Belinda's hand, and pulled her toward the door. A mischievous grin that may have once belonged to a much younger Belinda crept across the woman's face as she acquiesced, then practically skipped out of the house.

They reached the tire swing, which hung under a large tree in the front yard, and Rachel handed Belinda one of the pinwheel sandwiches.

"I think I've discovered where all those boys of yours got their spunk." Rachel bit into the rolled-up flatbread, as Belinda did the same.

After the last bite, Belinda plopped into the swing. "I needed that. I've been so busy, I haven't eaten much the past few days. And poor Mattie—I hope she eats today, but with all the excitement and feeling like she has to impress all of Winston's family, I don't know if she will. And Mark, he wouldn't be here at all if not for his love for his sister. Now he's gone. He left the second the ceremony ended. I barely got to say a word to him with all the commotion and his coming and going in such a rush. When Herschel and I got married . . . " She paused on a long sigh and switched her focus from a far-off place back to Rachel. "*Ach*, I'm talking too much."

Rachel leaned her back against the tree trunk, and Belinda spun the swing around to face her. "What about you, Rachel? What are you going to do about Noah?"

So, the word was out. A little sound of dread escaped her on a sigh.

"Don't worry, I haven't said anything, and Mark didn't tell anyone else that he'd delivered a letter for you. But if Noah comes to see Saul, he'll be coming to see you, too."

Not really. He seemed to want to avoid her. At least, at first. But then, he'd not run from her temper in the barn. "I was just Saul's

messenger, Belinda. Noah didn't come for me—*wouldn't*, I mean—
wouldn't come back for me."

Belinda dug a heel in the dirt, so that the easy twist of the swing
came to a sudden stop. "He's here? You've seen him already?"

Rachel bit her lip at the sudden stab of pain from the wound Noah's
appearance re-opened. If she spoke aloud now, the tourniquet of pressure she'd been relying upon to control the bleeding pain would fail
to hold.

Belinda didn't require another word. In an instant, she was on
her feet with her arms wrapped around Rachel. More than a decade
worth of pent-up sorrow spilled into the woman's nurturing embrace
before Rachel could do a thing to stop the flow.

"I suspected as much." Belinda spoke softly as she caressed
Rachel's back.

Rachel pulled away enough to look at the woman several years
her senior and wipe a hand across her face to dry her tears. "What
did you suspect?"

"Rachel, I was a young, married woman with twin babies when
you and Noah were youth. I'd found love with Herschel and noticed
it easily in others when it appeared. Noah's love for you was so obvious, but I always rather supposed you didn't know you loved him back
until it was too late."

Had everyone else seen it, too? She'd never imagined her deepest
secrets were so obvious. "I didn't realize. Oh, Belinda, has everyone
known all along?"

"Of course not. Though, I'd dare say Bishop Nafziger had an inkling.
He's bent over backward to make you happy because he is a kindhearted
man who wants what is best for his flock. But there's also plenty of

guilt to go around the whole community when it comes to our failures with Noah and Saul. Maybe *Gott* is giving us all another chance."

Rachel's heart broke for Belinda. Beneath her words, the ache of a mother's worry over her own child bled through. She knew Belinda wished Mark would return from the outside world. Her pacifist upbringing so at odds with his choice to join the military had turned her upside-down for weeks. But Mark kept in touch with his family, if not with the rest of the Amish.

"I should have known you'd understand me, Belinda. Our sorrows aren't so different, I suppose."

"It's the way of things. We suffer so we may comfort one another through the trials of this life. *Gott* will make a way for us both. I believe so with all my heart." Belinda stood and straightened her dress. "I've been a runaway mother-of-the-bride long enough, *ja*?" She laughed. "You think about what I said, though. Don't give up on Noah. Not now."

Belinda walked back toward the house, and Rachel followed deep in thought. Another chance with Noah. Did she dare believe it possible?

CHAPTER SIX

Noah ran a hand through his still-wet hair as he paced the floor of his father's narrow and sparse living room. He'd managed a much-needed shower, while Trudy had helped Saul dress in his Sunday best before she'd returned home. The man was determined to attend today's wedding.

Saul was proving more able-bodied than Trudy had led him to believe. Noah was almost convinced the man was milking his daughter's sympathies.

Noah had to wonder how his sister managed to care for their father along with all of her own responsibilities. She was perfectly convinced Saul wasn't much longer for this world—as Saul himself had reminded them both a few times over the course of half a day.

Of course, Noah had heard stories of folks who surprised their kinfolk with a sudden surge of life before their time came. Old Benjamin Nafziger, the bishop's father, had done so. Noah had only been a child, but the ruckus Old Ben caused wasn't a thing one forgot. He'd awakened from a coma, walked out of the room right after the ministers had prayed last rights over him, then died three days later behind his plow. Old Ben got his corn planted, though. And his widow sold the harvest for an unheard-of profit.

Now, his *datt* was determined to rope Noah into attending the wedding with him. Noah's plan to quietly sneak in a visit to his dying father, make what amends he could, and slip right back home to Alberta was unraveling faster than a wool sweater with a loose strand of yarn in the paws of a barn cat.

"You ready?" Saul asked from the dining table where he sat waiting for Noah to dress. Noah sighed and reached around to the peg on the wall for his father's lightweight jacket. The man might blow over in a strong breeze or freeze to death despite the pleasant temperatures. He hadn't an ounce of extra flesh to warm him.

Noah held out the coat and bundled up his father. "You really think this is a good idea, then? Look at me, *Datt*." Noah pointed out his clothing, an outfit he'd wear to church—a non-denominational *Englischer* church. "I don't know this Winston fella and haven't seen Mattie since she was a little girl, but I don't want to stick out like a sore thumb and ruin their day. You know people will talk."

"Talk—that's all you're doing when we need to get a move on. A little vain to think your showing up is enough to ruin a wedding, eh? You have a car to take us there, and I can't stay long to pay my respects. Anyhow, who's gonna recognize you after all this time?"

Anyone who knew his *datt* before he'd turned gray, that was who. Strong genetics was the reason Noah was forced to think about his old man every time he looked in a mirror.

"Rachel and a girl named Samy already saw me, *Datt*. I told you this already."

"*Ja. Ja.* So you said." Saul may as well have cotton in his ears for as much as he pretended to hear any rational reason for Noah not to make an appearance at this wedding.

"By the way, that reminds me of something the girl said. Who is Yo-yo?"

"Samy is Joel Yoder's girl. She had a bad speech problem and called him Yo-yo. She talks up a storm now, but the name stuck."

Interesting. He hadn't been surprised to learn Joel was a minister in the small Amish community. Rachel had given some details in her letter, and Mark had answered a couple of questions for him back at the ranch while they fixed his motorcycle. Noah didn't recall anything about Samy, though, and she'd piqued his curiosity with her appearance in the barn that morning.

"And who is Betsey?"

"One of my miniature ponies. I sold them. Probably should have given Betsey to the child, but the buyer wanted the whole lot and Betsey in particular, since she was pregnant."

"I don't expect that news went over easy." Noah might not know much about Samy herself, but he knew the heart of a child, especially one attached to an animal. His own heart twisted at the thought of her disappointment.

"The child keeps sneaking over here, anyway, to make sure Betsey hasn't come back. Rides that big horse of Joel's bareback across the fields. Stubbornest child I ever saw. Reminds me of . . . "

"Me, right?" Noah didn't need an answer. The real question was how his *datt* treated the constant reminder. Of course, the man was frail now. And sober. Besides, he'd never hurt a girl, which was why he'd sent Trudy to live with his sister after their *mamm* died and things got bad. "Does it bother you having her come around?"

"*Nay.*" The declaration held a level of shock at the suggestion. He must truly care about the girl. "Ask Joel. He says I encourage her too much."

The last thing Noah had expected was for his *datt* to go on the defensive over the question. Such a strong attachment struck Noah unexpectedly. Saul Detweiler was clearly a man Noah really didn't know anymore.

"Ask Joel for yourself at the Bellers," his *datt* continued. "If we don't get there soon, we'll miss the second meal. Trudy didn't bring supper, either, so let's get going. I don't have much longer, you know. And a dying man deserves a good supper."

"C'mon then. I'll help you to the car." But Noah wasn't making any promises to get out of that car himself.

When Noah was growing up, his parents often hired non-Amish drivers to take them to doctor's appointments and sometimes to shop. Hauling Saul to this Amish wedding in a rental car wasn't too far removed from the memory, except Noah was the driver this time.

"Over this next hill is Joel's place. We'll pass the school; then the Beller place is at the bottom on the right."

Noah had passed the place twice that day already on his way to and from the little village where the animal hospital, a local market, and Nancy's Bed and Breakfast were all clustered together. "It's easy enough to spot today, *Datt*. Every buggy on the island has to be parked along the lane." Not to mention a few fifteen-passenger vans. Even from the top of the hill, the dome of a large, white tent was visible, along with a mass of softball players gathered in a field.

"Did you say half of these folks are out-of-towners?"

"More than that. Winston's kin from Pennsylvania and Ohio have pretty near taken over," Saul muttered with a hint of aggravation.

"I'm sure all will be back to normal soon enough."

"*Everyone* will leave again, you mean."

Noah discarded an uncomfortable twinge of guilt. He refused to be as easily manipulated as Trudy. He didn't plan to hang around long enough to be touted as the returned prodigal. He'd been forced to leave and, honestly, felt somewhat arm-twisted to return.

His *datt* stroked his long, gray beard and stared out the window. "Could be lonesome for some here. Maybe for them that go, too. Depends what they return to, *ja?*"

"I'm not lonely, *Datt*. I have a good life back in Alberta. I only came because . . . because if God could forgive me for all I've done, then I have to find a way to forgive you. And I'm going to tell you the truth. I don't believe I've managed to do that all the way yet." Noah flipped on the right turn signal. The rapid click matched the beat of his pulse as they passed buggy after buggy parked along the drive.

Parking too far away from the festivities would make for an impossible walk for Saul. Noah had to get closer somehow, and a narrow opening between a buggy and a van enabled him to steer the car through and pass further up the field, where he could park at the head of the line.

Beside him, Saul crossed an arm over his body and gripped the seatbelt as the front tires came to a sudden stop in a ditch Noah hadn't expected to be so deep.

"Guess I forgot I'm not driving a truck."

"Strong-headed as always." His father's voice held more wistfulness than reprimand. In fact, there was no criticism at all—more regret than anything.

"*Datt* . . . " The name only he and Trudy claimed for Saul—*Datt*—came easier this time. Noah heard the change in his own tone from his earlier forcefulness, as his father's eyes locked with his own. "I hope we find peace before I go back. I truly do. But I won't be staying; you need to understand that up front. All right?"

The deep lines etched in the elderly man's forehead became more apparent as he turned his focus directly on Noah. "My greatest dying prayer is that you don't end up like me, Son."

Noah hesitated. No, he couldn't do it—drop his father off and disappear for an hour or two before coming back to collect him like some random taxi driver. "Wait here. I'll come around and help you out."

Maybe Noah could meander through that crowd without anyone taking much notice. And maybe his *datt* had a point. He might be thinking a little too highly of himself to suppose the shock of folks at his return would upstage a wedding.

Facing Rachel and his father was more than he'd have wished for one day. Fitting into a massive Amish gathering was not another emotional hurdle he desired to add to the day's list either. But with the Lord helping him, he was going to hurl himself into this Amish arena for his actions to be judged anyway.

From behind the serving table, Rachel attempted to serve the last guests in the line with patience. She was keeping an eye out for Samy, since Lydia had come through the house in a moderate panic looking for the nine-year-old. Towering a head above anyone else in the room, Tony waved to her from where he stood talking to Mattie and Winston at the bridal table. She offered Tony a friendly smile and tried not to worry. Samy would show up; she always did.

None of the church members, whom Rachel had queried as they collected their food, recalled seeing the child recently. She dished out the last plate and took comfort in the fact the crowd would thin out soon. A number of relatives and friends would stay late into the night, but most folks would head home after supper was finished.

More than likely, the commotion of such a large gathering had overwhelmed Samy's senses. She'd hidden somewhere to control the unpleasant feelings which raged through her autistic nervous system. Once everything calmed down, she'd come out.

Before another hungry guest could get in line, Rachel set down her serving spoon and slipped out of the room to check the rest of the house. When Samy needed a quiet place, she naturally migrated to a space where she could be alone. Since no one should be on the second level of the farmhouse, Rachel climbed the stairs to search the bedrooms.

Opening the first door, Rachel called, "Samy?"

No answer.

Rachel walked closer to the bed and peeked underneath. Every room yielded the exact same results—no Samy. Rachel's heart began to beat faster as she returned downstairs and slipped outside.

Surely, Lydia had found her daughter by now.

"Can I help?" Tony's familiar voice came from behind her. She turned as he walked across the porch with purpose. "What are you looking for?"

As she expected, Tony was more than happy to help after she explained the situation. Tony knew Samy. Who didn't? She'd stolen a piece of almost every heart in the area, Amish and non-Amish alike. Her love for horses and fascination with any work Tony did at their farm had made her one of Tony's favorite children among his customers.

Plus, his height sure would give her a better advantage in her search through all these people.

"Can you head over to the softball game? Samy would normally hover near the outside of the crowd, maybe even wander off alone beyond the outfield. And keep an eye out for Lydia. Maybe she's found her already. I'm going to check the barn."

"I'd guess the barn as the first place she'd go. I'll come to you there with any news or after I check the ballfield."

The temporary tent erected for the wedding blocked Rachel's view of the barn, where the Bellers kept their horses. Further to the side, the dairy shed was visible. Since she rather doubted the noisy tent would appeal to Samy, Rachel skirted around to the dairy shed first.

Two of Hershel's boys were inside finishing the second milking of the day. But according to the boys, Samy hadn't been there, either.

"Martin. Myles. You're sure neither of you saw her at all?"

"Can't say I've seen her all day, Rachel. But I wasn't looking either." Myles shrugged. Of course, the eleven-year-old hadn't been on the look-out for a girl.

Rachel glared at him anyway. This was serious.

The older, Martin, gave his brother a fake punch in the arm. "If she'd come through here, I would have seen her. Soon as we finish cleaning up, we can help you look."

"What? I'm hungry. We already had to be last for supper."

Martin answered his brother's complaint with a low growl. "Think of someone other than yourself for a change."

"*Danki* for your help, both of you, but you should go eat." She didn't have time for their fighting and headed straight to the barn with a fading hope of finding Samy there.

As she neared the horse barn, Joel's profile came into view at the open doors. Had he found his daughter already? A wave of relief crested in her heart, only to recede at the site of three more men in animated discussion with Joel. The grim line of Herschel Beller's mouth, alongside Bishop Nafziger stroking his beard, didn't bode well. Then, Joel's head bowed, and his eyes closed, as he massaged his forehead with a thumb and forefinger.

The fourth man, with his back to her, turned at her approach, confirming the person she already knew it to be. Noah held his cowboy hat close to his abdomen. His eyes, dimmed grave with concern, met hers. He stepped away from the circle of men to speak to her in a quiet voice. "Samy is missing, and so is one of Herschel's horses."

No one needed to explain the fear in their hearts. Everyone knew Samy loved to ride bareback across the fields. Yet she was always on Amazon and always followed the same path from the Yoder's farm to Saul's.

On an unfamiliar horse . . . across a mile of different terrain than her normal route . . .

"You haven't found her yet?" Joel's question pulled her attention back to the men. Rachel shook her head when the answer stuck in her throat and watched the last of Joel's hope drain with the color from his face.

Hershel's giant Percheron's munched on their feed in the background as the group of men grew thoughtful.

A gentle touch from Noah's arm across the back of her shoulder directed her into the circle with him. Noah stood at one side and Joel on the other. A day ago, she wouldn't have imagined the three of them together again in any scenario, but there wasn't time to examine the strangeness of having Noah here with them now.

Noah looked at Herschel. "If you have another horse agreeable to riding, I have some tracking experience."

Herschel nodded, then focused his attention on Joel. "Anything I have is yours. And I do have one horse used to being ridden with a saddle."

"I could go right now. The sooner, the better." Noah's spoke with more comfort than urgency, as if he didn't want to spook Joel or any of the men listening. "Do you have an idea where she would try to go?"

"She always goes to Saul's but never from this far. And Amazon knows the way from our house. From here . . . I don't know." Joel tapped his straw hat against his thigh.

"My other buggy horse, Silver Star, was a trail-riding horse before I got her. She'd have been a better choice for Samy." Herschel cleared his throat. "I don't want to cause unnecessary concern, but Thaddeus was a racehorse and prefers the road. I don't know how far Samy will get on him. I don't think he'd throw her, but he may not cooperate. He'll go his own way."

"We have only an hour or so until dark." Bishop Nafziger spoke for the first time, taking charge for Joel, who looked shaken. "If Thaddeus decided to bolt or throw her, then we have a short time to find her. Like Noah said, the sooner someone heads out on horseback, the better."

Rachel had to help. They might be hesitant to trust Noah, but she could feel his quiet confidence. He knew what he was doing. "I could go with Noah. I can ride Amazon. I don't need a saddle." She had Joel's attention now, but he looked as unconvinced as the rest of the men around her. "If Samy is trying to get to Saul's house, then she'd most likely head toward the school because she knows the way from there. There are more than enough people here to start out on foot to search between here, the school, and your farm. Noah needs someone who knows the area. Together, we can cover the trail Samy usually takes to the Detweiler farm. Between Noah's skill and Amazon's instinct, we will find her, Joel."

She knew the look on Joel's face. He wanted to say no, but he was backed into a corner. The bishop was quiet, and beside her, Noah kept his peace, too.

Herschel spoke up. "I can get the boys to the fields between here and the school. They know them like the back of their hands." At least, Herschel was convinced and ready to get moving.

Joel looked back at her with more focus now. His shoulders straightened. "I appreciate your offer, Rachel." Then he spoke directly to Noah. "*Gott* was gracious to send us a man with experience in these things for today. I'd prefer to go with you myself and bring my daughter home. But I think I must be available here to help make decisions."

He paused without breaking eye contact with Noah. Rachel had witnessed a change in Joel as the burdens of being a minister tested him over the past few years. No test had been as personal as this one.

"I'm trusting *Gott* has sent you for this purpose today, Noah." Joel darted a meaningful glance Rachel's way. "Be careful."

"I'll do all I can." Noah hadn't always liked Joel when they were young, but his words showed respect now.

Herschel spoke next. "*Kumm*, we should hurry." He motioned to Noah and Rachel. "I have a blanket you can use on Amazon and a saddle for Silver." He looked down at Rachel's dress. "Maybe you should go see what Belinda has for you to wear."

Herschel's no-nonsense attitude saved her from embarrassment in front of the other men. He was right, too. Her Sunday-best dress was not appropriate for riding around on horseback. Mattie and Belinda both wore leggings under their dresses for various farm chores. She'd borrow a pair and be ready in a snap.

She caught up with Joel, who was going to find Lydia. "Dr. Drake is here. He can drive people to the school and your house to check faster. We will find her, Joel."

"*Danki*, Rachel. Samy is in *Gott's* hands. He will help us." He leaned a little closer to her then. "After this is settled, we must talk."

He was overreacting to Noah's arrival, but this wasn't the time to point out the fact. "All right, Joel. Don't worry. We are going to find Samy."

Joel grimly nodded and walked ahead. Come to think of it, Joel hadn't ever cared so much for Noah either. She watched as Joel approached Tony, who stood just a few yards away. Tony's head was shaking in concern. Her overprotective boss wouldn't like the idea of her riding off with a man he'd consider a complete stranger. Neither of them would understand how she knew she was safe with Noah. She couldn't explain herself how she'd fallen right back into step with Noah so fast.

She glanced backward as she left the barn. Noah was already preparing Silver Star for her saddle. "I'll be ready as soon as you get back," he called to her.

She'd better hurry before Joel changed his mind.

CHAPTER SEVEN

Noah held the reins of Herschel's Appaloosa and Joel's Morgan mare—both gorgeous animals—while he waited for Rachel to return. He was still astonished at how quickly he'd found himself in the middle of a rescue party. He'd been talking to Herschel in the hope of seeing Mark. He hadn't thanked the guy properly at the time he delivered Rachel's news about Saul and was disappointed to learn Mark had already left.

Before he knew what was happening, he and Herschel were searching the barn for Samy. Herschel had discovered the missing horse, and then Rachel showed up. Rachel clearly believed Joel's horse would assist their search, and Noah agreed. Even if Amazon wasn't a trained search and rescue animal, her senses were still more powerful than a human's. If Amazon already knew Samy's scent and voice, as well as the path Samy normally traveled from her house to Saul's, then Rachel was absolutely right to insist the horse join the search. Once they reached the Yoder's farm, Amazon was going to be a huge asset.

Still, they had no time to waste.

Amazon shook her head at the reigns. Both horses were getting jittery, likely from the tension pouring off Noah. Inhaling a long, slow breath, he let the anxiety settle. As the person furthest removed from Samy, he had to be the one to stay calm.

"You're going to need a flashlight this close to dark." A man's voice turned Noah's attention to the open doorway, where the local veterinarian stood holding out a large light in one hand and a walkie-talkie type device in the other. "I only have two portable ham radios. I gave Rachel the other one. Can't say as I like sending her out there with a stranger."

Noah had noticed the vet earlier mixing with the Amish. He must be on good terms with them, as he'd witnessed several hearty laughs coming from the man's direction. But when it came to Rachel, he was becoming a nuisance. At least, Joel had been protective in a way Noah respected. This guy had something to prove. Maybe it shouldn't get under his skin, but Noah bristled, anyway.

"I believe she volunteered." Noah already had a light but accepted Tony's for back-up. "No one is sending her anywhere she doesn't want to be."

"That's true." Rachel interrupted the man-to-man stare-down. She stepped up beside the vet and placed her hand on his forearm. "Don't worry about me, Tony. And I'm very grateful to you for staying to help."

The softness in her voice melted the giant into a puddle and re-minded Noah how little he knew about the Rachel of today. Maybe the man had some right to be so protective. Would Rachel really form an attachment to a man outside her faith?

Noah tossed aside the notion—one too dangerous for him to entertain. Tony ought to as well because it wasn't going to happen. People might change—but not down to the core of their being like that. Growing up, Rachel never questioned joining the church. She'd been baptized and taken her vow as soon as their bishop allowed. She wouldn't leave the Amish. Not for anyone.

Noah walked the horses closer and handed Amazon's reins to Rachel, then squared up to face Tony. "I get your concern. If I were in your place, I'd be cautious, too. But in this case, you'll have to trust Rachel. I might not know the island, but I know the back of a horse, day or night. And I've a good tracking sense that served me well over the years on the Albertan prairie. We can pray it serves us well tonight, too."

Tony didn't argue or agree. And really, they didn't have time for more discussion. Instead, in one smooth move, the vet swept Rachel onto Amazon's back. A pair of black leggings kept her modest as her borrowed dress flared up, but her face was as scarlet as a Rhode Island Red. Tony had a lot to learn about Amish women.

For Rachel's sake, Noah was glad no one else saw the man's arms around her. He could imagine the rumors. Truth be told, she had to get up on the horse somehow, though. A relative or a husband would have saved her embarrassment, but he hadn't seen either of her brothers. If Reuben or Albert were here, they hadn't made themselves available. Another thing that hadn't changed. Noah should have been the one to offer the favor himself.

"You ready, Raye?"

Rachel clicked her tongue and maneuvered ahead. She couldn't go far or fast until she'd cleared the area around the house, but Noah sensed her intent to leave both men behind as fast as possible. She never could abide discord.

Noah leaned forward in the saddle and went after her.

Rachel strained to see across the furrowed field where Joel's potato crop lay buried beneath the rows of raised, red dirt. She'd managed to put aside her frustration over the two men and their petty wrangle over which one got the final say over her well-being. To her way of thinking, she hadn't given either the privilege.

At least, Noah had the decency to apologize once they were well beyond the Beller farm. They'd progressed in tandem until Amazon had led her to the left around Joel's fields, so Noah had gone to the right and called out to Samy from the other side.

After each call, they paused to listen. Samy's name bounced back and forth across the field between them with a steady beat of silence in between. Rachel squinted to see Noah's shrug; then they both drove their horses onward. They'd ridden to Joel's in a hurry and left the area between the dairy farm and the schoolhouse across from the Yoders' for folks on foot to join in the search.

Now, as they meticulously covered the trail from the Yoder farm to the Detweilers', Rachel prayed Samy had safely arrived at Saul's long ahead of them. Still, the time before dark was short. If something had happened to the child on her way, they had to find her soon.

As they reached the north end of the field, Noah rode to meet her. Noah eased his horse beside hers so that he faced her directly when he came to a halt. The two-way radio in his saddlebag beeped.

Noah handed her the radio. Tony's voice mixed with static while she bent forward to grasp the handheld device, then raise the antennae. She and Tony occasionally used the radios when they were both out on house calls. He'd insisted she take a class and get an operator's license because cell service was often unreliable on the farms he served. Thank goodness for his forethought tonight. If only she wasn't afraid of the message his call would bring.

"Do you copy? Over." Tony's voice crackled through the speaker.

She looked down at the radio in her hand, then to Noah. His eyes shifted from the radio to her face. "You have to answer, Raye."

She knew that. And once she did answer, the news was exactly what she had feared. Tony and Saul hadn't found Samy at the Detweilers' farm.

Rachel felt she was going to be ill. She'd been convinced Samy had headed in this direction. Where else would she go on horseback?

"Raye, we have to try to think like her. It's possible she just hasn't gotten there yet. And if she does arrive, *Datt* will be there. But what might have distracted her or led her to wander from her usual path?"

"I don't know. She goes to school and Saul's house every day, but they haven't found her at either place. Other than that, she might try going to the bishop's house."

"Well, if she's gone to the bishop's, she'll be found, right? I don't know her, but from what I saw, she's a smart girl." He'd worked with enough children with autism to respect their intelligence. True, she'd taken off on an unknown horse on impulse, but Samy had a skill set to help her. "Joel has obviously taught her to take care of herself on a horse. We just have to find her."

"It's not only all the things I can imagine going wrong for Samy. It's Lydia. I can't explain what this is doing to her. She's blaming herself. And she'll never get over it if anything happens to Samy."

Noah was swinging a leg over his horse. He dropped to the ground and put out a hand to help her down, too. What was he thinking?

She looked ahead at the trail Samy and Amazon had blazed over months of afternoon rides through the pines toward Saul's house. "We need to keep going."

Noah wasn't listening. He just stood there waiting to help her down. "We need to pray first." A calm assurance passed from his gaze straight to her fear-riddled heart.

Taking hold of his offered hand, she dismounted. The warmth of his touch comforted her. So different from the embarrassment earlier when Tony had lifted her onto the horse.

Noah let go of her hand but held her eyes with the tenderness of his bold, blue ones. He removed his hat; and when he bowed his head, the long wave of his hair falling across his forehead brushed against her prayer *kapp*.

Her eyes closed, but she didn't dare bow her head as it would land flush against his chin. A few seconds ticked passed, maybe less, when a peaceful aura settled around them, calming her soul.

"Dear God," Noah began, echoing a reverence to match the peace, "We are afraid for Samy and for Lydia. And yet, we know nothing is lost to you, especially not your children. You see what we cannot envision. You hear their cries while we are deaf to them. Open our eyes and our ears, Lord. Show us the way to Samy."

Silence drifted between them. Noah remained still, as if listening to some unheard voice. The prayerful attitude overpowered her desire to hurry ahead with their search and pulled her thoughts to a higher place—a realm of prayer she'd visited only a few times in her life—a place where *Gott* was more real than the world around her.

Gott, I know You want what is best for Lydia. Let it be Your will that she not suffer unnecessarily. Watch over Samy and lead her to safety. Help me trust You to do what is best.

A firm and calloused hand brushed across the palm of her hand, making her aware once again of Noah's presence. When her eyes opened, he was stepping back a pace.

"We're going to find her, aren't we, Noah?"

He nodded, then offered a boost to help her get back on Amazon. Rather than toss her like a rag doll, he cupped his hands to make a step for her foot, then gave a gentle boost.

Strange that these moments with Noah weren't the least bit awkward, as if their friendship had never been placed on hold.

Rachel gave the horse her head, fully expecting Amazon to take the route she'd worn through the woods. Instead, Amazon bolted at the entrance to the woods. Her ears perked upward, and she veered left toward the road.

"Let her go," Noah called from behind, as he came up beside her so that the animals were head-to-head. "Silver heard something, too. Let's see where she leads us."

"All right, Amazon." Rachel stroked the animal's neck. "Take us to Samy."

Amazon carried them back to the main road on the opposite side of the hill from the Yoder's farm. At the point where the hill bottomed out into a dip, she stopped. If they crossed over the road, they'd be on the far end of Abe and Sarah's farm near a pond where the horses often watered.

Rachel twisted around to see Noah waiting behind her. "I think I know where Thaddeus has taken Samy. We have to cross the road here."

The dusky light was rather dangerous for riding on the road, and Rachel was relieved once they crossed to the other side to ride across her brother-in-law's pasture. The pond, less than fifty yards from the road, had to be close now. In full daylight, they might have seen Samy anywhere in the wide-open space of Abe's pasture; but Noah had to turn on a flashlight to search ahead of them, slowing their progress.

"Samy!" Rachel forced all the power her lungs possessed into the frantic call. Yet silence was the only response.

A few heartbeats later, Amazon came to a halt and whinnied in the way a horse calls to another horse.

Noah reigned in beside them and dismounted. "I think I see her. She's coming to us." He extended a hand to Rachel. "Stay here with me and let Amazon go to her."

As soon as Rachel was clear of the horse, she released the reigns and watched as Amazon walked ahead. Several feet away, the horse bowed her head low and nickered as a child's thin arms wrapped around her neck.

Noah touched Rachel's elbow as she was about to lunge toward Samy. "Give them a minute."

He was right. Amazon deserved the reward of the girl's love, and Samy needed time to comprehend she was safe.

Only when the warmth of Noah's arm wrapped around her shoulder did she realize she'd allowed herself to lean into him as they watched. Joel would worry—and Tony, too.

She'd work out the meaning of it all later. And very soon, she'd call on the radio to alert the others of the good news. But for a precious minute, she allowed herself to lean into the security of the moment and the precious gift of answered prayer.

CHAPTER EIGHT

Noah watched out the kitchen window. Midday was approaching, and he itched to be outdoors. It had been three days since Samy's rescue, and Noah had spent them all at his *datt's* house. The wedding guests at the bed and breakfast had all gone back to Pennsylvania, but he didn't much feel like checking in there when he'd be going back to the ranch soon, anyway.

But for the dying man in the back bedroom, he'd have been back on his way already. Saul had refused to eat more than a little oatmeal and drink some sips of coffee each morning since returning to the house during their search for Samy.

By the time Noah came back that night, Saul had taken to bed. Noah hadn't been too concerned the first day. All the extra exertion was bound to take a toll on the man. But now, well into the third day, Noah saw no sign of improvement. He'd rallied enough this morning to refuse Trudy's insistence they go to the hospital but hadn't said a word since she'd gone home to her family.

He'd promised Trudy he'd stay at least through the weekend. But today was Saturday, and he was still far from any sense of resolution from this trip.

He reached in his pocket for his cellphone to call Stedman. Reception was spotty. He'd have to walk to the end of the drive to get a good enough signal to place a call.

On his way out the door, he grabbed the pot of congealed oatmeal off the stove. He'd told Trudy not to pitch the leftovers earlier. May as well make the chickens happy.

Noah had a nagging idea of what the old man needed to motivate him. But who was he to go tell Joel he ought to let his daughter visit? Noah understood the need for a consequence. And since Noah was around to do Saul's chores, he supposed the discipline made sense to a father like Joel. But Saul was paying the price as much as the child.

Pot and wooden spoon in hand, he eased into the henhouse.

How many more days of this could he take? Alone on the prairie, he hadn't much minded the solitude. Hard, physical labor took care of sleepless nights. He could fall asleep with a boulder for a pillow after a day rustling cattle.

Another day of cooking oatmeal and twiddling his thumbs was bound to mean another night of staring at the ceiling until the wee hours. Worse was remembering Rachel's soft form resting against him when they'd found Samy. Yep, he needed some good, hard labor to wear him out.

If he found the right project—one he could complete in a few days with some muscle—he could still watch out for Saul and work at the same time. He dumped the oats for the hens, then set the pot down and pushed the levered lock back into place on the cage door. Around back, he'd seen an old garden spot when he'd mown the grass the previous afternoon. But a garden would just make more work for Trudy when he was gone.

He walked down the drive a bit to survey the farm as a whole. The yard around the house was tidy. Thanks to help from the church, if he was to guess. The roof appeared to be in good shape—less than five years old.

Before long, the hayfields would be ready to mow. Several head of steer wandered through the other fields, and he'd learned Saul rented the fields to a church member for raising his Angus beef. Likely, the same farmer mowed the hay.

Saul hadn't ever cared much for cattle. He was a horseman through and through. And Noah still didn't know what had happened to his *datt's* once-successful horse training business. He'd mentioned selling miniature ponies—the ones Samy had loved and still missed. Maybe the minis were something of a hobby. They certainly weren't the thoroughbreds, quarter horses, or Morgans on which he'd established a reputation in Ontario.

Maybe his *datt* would rally enough to answer a few questions. Would he even share his story with Noah if he did?

Closest to the house, the outbuildings and the barn had all seen better days. Roofs needed repair; boards needed replaced; and a whole lot of paint wouldn't hurt either. Noah's bank account could handle the cost. He'd consider it a gift to his sister, who'd benefit if the property value increased a tad from the improvements. He could finish the work in a couple weeks. And if he was being reasonable, he probably couldn't haul himself out of here much sooner than that anyway.

Hitching up his *datt's* horse cart and making a trip to the hardware store might require more Amish than Noah had left in him. Then again, he might keep his sanity, and Trudy would be relieved for him to stay a while longer.

At the end of the drive, his phone registered reception of full service. He dialed Stedman and kept walking toward the crest of the hill, enjoying the scenery change.

Stedman answered the call and assured Noah there was no hurry for him to return to the ranch. He had everything under control, the man insisted, even if this was the busy season.

"This is something you have to see through, Noah. I'm not getting in the way. Don't you let the ranch be an excuse to keep from doing what God wants you to do."

Knowing what to do was his problem. He didn't think God had brought him back here to attend to a bit of farm maintenance. Nope. God was in the people business. Unfortunately, relationships were precisely where Noah struggled.

"Keep praying, Stedman? I haven't made much progress with *Datt*." Only about as far as thinking of the man as his *datt* again. "And as for Rachel . . . " Why had he brought her up?

"What about Rachel?" Stedman wasn't going to let him off that hook.

"It's a little more complicated than I hoped." Or rather more difficult to avoid than he'd let himself believe. He'd known all along she had the power to rope his heart right back into her hands if he got close enough.

"Love is like that."

His boss sure enjoyed stirring up a hornet's nest. "Stedman . . . "

"Listen, Marilyn and I will keep praying, and don't you fret over getting back here before you know your work there is done. God will work everything out on this end. And, Noah, He'll do the same on yours as well. Trust Him."

After saying goodbye, Noah pocketed his phone and looked up to see he'd reached the neighboring farm—Joel Yoder's place, to be exact, with a hand-carved sign beside the barn marked Lydia's Amish Shoppe.

An open sign hung in a window. Curious, he stepped through the door. Neat as a pin, a reading nook stocked with shelves of books drew his attention. A magazine rack filled with Plain newspapers and periodicals stood between two cozy chairs like an invitation to sit a spell and catch up on Amish and Mennonite news from around the world.

"Can I help you?" A tall, slender, Amish woman approached from the back of the store. She must be Lydia, whom he'd only seen once before from a distance and in the dark. "Ah, you're Noah, I think. I never got to thank you properly for finding our Samy."

As he searched for the right words to respond, two youngsters ran around the corner. Samy he knew, though she hesitated as if a little shy. The other child, a boy a couple of years younger, walked right to him.

"I've never seen a cowboy before, but you look normal to me." He gave Noah a thorough perusal. He didn't speak English like an Amish child, making Noah wonder if both children were adopted. "Where's your cowboy hat?"

"I wear it on the ranch. Doing cowboy stuff."

"Oh." The boy's shoulders sagged, and he stepped back.

"Amish farmers do plenty of cowboy work, too, you know. I'd be proud to wear that Amish hat of yours. Everybody knows the Amish are the best farmers."

The boy's chest puffed up, and Lydia frowned a little. "Owen, why don't you go pack up your crayons and books?"

Too late, Noah realized he shouldn't have used the word proud. He ran his fingers through his hair and scratched his head before addressing Lydia. "I didn't mean to bother you. I was just stretching my legs a bit and got curious when I saw your shop."

"You're welcome to browse. I'll be closing up for lunch in about ten minutes, but I am glad you stopped by. We've been meaning to get over to Saul's to see if we can help." She looked down at Samy, who gazed at her *mamm* intently—hope radiant in her large eyes.

"There might be one thing. Is there any way I could speak to Joel for a minute before lunch?"

"Of course. In fact, why don't I just close up already, and you may join us, too."

Noah tried not to squirm. The invitation was kindly meant, but he'd meant to speak to Joel privately. "I can't leave Saul for too long."

"It's nothing but a sandwich and a few fixings. Won't take long but will give us a bit to talk."

Talk. The very thing Noah couldn't seem to do without saying something he'd regret. How was he supposed to refuse without being rude? He caught sight of Samy waiting for his answer.

"Can I sit next to you, Squirt?"

"What's a squirt?"

He laughed. "A squirt is a bright, little girl with red hair whom people love the second they meet her."

"Oh." Her head tilted and her finger rested on her bottom lip. "I think you mean me. My name is Samy, but you can call me Squirt, like my *datt* is Yo-yo."

Lydia smiled then. "Go on ahead with your brother and wash your hands for lunch. I'll be right there, but go ahead and set the table, please."

A bell jingled as the kids ran out the shop door and left Noah unsure how to proceed with their *mamm*. She'd gone to a small desk and shuffled around some letters, then pulled a set of keys from a drawer.

Walking back toward him, Lydia clasped the keys and folded her hands together in front of her. Her posture reminded him of a schoolteacher bringing order to a rowdy classroom after recess. Serious not stern, he noted. If she'd been a teacher, she'd have been kind and patient, even if no-nonsense. He decided he liked her already.

"You seem very *goot* with children, Noah."

"I work with kids at the ranch." And usually understood them better than adults. Should he mention his therapy for special needs children? Maybe not yet. He wasn't even sure if Samy had ever been diagnosed on the autism spectrum.

Lydia pressed one hand against her dress, then place it right back overtop the other so that her arms hung down with her hands below her waistline.

"Rachel is my dearest friend. And I am truly not one to meddle." *But* . . . Her eyes pled for understanding, and now she appeared as tongue-tied as he often became. That made two things he and this woman had in common. Rachel had once been his dearest friend, too.

"Even to me, she's never confided much about you. Now that you are here, the pieces are falling together. Rachel could be married to Joel, you know. But she called it off before I'd ever met either of them." The poor woman's face burned red with some combination of frustration and embarrassment, likely from being so forthright to a stranger, but she continued. "No one ever really knew why. I think they might start to see the full picture now, just like I am. And some of them—her family especially . . . *Ach*, I just don't want unnecessary trouble for her."

Noah's heart thumped hard in his chest. He'd believed his youthful love unreturned and that he was the only one suffering by his leaving. Or had he convinced himself Rachel would soon get over any feeling for him merely to ease his own conscience?

"The last thing I want to do here is cause problems for Rachel, I assure you." On his seventeenth birthday, the solution to a similar mess had been to leave. Confused or not, he'd done so for Rachel's sake. So far as he could tell, he wasn't going to have any other choice this time either.

"What I'm asking is for you to please be gentle with her heart. Don't give her any false hope or cause for others to gossip."

Was she saying he actually had a shot with Rachel—even now?

"I've always cared deeply for Rachel. I'd do anything to protect her."

Lydia's lips pinched, but she nodded. "We have to trust *Gott* with the rest then, *ja?*" She offered him a polite kind of smile as she walked around him to the door, but the worry hadn't left her eyes.

If Samy weren't expecting Noah at the table, he'd bail out of this lunch with Joel. The man never cared much for Noah growing up and likely hadn't changed his mind for the better. Asking him to let his daughter come visit Saul may not have been Noah's most brilliant idea.

Just to make everything more fun, now Joel was the minister. And the minister's wife already had some serious concerns about gossip going around the community. Gossip he'd brought by coming here.

He stepped out of the shop behind Lydia and followed her to the house. Talking with Joel might get uncomfortable, but that was nothing compared to what he owed Rachel. He had to make sure Joel understood he'd be on his way after doing what he could for Saul. He wasn't here to stir up trouble.

CHAPTER NINE

Family suppers at the Erbs' house were a Saturday tradition. Week after week, year after year, nothing really changed after her father's death, except her brother led the silent blessing on the food from the head of the table in *Datt's* chair.

Rachel and her *mamm* continued to host the rest of her siblings and their children for a potluck-style feast. Her sister, Sarah, never offered, likely never even considered she might. Her two brothers' wives must have been content to leave things as they'd always been, even though Reuben as the eldest might have claimed the tradition as head of the family.

If Rachel had married and left home, maybe Reuben would've felt the need to step in more. But as things were, he never interfered. Laura, his wife, was always happy to help with the meals and brought twice as much as her own clan would ever consume.

Reuben tapped on the table to indicate the prayer had ended and the feasting could begin. Goodness, Rachel was distracted. Instead of giving thanks. she'd spent the whole prayer time pondering her family. Over the past few days, she'd spent far too much time speculating over the what-ifs of her life.

Serving bowls were passed. In the next room, the grandchildren, seated around card tables set up for them each week, filled the silence with laughter and giddy chatter.

"Well then, Rachel, what do you have to say for yourself this time?" Her brother Albert's glare all but made her choke on the pickled beet she was chewing.

Albert and his wife, Vonda, rarely spoke to Rachel at all, since she'd bent the church rules to become a vet tech. Or maybe it was since she'd broken her engagement to Joel Yoder. Never mind, the bishop had never seen fit to reprimand her for either action. Those two kept themselves and their *kinner* at a safe distance, lest Rachel's independent streak infect them from close contact.

"What . . . ?" She grabbed her water glass to wash down the stuck food so she could respond, but Albert wouldn't wait.

"That's about right. There's nothing for you to say. Have any of the rest of you heard the shame she's brought on our family this time? Why can't you behave like an Amish woman for once?"

"What do you know about being a woman, Albert?" Sarah snapped. Rachel may as well sit back. Once Albert and Sarah got going, there was no room for anyone else in the fray.

If *Datt* were here—but he wasn't.

Mamm was as depressed as her two middle children were disgruntled. And Reuben, he had yet to ever interfere one way or another. He always chose a safe, neutral position, if any position at all. Rachel was the lone peacemaker, since her *datt* was gone. And tonight, she didn't care to try. Maybe Reuben had the right idea.

There was an opportune transition in every gathering when Rachel could slip away without notice. In the hectic moments when dishes were being cleared and dessert served to happily filled bellies, Rachel could back her way entirely out of the kitchen and through the back door.

The peace-loving half of her family never gave her away if they noticed. Vonda and Albert were likely too relieved to have her gone to say anything. She'd always returned quietly before the last buggy full of relatives departed, so her *mamm* would not be alone.

But why wait? She'd no appetite left, anyway.

A stupid, silly notion to walk over to the Detweiler farm popped into her mind as it had done every evening since the wedding.

She pushed away from the table. "Excuse me, *Mamm*. I believe I'll take a plate of food over to Saul. It's been a while since one of us checked on our sick neighbor, hasn't it? Seems like a very Amish woman kind of thing to do, don't you think?"

Her *mamm* hadn't always liked Saul too well. But her attitude changed after Rachel's *datt* died. Namely because Saul practically gave her this piece of property, so she and Rachel could move to the island.

Her *mamm* nodded in approval, and Rachel let out a breath she'd been holding. "That's a *goot* idea, Rachel."

Albert jumped to his feet. "You're not fooling anyone. You're going over there to see Noah, that good-for-nothing who's only here to ruin whatever scrap of reputation you have left."

"Stop, Brother. I'll handle this." Reuben's unexpected assertion of his place at the head of the family shut Albert's open mouth before he could continue. "Take Drew with you, Rachel, and let Saul know we are praying for him."

Before Albert could explode, Rachel hurried to fetch Drew from the adjoining room and ran upstairs to get a cardigan and flashlight. Reuben's wife, Laura, met her and Drew at the kitchen door with a basket already prepared.

"*Danki*, Laura. What would I do without you?" Rachel discreetly slid the journal Saul had given her under the towel in the bottom of the basket.

"Get going now; it'll be turning dark. Drew can carry the basket and the lemonade." Laura hurried the on their way.

Rachel paused as her nephew shut the door to the fracas behind them. They walked as far as the old root cellar dug into the hillside generations ago for another family of island farmers. The sun's last rays touched the stones of the retaining wall beside the cellar door. The warmth recommended the seat. "Drew, do you mind? I just need a minute."

"I'm not in a hurry." He leaned against the cellar door with the load his mother had given him to carry. Drew always held a soft spot in Rachel's heart with his kind ways like Laura. She longed to hug him now, but he was at the age he felt himself a man already—much too old for such shows of emotion.

From her vantage point on the stone wall, she could see straight across the Detweilers' hayfields and over the top of the pine forest to the silos on the Yoders' farm and Lydia's Amish Shoppe.

Funny that Noah was there on the farm between hers and Joel Yoder's. Noah, who had stood between them during their engagement, even though no one knew where he was.

Rachel had been vague in her explanation to Lydia after she'd married Joel, but she'd shared enough for Lydia to understand she had no romantic feelings for Joel—ever. And truly, he'd never had any for her, either. So far as she knew, only Belinda Beller had guessed at Rachel's reason for not marrying Joel, but Albert said everyone was talking.

Did she even want to know what people were saying? Albert never showed any scruples against exaggerating to benefit his arguments. Hopefully, he'd done the same in this case.

All Rachel ever wanted was someone who made her feel loved the way Noah did. She'd realized it before she married the wrong man. But too late, nonetheless. She was sick to death of thinking of it. All the reasons why she couldn't hope for love with Noah had hammered through her skull the weeklong now. He was here, but she had no reason to believe for any outcome different than the way things had been. Week after week. Year after year. Was her course so set? Was she truly so powerless to change it?

She'd changed direction before. Doing so again couldn't hurt any worse than breaking an engagement or alienating her own kin by taking online courses to get a job she loved. She didn't like to think she was as hard-headed as Albert and *Mamm* or as insensitive as Sarah. Heaven knew, she tried hard not to be. But something in her life had to change, even if Albert didn't like it.

She pushed up from the comfort of the warm crevice in the rock. Well, there was one thing she wasn't going to be—a sad, mopey, old woman. Sometimes, life could use a little stir.

"You ready, then?" Drew slipped a phone into his pocket and picked up the gallon jug of lemonade. She'd wondered at his silence. Drew was never quiet.

"Don't let Albert catch you texting." She pointed to the phone's hiding spot.

"*Datt* lets me have it, so long as I pay the bill—but only until I join the church."

"I was teasing, Drew."

"Oh, well, you're right, though. Who'd want to listen to one of Albert's lectures by choice?"

By the time they reached the Detweilers' driveway, Rachel was sure Drew had shared every speck of newsworthy information he'd seen or heard—and then some.

"Martin Beller told me he bumped into Noah at the hardware store this afternoon. Says he loaded up Saul's wagon full of tin roofing supplies, paint, and lumber. I reckon Mr. Jackson at the hardware store weren't sure what to make of it. Didn't know if he was waiting on a cowboy or an Amish man." Drew snickered at his own joke.

"Hmm?" Rachel inserted the same syllable every so often. Drew needed very little participation from her to continue. He'd kept the conversation fluid the entire walk without much more than a phrase or two on her part.

"I reckon it's nice of you to take this over to their place. A man's gonna get hungry working like that by himself. You don't suppose we ought to talk to Joel about getting together a group of menfolk to help him, do ya?"

"What does your *datt* say about that idea."

"I didn't ask him. Just now thought of it. Although, I did think something felt strange about Saul's son doing all that work himself. Him not even being Amish anymore. But that don't seem like a reason not to help one of our own."

"Or choose to be salt and light to one who isn't?"

"*Ja*. That, too. What do you think Uncle Albert would say to that? Some folks are pure hard-headed, you know? Like as if helping a body means you agree with them on everything. I'm glad Joel's not like that.

I wouldn't want to join up with a church if the minister was as block-headed as Albert. When Emmie and I . . . I mean, if I ever get married, there's going to have to be an understanding. Because if I ever draw the lot to be a minister, my family won't be thinking they're better than others. Don't you agree, Rachel? I don't think that's how *Gott* meant for us to act to one another. A minister ought to be the humblest around, don't you agree? Sure as shootin', I pray that Albert never draws the short straw. Can you imagine? Makes me *narfisch* to say the vows, the idea a thing like that could happen."

"You've sure done a lot of thinking on the subject." Joining the church for all the young men included a commitment to accept the role of minister were they to ever draw the lot. "Just don't miss the real question, Drew. What matters most is how you will handle the duty and responsibility if *Gott* chooses you."

"*Ja*, I see your point," her nephew acknowledged as they crossed the last few yards of the way.

Rachel stepped up to the back door of the house. "I don't see any light coming from inside." Apparently, she ought to have done a bit more thinking things through herself before showing up with a basket-ful of food near dark. "Here, I'll take the basket and just slip it inside."

"Can I help you?" Noah's voice came from behind them. She and Drew turned at the same time. Noah looked from Drew, to the basket, and then to her. "Hello, Rachel. Come on in."

Drew stepped back so Noah could pass and open the door, which he then held for Rachel to enter. Noah flipped a switch, and the propane-powered lights hummed as they warmed up to brighten the room.

She'd been in Saul's house a half-dozen or more times in recent weeks but not since Noah had arrived. The feeling of the place was different. Her spine didn't shiver at the cold emptiness of it this time. In fact, she didn't feel cold at all. *Nay*, she felt at home, rather than a visitor in a simple dwelling for an old man.

Did Noah do that? Make it feel like home?

Ach! He probably just turned up the heat or lit a fire in the still cool nights, whereas Saul was too thrifty.

"Thank you." Noah drew her attention back to reality and the food she was naturally setting on the counter, as if she were in charge.

What was she doing? She looked around for Drew and wished for his incessant chatter to fill the awkward moment. "Where's Drew?"

"He stayed outside." No long-winded explanation was forthcoming from Noah. "Is that amusing?"

"*Nay*." She tried to erase the smile from her face, but the thing had a mind of its own and remained in place. "He's a talker. I'm just enjoying the momentary break."

Noah reached across her and lifted the lid on the creamed potatoes and whiffed the aroma escaping the container. "I need to *redd up* a bit and check on *Datt* before I eat. Will you wait?"

She thought better of teasing him that she wouldn't run away and gave a nod instead. She wasn't sure exactly what she expected to happen when she announced she was taking a basket to Saul. Her brother was right about her wanting to see Noah, but even she didn't know why. Not exactly. Except that she'd felt so at home in his arms the other night. And with all the quarreling over her, she'd just wanted be held safely there again.

Of course, she knew he wasn't going to do anything of the sort. Still, even as children, simply being with Noah soothed her. That's really all she needed—to talk to him. She'd feel better then.

When a floorboard creaked, she looked down the hallway to see Noah coming back. He was wearing a clean shirt. His hair was wet and slicked back. The stubble on his chin indicated he hadn't shaved for at least a couple days. Not that she knew much about men and shaving. And suddenly, he was close enough to sweep her into the stormy blue of his eyes. Her heart beat an unsteady rhythm, and her knees buckled.

Noah's firm grip enclosed around her elbow as he slid a dining chair behind her. Her backside hit the seat hard so hard, Noah grabbed for the frame behind her shoulders to keep the chair upright. The front thudded back down on the floor. For fear of falling, she gripped her seat with one hand and Noah's upper arm with her other and landed so close—ever so close—to his face.

His eyes burned into hers. She dropped her hold on him, but he didn't move. His Adam's apple dipped. The hair he'd combed back fell back in its usual wave across his forehead.

"I'd never have left you, Rachel, if only Joel had met Lydia sooner."

Really? And if he didn't loosen his gaze, she might stop breathing.

As though he read her mind, he drew back a short couple of inches. "Why didn't you marry him, Rachel? I need to know."

She couldn't hide the truth from Noah. And if he still wanted her the way his whole being was telling her at this moment, then no pity from the bishop was going to save her this time. Unless Noah would come back—all the way back to the Amish again.

She was in trouble. So much trouble.

Noah had been desperate for answers before in his life—when he was younger mostly and most often before he'd put his trust in Christ. Rachel's response to his question shouldn't hold so much power over him. He hadn't been fair to ask her. She owed him no explanation. Yet, now that he'd spoken, he couldn't take the words back.

She was pale, and her bottom lip trembled.

"I'm an oaf. You don't have to answer." He pulled out the chair beside her and sat at a respectable distance, where she'd set a plate and fork for him. "Aren't you going to eat with me? You brought enough food for four or five people." His attempt to lighten the mood stopped her trembling at least. "I'll get you a plate. And your nephew, too."

"*Nay*. We've eaten." She reached out a hand to stop him, then pulled back before touching him. Smart woman.

He loaded his plate to satisfy her. Maybe if he started to eat, she'd stay. But she pushed back her chair. "Don't go yet. Please. I'm tired of eating alone."

"I just thought you might like some lemonade." She raised a brow at him. "Well, would you?"

"That's nice, Raye, but you don't have to serve me. I just appreciate the company. Sit a spell and rest." He shoved a forkload of potatoes in his mouth and wiggled an eyebrow.

He was flirting with her. He almost choked, and she thumped him on the back.

"I'll get that lemonade, Cowboy." Her voice was normal again. The take-charge-of-the-situation girl he'd once known now filled a grown woman's body.

He nodded and looked away before he choked again.

The screen door creaked behind them, and Rachel turned around. "You may as well go on back, Drew. Take the lantern and don't walk on the road. Tell your *datt* not to worry. Noah will bring me home as soon as he finishes eating."

"You're going to get me in trouble, *Aenti*." The teen held the door open, so a draft eased across the floor.

Noah could still imagine what Saul would say. *In or out, Boy; I'm not lighting a fire to warm all of creation.*

"And I'll tell Reuben I'm a grown woman. He should be thankful to have a son who minds his elders. Now, hurry up; tomorrow's the Lord's Day, and your *mamm* will want to be getting home and the *kinner* to bed."

When he heard the storm door shut firmly after the rusty hinge of the screen door behind Drew, Noah turned around to see Rachel pouring his lemonade. "That boy is almost a man, you know."

"He's seventeen." She put out the drink for him to take and perched her other hand in the curve of her hip.

He couldn't help but grin at the sight of her like that. She sighed and sat down again with her hands folded together on the table in front of her. After a minute, she looked up at him, misty-eyed. "I see what you mean."

Were they both remembering himself at seventeen? He set his fork aside and leaned over his plate so that her full attention was on him. "An Amish boy has a world of life choices on his shoulders at that age. Other kids can still enjoy the freedom of being almost grown while their parents handle all the responsibility. They've got time to figure out the course they want to take, maybe after high school or halfway through college. Later than that, even, they still have choices. But Drew will likely be married by then, vowed for life to both a wife and a faith."

"I know." Of course, she did. "I didn't exactly . . . back then, but I do now." The sincerity of her words squeezed at his heart. "And with

Drew, it's hard to believe he's so grown already. You're right; he needs respect. I wasn't aiming to shame him."

"You didn't shame him, Raye. Just got a little sassy is all. Some men like that, you know."

"*Nay*, they do not."

He could offer himself as evidence she was wrong, but he let it go. She'd reached for her picnic basket and was rummaging around the bottom of it, so he tucked in to the rest of his supper.

"Do you want milk with your cake?" she asked, and he realized she'd been very quiet while he finished eating.

He pushed back from the table. "Yeah, that sounds great." Stedman and everyone else he knew poked fun at his habit of pouring cold milk over his cake into the bottom of a bowl. "Want some? This is a huge hunk of cake you brought. Saul won't eat any."

She hesitated.

"You didn't have any yet, did you?" She shook her head. "You're not on a diet, are you? 'Cause it's been a long time since I enjoyed chocolate cake and milk with someone who wasn't laughing at me."

"Why would I laugh at you?"

"Because most people think cake and ice cream go together, not cake and milk."

"Makes no never-mind to me. Eat it the way you like, I say."

No need to tell him twice. He lobbed off two pieces into bowls and poured cold, cream-heavy milk over them. Rachel's spoon clinked against the edge of her bowl as he scooched it across the table to rest beside a red, leather-bound journal. Was that what she'd dug out of the basket? He nodded at the vaguely familiar red leather. "What's that?"

"The answer to your question."

Come again? The cake held more appeal than the mystery. He shoved a bite in his mouth from where he stood, then leaned over her shoulder to read the writing etched into the cover.

Recollection dawned. He knew exactly what was in this book. "Where'd you get that?"

"Saul." She snatched the journal off the table, as if sensing his desire to destroy it. "He gave it to me just before Joel and I came to the island to look for a farm. Just before we were supposed to get married."

The answer to his question, eh? Sure, as shootin'. And now he had so many more.

"I could insist you give it back, you know."

"I don't think so. More than half of it was written to me, so I have a fair claim."

"Shall we use Solomon's sword and slice it in half, then?"

She pulled it to her chest and crossed both arms over it. "*Nay!* And I won't offer it up either." Her eyes twinkled with mischief.

But for her smile, he'd tell her she ruined his dessert by resurrecting those old memories. In truth, Rachel hadn't ruined anything. He'd done that. And being with her again, he'd do almost anything for a second chance to get it right. Anything other than go back to being Amish. It was the one thing he couldn't do. And without asking, he knew she'd never settle for less.

"Raye, I better get you back home." The kitchen was a mess. She'd want to fix it, but he'd do it later. The longer she hung around making the place feel like a home where they belonged—together—the harder the inevitable would be.

"I only hoped . . ." Her voice drifted. She must realize his point then. Right?

"It's better this way, for both of us. I'll clean up after I take you back. And you can keep the journal. I don't have any use for it." He hadn't intended to sound so cold and heartless. He did, though, even to himself.

What would he do if she cried? Comfort her. Hold her. Lose himself and all his resolve. He hazarded a sheepish glance her way.

Far from a tearful, broken spirit, she sat cross-legged and straight-backed, flipping through the pages of his journal. *His* journal, as if it were loaded with ammunition and ready to fire. And he had it coming to him.

"Raye . . . "

She held up a finger to silence him. "There's one in here about cowards. I'll find it, just a minute."

Ouch.

"I don't see it right now." She shut the book and placed it in the basket, which she then slipped over her arm. "Ready?" She stood.

He hadn't intended to end the visit so abruptly but grabbed his hat and rental keys, then flipped off the gas lights. Once more, he felt like he was eating her pretty, little dust as she shut the back door of the car before he got there. So, he was merely the taxi driver now.

He climbed into the driver's seat, buckled up, and adjusted the rearview mirror to see her. "This isn't what I meant."

"Isn't it?"

"Raye, you know it's not. Please come up front. This is Saul's doing, not mine. I didn't like his meddling any more than you."

She held onto the latch of her unhooked seatbelt like a lifeline. He knew she didn't really want to sit back there.

"Fine." She got out. Noah pushed the passenger side door open for her. She plopped down and buckled up next to him. "You could have stayed in Alberta on your ranch. You didn't. You could have stayed here. You didn't. You still have choices every day because you never committed to anyone. Drew might only be seventeen, but when he decides he loves Emma and wants to marry her, he'll stick to it. And if he decides to join the church, he'll stay. And Emma won't be wondering 'what if' for the rest of her life. And neither will Drew. They'll forge ahead making a life. I tried to do that. Without you. Without Joel. And I was doing fine. And I will do fine again. I vowed to the Amish church, but I won't pretend I expected to end up alone. All I ever wanted was someone who would love me the way you *did*. Except for now. Right now, you just make me foot-stomping angry. And I want to go home."

"I'm sorry, Raye."

"Do not, Noah. Do not say—that."

The engine filled the silence between them. What else could he say? And then he remembered the last words he'd written in his journal.

I'm sorry, Raye.

CHAPTER TEN

Every other Sunday was visiting Sunday for the members of the New Hope district. On those mornings, Rachel enjoyed the quietness of the sunrise and relished the slower pace of a day of rest. She'd gathered the eggs for breakfast a smidge early and taken her usual moment to reflect from the front porch swing while God adorned the sky with color. On any other off-Sunday, the habit relaxed her. But not this morning. Instead, a troublesome feeling persisted at the back of her thoughts. She was going to be alone forever.

She tried to tell herself to snap out of this funk. Believing such a lie was utter nonsense and self-pity. She knew so because she had family, friends, and a job she loved. Still, she couldn't shake the sadness—or maybe it was grief—suffocating her heart.

She had to let Noah—the idea of him—go. It hurt. Like cleaning out an infected wound. It would heal, then, right? That's what was supposed to happen. She'd cleansed and dressed many a sore, even deep surgical openings, and cautioned many a caregiver of the necessity for patience, time, and gentleness.

Today, she needed gentleness. *Mamm's* worries and Sarah's bluntness would sting like vinegar, and she couldn't take it. Not today.

What she needed was the compassion of a friend like Lydia. As soon as breakfast was finished and she'd read the weekly Bible reading with *Mamm*, Rachel could go visit the Yoders. Besides, she'd been awful neglectful of Lydia this past week, considering the news a baby was on the way.

There'd be no avoiding Joel, though. She'd taken a wide berth around him since his ominous declaration of needing to talk to her. Joel was never unkind. Surely, he'd offer some understanding, and now, she could assure him he had no reason to worry about her and Noah.

After breakfast and prayers with her *mamm*, she decided to walk to the Yoders. Of course, Drew had washed their buggy the day before for visiting—a kindness he paid his *gammi* every Saturday. But Rachel preferred to walk the short distance on such a cloudless day.

It was Joel whose path she crossed first on the walk to his farm. His best felt hat caught her attention as he strode over the crest of the hill, then his dark jacket, crisp, white shirt, and black Sunday pants. He dressed no differently than any other Amish man, but she knew his face and his stride from a distance. She'd known him all her life, after all.

"Hello, Rachel." He greeted her where they met and stopped a few feet from one another. "I was coming to see you."

Alone? For sure, he appeared every inch the minister before her now. "Not exactly a friendly visit, I take it."

His brow creased, and he glanced away toward the other side of the road as he cleared his throat.

"Joel, we are friends. What is the trouble? You can tell me."

"I didn't plan to talk about such personal things out here on the road." He looked back at her. "Although, it doesn't make much difference where we speak; this will be awkward and maybe not even proper. Would you like me to get Lydia? She thinks we can have this discussion without her, that you need the freedom to speak your mind, but . . . "

"You'd rather have her present."

"*Ja.*" His shoulders relaxed as did the forced sternness of his jaw. "But would you?"

She could talk about anything with Lydia, much easier than Joel. Of all the people in the world, she'd come closest to sharing about Noah with Lydia. "The thing is, Joel, maybe it's long past time we were honest with each other about what happened. And Lydia wasn't here for all of that."

"But she is here now. And we cannot change what is past. It is what we are going to do now that is important. My concern is for the future, Rachel. Your future."

So, they were going to continue to plow ahead and never address the cause of anything. "I appreciate the wisdom in that, Joel. I truly do. But don't you think sometimes we have to learn from the past, at the very least?"

"I don't know if we're talking about the same thing here."

"Exactly. You've never heard my side of . . . of anything. And the longer that goes on, the less and less we will understand one another."

His jaw tightened. Clearly, whatever he had to say, he'd expected it to be dutiful, succinct, and done. She didn't relish making his task difficult.

"Are you sorry you drew the lot, Joel?"

"Sometimes, I am."

"Like right now?"

He looked away. A shadow fell between them as the sun passed behind a cloud. With a deep breath, he looked up to the sky, then back to her. "I'm not so much sorry as I am fearful, Rachel. I'm afraid this is only the beginning of the trouble about to come between us."

He spoke the plainest of his inner thoughts as he'd ever done and stunned her. *Nay*, frightened her. In all their lives, nothing had ever happened she couldn't smooth over—not even a broken engagement and his marriage some few weeks later to Lydia.

"Rachel, I have been slow about a great many things in life. But I noticed more than you may think, even before you broke our engagement, as self-centered as I was. And one thing that never escaped my notice was Noah's obsession with you when the two of you were but children and youths. I didn't like it. Reuben was newly married, and Albert was too . . . too . . . ."

"Thoughtless," she supplied.

"I'm not the judge of his motivations, but he wasn't paying attention, so I took it on myself to protect you as a big brother ought to do. I'm not proud of the fact, but I was relieved when Noah ran away. Relieved, Rachel, that you wouldn't end up with a man like Saul. Now, he's back, and I can't figure any reason more than that he still wants you."

"He came for Saul. And even if you were right, it doesn't matter. Noah will leave just like before." Her voice sounded snippy. She'd wanted him to talk to her about the past, but his revelations were not making her feel better.

Joel shook his head. "I'm not a blind man. Your feelings run deep, too. After all this time, you and he fell right in step together to find Samy. And you know, I am thankful. The problem is that I can't protect you this time, Rachel—not if you choose him over the church. No matter how much I want to, I can't stop four hundred years of tradition for you."

Joel was right—the side of the road was not a great spot for this conversation. She felt exposed to the world with her innermost feelings and fears spewing out of Joel's mouth. First Belinda, now Joel. Was she truly so transparent all the way down to her soul?

"How long have you known . . . known he was the reason?"

"Not until I saw you together in Herschel's barn. I knew you were upset when Noah left, but I didn't realize . . . Well, I might have gone on forever without any idea as to what drove you to break our engagement. After all, things worked out for the best, it seemed, for us both. But it only worked out best for me, didn't it? You still don't have what you want. And I'm sorry to have been so clueless; that's the word Lydia used." He lifted his hat a few inches off his head and repositioned it, then glanced up to the clouds quickly overtaking the beautiful morning. "*Datt* Nafziger and I . . . Well, we figured your work was making you happy. If it gave you fulfillment, we could let the extra bit of education slide. Lydia says we're wrong to believe that's all you wanted."

She suddenly didn't like Joel much in this moment of revelation. And even though his apology did help, he probed like a surgeon into the recesses of her wounded heart. Joel, whom she'd always admired and trusted and loved more than either of her brothers, was once again being a true friend to speak the truth. But it hurt. She wrapped her arms tightly around her waist.

"Rachel." A light touch nudged her elbow—only enough to jar her attention back to Joel's face. Her gaze had wandered with the painful memories. "Are you yet so unhappy?"

The brotherly concern in Joel's voice chipped a crack in her defensiveness—a very small one. Still angry, she shot back with unexpected force. "Who is happy all the time? And Noah is not his father, Joel; you have to at least give him that much credit."

"That's not what I meant. And I regret my judgment of the past. I was wrong about Noah *and* Saul." He looked down at her with an expression she imagined similar to her own when tending a wounded animal. "Remember when Lydia and I were first married? You sensed she didn't feel accepted—that she didn't feel like she belonged here. And you did something about it. She'll love you forever for that, Rachel, and I owe you tremendously. How is it that you knew so quickly, so innately, what a stranger needed?"

"I don't know." *Ach*, but now he was going to make her cry. Why did she ever wish he'd open up?

"You will if you think on it, Rachel. You didn't need to know Lydia because you knew Sarah. All your life, you'd lived with your sister's barbs and prickles. But more than that, you understood there was a big hole in my dearest Lydia's heart that only love could fill. You made *Gott's* love visible to her through your kindness and friendship."

She rubbed at her nose and swiped a threatening tear to hide her emotions. Hopefully, he thought she had an itch.

"Loving Lydia was easy, Joel. Besides, your love was what truly led Lydia to the love of the Father in Heaven. Noah's situation is different, and I don't think any of this matters as much as you fear. He's going to leave again, you know."

"For sure, he promised as much to me yesterday. But will he be alone this time?" The question in his eyes held no judgment, no ultimatum. Only worry.

"Of course," she stammered before the full meaning had time to take hold in her heart.

"I'm not so sure." Joel bowed his head and ground the sole of his foot back and forth in the gravel before looking back up at her. "I don't think you can answer with such certainty yet either. The heart is never easily understood, Rachel, and its power to change the course of a life, for *goot* or bad, is unequaled."

"What of *Gott's* will, then, Joel? We do not control things so much."

"I am praying for *Gott's* will to be done, Rachel. That's all I want for you. I've been slow, but I've finally come to realize that I can't figure

His plan out for you. You have to listen and follow Him for yourself. Some days, that's not so hard. Others come with difficult testing. I think you know this is one of those times."

Did she? After last night, she hadn't felt she had any choice to make, as if it was all predetermined. Joel could not have any idea how he was tempting her to change course, to consider the unthinkable. And she had no assurance Noah would even want her to go with him.

She couldn't bear the conversation any longer. "I think I need to go."

"You may still come to visit with Lydia and the children." He gestured in the direction she'd been headed in the first place and waited, as though for her to pass him.

"*Danki*, Joel, but I need to be alone right now."

He nodded and stepped away, then paused before turning toward his home. "This time, the choice is yours to make between you and *Gott*. Don't allow others to decide for you. You will only have peace if you are confident you have followed *Gott* in this. His love will not fail you, Rachel, even if others do."

Rather than heading home herself or in the direction of the pond with its reminder of finding Samy and resting in Noah's embrace, she headed the opposite way toward the schoolhouse. The Beller farm was only a mile down the road. She'd visit with Belinda and have time to clear her head on the way.

Joel's fears were unfounded. Weren't they? She'd never leave. She wasn't a quitter. He may think so because she'd broken their engagement. But he was wrong. What she'd done was the opposite of quitting. She'd been fighting for what she knew was right for her—for them both.

The wind shifted, bringing the scent of a coming storm. She picked up her pace to reach the shelter of the schoolhouse.

Moments after she huddled under the school's small, covered porch, the heavens opened with a drenching rain. The wind left her damp and chilled, but the force of the downpour decreased in only a few minutes.

She leaned over the railing to check the sky. Island squalls often passed quickly. Sure enough, blue sky was already breaking through the clouds. She'd be able to walk the rest of the way to the Bellers' soon.

Belinda had mentioned they'd all failed Noah and Saul to a degree. Maybe *Gott* was giving them all a second chance. If love was powerful enough to make her leave, as Joel proposed, why not bring Noah back to stay?

The hope wasn't entirely new. Hadn't she hoped in vain Noah would return for years? But he was different now. He had a new life—one she very much doubted he'd consider leaving.

Either way, one of them stood to lose almost everything. She just couldn't figure how love was going to win for her and Noah. Too much had changed, while too much stayed the same.

As the Bellers' farmhouse came into view, so did Reuben's horse attached to his buggy and tied to a post. Of course, Reuben stood a good chance of showing up here on a visiting Sunday. He and Herschel had been close friends since grade school.

A visit with Laura, as well as Belinda, suited her fine. So long as they didn't get too curious about her visit to the Detweiler home last night. Reuben hadn't appeared pleased with how late she'd returned home. Laura, bless her, had shooed him out the door, so the children could get to bed. No one else had waited for her—another blessing.

She walked around to the kitchen entrance at the far side of the house, rather than the front door where the men would surely be talking in the living room. But when she popped her head into the kitchen, the room was empty.

"Herschel, now, there's no cause for getting so upset with Reuben. You can't be blaming him." Belinda's voice came softly from the other room.

Stunned because she had never known the two men to be at odds, Rachel forgot to make her presence known. She was as rooted to her spot on the floor as unripe fruit to a tree stem.

"*Nay*, he's right." Reuben sounded bone weary. "Albert has gone too far. I should have talked to him about his issues long before now. Not sure how you expect me to defend Rachel against all this, though. She's a grown woman. Our *datt* spoiled her, *ja*, but she's a kind, faithful sort."

Spoiled? *Datt* had loved her, not spoiled her. About to march right in and say so, she reversed course. This was a private conversation not meant for her ears. And whatever Albert had done . . .

"I think"—Herschel's voice reached her before she reached the door—"What you can do for Rachel is give Saul's son another chance. If enough of us stand up to the gossip, he might stand a chance."

A chance for what exactly? Rachel wanted to know what Herschel meant, but her conscience refused to let her eavesdrop any further. And the last thing she wanted to do was join the discussion. Nor was she in the mood for the long, uphill walk home, but what other choice did she have?

All her choices were limited. And she was sick to death of everyone supposing they knew her heart or her mind. Herschel was right. Noah deserved another chance. And if no one else was willing to let him have one, she most certainly was.

CHAPTER ELEVEN

The hope of receiving Sunday visitors had perked Saul up in the morning. Noah helped him dress and carried him to his reclining chair in the living room. Noah had read from the Psalms and then the passage of Scripture all the church members would be reading in preparation for next Sunday's sermon.

Bishop Nafziger showed up not too much later with Samy right beside him. Being both bishop and Samy's *dawdi*, Noah supposed Joel had relented if Abe Nafziger decided the child should come. However it came to be, Noah was grateful.

The two stayed nigh an hour. The company must have done Saul good. At lunch, he'd actually taken a few sips of the chicken soup Trudy had left for him. But as the early afternoon ticked away, so had his *datt's* strength, until Noah returned him to bed before two o'clock.

"*Datt.*" Noah stood over the bed where his father lay, eyes closed and mouth twisted. "Are you in pain? I can get you some medicine."

"*Nay.*"

He sensed the man trying as hard as he could to forebear the past, so he could pass to the next life with some sense of peace between them. And Noah found it difficult, nigh impossible, to remain angry with a man in such a pitiful state. It was a painful sort of pity aggravated with lingering regrets.

Things needed to be said, but neither had found any words. For now, they only had the motions of a sort of acceptance of one another.

"Sing."

"Me, *Datt?*" Noah couldn't carry a tune, not even an Amish dirge. No one ever requested him to sing.

"Sing up to heaven. A joyful noise."

Those were his mother's words. *Gott doesn't ask for a beautiful voice, only a joyful noise. He judges the heart, mei sohn, not your voice.*

"Noah?"

"I'm here, *Datt.*" He pulled the cushion-less, wooden chair from the corner up to the bedside, then lay his hand on his father's shoulder. "I'll sing for you.

This world is not my home.
I'm just a-passing through
My treasures are laid up
Somewhere beyond the blue.

The angels beckon me
From heaven's open door
And I can't feel at home
In this world anymore.

Oh Lord, you know
I have no friend like you . . . "[1]

Noah couldn't say whether his voice cracked first or his heart, but he couldn't go on.

"Is Jesus your friend, *Datt?*" The powers of pain, bitterness, and anger were no match for the longing within Noah's soul to know his *datt* would spend eternity with God. At the end, nothing else mattered.

---

1 Jim Reeves, "This World is Not My Home," 1924, Public Domain.

With more strength than Noah realized the man had left, his *datt's* hand wrapped around Noah's wrist and squeezed. "Take the cross, Noah. Follow."

The phrasing tugged the most tender places of Noah's heart. The response didn't exactly follow the question, but the meaning behind the words comforted Noah with a sense of assurance, as if to say he and his *datt* were on the same path with their Savior.

Further discussion would have to wait. His father's chest rose and fell in a deep sleep. He appeared at peace as Noah backed slowly out of the room.

The projects Noah had begun during the week now lay still for the day. He'd never outgrown the desire for a day of rest thoroughly ingrained in his Amish childhood. He wasn't one to leave his ox in the ditch; chores had to be done, and some ranch work couldn't be put on hold just because it was Sunday. What work could wait did. He'd do a better job the rest of the week if he took the one day to replenish both body and soul.

Still, he didn't have long to finish the work he'd begun. He could only hope to have the place presentable before a funeral led Amish and Mennonite alike from at least as far as Ontario to say farewell to Saul Detweiler.

"Hello," his sister's voice called from the kitchen.

He met her there, as she lifted a basket onto the counter with one hand while holding baby Isaac in the other arm. "I thought you were taking off today to be with your family." That was their agreement. Trudy's stress throughout the week bothered him, and he'd wanted to help her more.

"I know *Datt* won't eat, but I thought you might be hungry." She set a plate of food on the table. Too bad he had no appetite. "I meant to stay home today, but something inside of me kept nagging me to come. I brought Steve and the kids. They'll be in shortly."

"I understand. You have to do what you feel is right. *Datt's* asleep now, but he'll likely wake soon and be happy to see the children." Probably better not to mention his only visitor had been the bishop.

The door creaked open. Noah marked greasing the hinges on his mental checklist of things to do. Trudy's husband held the screen door open wide as the children filed into the kitchen.

"Noah." Trudy caught his attention. "Go get some fresh air, if you need. I can tell by the way you looked at that plate, you're not hungry. We will stay with *Datt* for a few hours."

Seemed his little sister couldn't stop herself from taking care of everyone else. "Thank you for the food, Trudy. I'll eat it later. Some fresh air does sound good."

He pulled on his boots and hat and headed in the direction of the hayfield. The farm was a little run-down, but the land was green and fertile, ripe with potential, and full of the heritage of generations of labor.

Why did a man long past his prime buy such a spread? Noah couldn't figure his father's motivation. He'd been a horseman—not a farmer, but an outdoorsman who loved his animals more than people. Supposedly, he'd moved to the island to be near Trudy and his grandchildren, but only Trudy ever came to see him. Not that Noah was judging. But he had to wonder whether she was really Saul's reason for coming to the island. Trudy did her duty by him and seemed to hold no ill-will, but that was the extent of the relationship as far as Noah could tell.

The long grass beneath his boots would soon be ready to mow for hay. Again, he wondered who did the job. If the burden lay on Saul, the field was going to go to waste. He came to the fence where his *datt's* property lined up against the Erbs' neatly landscaped yard. With an elbow propped on a wooden fence post, he counted the buggies parked on the side of the drive. Two covered and one open wagon.

Only when he recognized the local vet's dark blue truck did he jump the fence. He wasn't about to study on his reasons too hard, but Noah wasn't leaving town just to surrender to this guy. If Rachel was going to fall for a non-Amish fella, it had better be Noah.

All his best intentions not to cause trouble held him back as well as a twine lasso around the neck of a bronco. Noah didn't know anything about the relationship between Rachel and Tony, but she'd been angry—mighty angry—at Noah last night. Emotions that powerful meant something. And Noah wasn't the coward she took him for.

She answered the door, her eyes opening wide in surprise, and glanced over her shoulder, then quickly pulled the door shut and stepped onto the porch beside him. "We have some company. Tony was just about to leave. And, well, I don't know if this is a good time to invite you inside. *Mamm* is a bit emotional."

"Can I help?"

Her eyes were puffy, and she kept twisting the strings on her prayer *kapp*. She still didn't answer.

"Should I go?"

"*Nay!*" She grabbed his forearm as if he planned to dash away that very second. "Can you wait for me? Not here. Around back, there's an old root cellar. I'll meet you there."

"Of course, Raye."

"*Danki*, Noah. I won't be long." She slipped back into the house with care not to open the door wider than necessary.

He didn't like slinking around back as if he had done something wrong. She'd been so anxious, though, so he'd wanted to appease her. About the time he found the old cellar, the sound of Tony's truck could be heard rumbling down the lane. And then, Rachel appeared out the back door of the house with a shawl wrapped around her shoulders.

"You that worried about me and the vet seeing each other?" He aimed to sound as if he were teasing, although the tone didn't quite hide his suspicion.

"What?" She raised an eyebrow at him. "*Nay,* it's just easier to slip out the back door without being noticed. And I can't take another single question today, Noah, so I snuck out the back door to avoid being interrogated."

Interrogated? A strong word that definitely invited questions. First off, he'd like to know who was making her so miserable.

Her eyes begged for understanding. She looked as tired as his soul was weary. "Tony only needed to give me a key to open up tomorrow. He wouldn't upset me for anything. And now, you're here, right when I couldn't take the rest of them another second. I'm happy to see you. Honest. I just can't talk about it right now."

He held up his hands in surrender. "No questions, then. Promise."

She studied the sky where the sun still promised a few hours of daylight. "Can we go somewhere? Anywhere?"

He'd take her anyplace she wanted if only he could. But for now, he couldn't leave Trudy with Saul for very long. "I haven't been to the beach yet. Would you like that?"

"Very much." The way her sad eyes sparkled with a hint of joy made his heart leap into his throat. Had he given her that glimmer?

Their side-by-side walk through the hayfield with her arm linked through his was easy, gentle, and tickled with a breeze that smelled of pine and salt water. No words were needed. And the knowing he'd lifted her spirits with nothing to offer but himself soothed the burning ache from watching life slowly ebb from his father's body.

The drive to the beach was quiet, except for Rachel's occasional offer of directions. Her hands remained lightly folded in her lap, her posture relaxed against the leather of her bucket seat. Content to watch her in the short glances possible while driving, he left her alone with her thoughts. Every once in a while, her eyes closed for a moment.

"Don't fall asleep on me, Raye."

Her head twisted to face him, and she opened one eye. "I wouldn't dare. I was just asking the Lord to give us time to get to know each other again."

His heart stuttered. "I'd like that. I'd like it a lot."

The deep connection they'd shared growing up had been a strong bond, but a great chasm of both man and womanhood had separated them in the interim years. Could he bridge that gulf to befriend her? Rachel, the woman who knew her mind and set her course with determination despite the obstacles. She was no longer the girl he'd loved so ardently. Who was the woman she'd become? Did he have the courage to find out? If he loved this woman as he had so completely the *maydel* in his youth, his life would never be the same.

Even if he hadn't promised Joel he'd never take Rachel away from her faith, he'd never to do that to her. If she captured his heart again . . .

"In a little way, there's a spot to pull over and a path we can walk to the shore." She pointed to the right side of the road. He slowed down. "Just there. See?"

He eased the rental off the road onto a rutted parking spot worn into the island's red dirt.

"Raye." Her head turned, her fingers remaining stretched out to open the door. "I was wrong." Her hand dropped back to her lap, and her eyes opened wider. "Whatever time God allows for me to spend with you now is too precious to waste." Her lower lip quivered slightly, and her eyes misted. "Raye?"

She sniffed and sucked in a deep breath. "I'm all right. Really." She waved a hand and opened her door. "Let's go for a walk."

He followed her along a footpath off the road. Crossing a grassy knoll, the road soon disappeared behind them as they edged onto the sandy eastern shore. To the south, storm clouds were building into a dark mass, and behind them, the lowering sun warmed his back.

Rachel bent down to remove her shoes and stockings, then turned northward. After pulling off his boots, Noah fell into step beside her.

The tide appeared to be going out to sea, but the wind behind them increased. He removed his cowboy hat before the wind snagged it, and Rachel's hand flew to the back of her head to hold her *kapp*. Her dress whipped around her legs in the wind. A shock of cold washed over their feet, and the unexpected wave rose calf-high, soaking his jeans and her hem.

"Maybe this wasn't my best idea." An apologetic pout turned her mouth in a twist.

Before he had the chance to think better of the idea, Noah scooped Rachel into his arms and returned to the grassy area to set her on dry ground. The astonishment in her large, round eyes met his gaze as he plopped down beside her and leaned back on his hands. He was on the cusp of offering an apology when her sweet laughter caught on the wind, and she fell flat on her back into the grass beside him.

"I'll take whatever moments *Gott* sees fit to give us, Noah; each one is an answer to my prayers."

They lay there—side-by-side, fingers entwined—until the rain came and ended their peace. He stood then and offered her a hand-up. As she stood, the rain washed in droplets down her face. No make-up to mar. No mascara to run. Clear, pure, heaven-sent drops cascading down her forehead, along her straight and slightly up-turned nose to land on her pink lips.

He kissed her. Once. Only long enough to dispel the droplet that teased him there.

But then her brown eyes pulled him back for a longer drink of her until they both gasped for breath. He leaned his forehead against hers, not willing to let go yet. They were soaked through to the skin. He wasn't cold; though, he ought to be. Still, he needed to get her somewhere warm.

"I reckon this changes things."

She shivered but smiled back at him.

Taking her hand, they ran together to his car. Soon enough, the car's heat was warming them. "I can take you home or back to Saul's to dry off first."

"I think I better go home. Or else . . . "

Or else, they may cross lines for which there was no erasing. He'd felt as much but assumed Trudy would be there until he returned. Another reason to get back.

"Raye, I won't run off on you again. I mean, I have to go back to the ranch." At least at some point, and he'd no idea for how long. "But

I won't leave loose ends. I won't disappear. I'll be in your life as long as you want me. I want you to know that." He paused to look her way. He was creeping along the road in the almost-dark with the wipers scraping across the windshield. She was staring at him.

He had to look back to the road but not before he saw a myriad of questions looming in her eyes. "I don't know what God's plan is for us. I can't see the future—our future. I just promise to do my best to follow Christ through this. He's the only One Who knows what is best for us both."

He paused, hoping she'd say something. Anything. Then she began to hum a tune he recognized.

> *"My hope is built on nothing less*
> *than Jesus' blood and righteousness."*[2]

An old hymn—though not as ancient as the seventeenth century hymns from their childhood—but a hymn often sung in Mennonite and other churches. He'd no idea where she'd picked up the song. He sure wasn't about to dispel the quiet understanding or the beauty of their kiss with such an unimportant inquiry now.

> *"On Christ, the solid rock, I stand;*
> *all other ground is sinking sand."*[3]

He'd rather listen, anyhow, allowing the words to flow over his soul.

As she came to the end of the song, Rachel wondered again how to tell Noah about all that had happened that day. First, the heart-rending

---

2 Edward Mote, "Solid Rock," 1834, Public Domain.
3 Ibid.

talk with Joel, and then the conversation at the Bellers no one intended for her to hear.

She was still wrapping her mind around the fact Herschel had defended Noah. Of course, after all the Bellers had been through with Mark, she supposed it wasn't too surprising even Herschel was more inclined right now to give Noah some grace.

The gossips had taken no short time to fill her *mamm's* ears with their rumors, either. And when Rachel arrived home, she'd discovered just what had fired up Herschel. If anyone had ever spoken such about Mattie . . .

The worst was her own mother's questioning as though she might actually believe the lies. It was all too much for one day. Poor Tony walked right into it all. Although from his lack of surprise, she suspected he may have exaggerated the excuse about an early appointment off in Montague in order to check on her.

And then, Noah showed up. She turned her head to watch him driving beside her. And all those worries melted at the sight of him and the lingering tingle on her lips from his kiss. Oh, that kiss.

"What?" He caught her staring, and she didn't care.

"You're a good kisser."

He laughed and took her hand in his. "That makes two of us."

She'd been so relieved when he'd come to her house. And she meant to tell him what folks were saying—just as soon as she'd collected herself—but the right moment never came. And now, when they'd just agreed to a new beginning, did it even matter what a few spiteful tongue-waggers thought of them?

They were almost home. She didn't want to start off with secrets. They'd had enough of those.

"Noah."

"Hmmm?"

"You came at just the right moment today . . . " An Amish buggy caught her attention as they crested the hill beyond the Yoder's farm. "Is that Joel's buggy turning into your *datt's* lane?"

"I wouldn't know one from another, but it is strange that a buggy would be arriving this late and in this storm." If he felt the same foreboding as she did, he kept it to himself.

"Go ahead and follow them. I can wait to go home."

Without questioning, he slowed to turn down the drive, keeping a safe distance between his car and the buggy.

Unsure whether he'd considered the possibility she'd reached with near certainty when both Joel and Bishop Nafziger exited the buggy, she lay a hand on Noah's arm before he opened his door. "Would Trudy request Saul be anointed?"

"Without me?" His eyes widened; then he hung his head. "I guess I shouldn't expect to be included."

"You're here now, Noah. *Gott* brought you back in time. I'm not fit . . . " She pressed a hand to her messy hair. "Or family. But I'll go with you if you want."

"I would like that very much."

She followed him through the rain and up the front porch stairs.

"We'll slip in this way, and you can go *redd up* in the hall bath."

"*Danki*, Noah." She could hear Joel and the bishop in the kitchen as she stole quietly down the hall. Noah blocked her from anyone's view by propping himself in the doorway between the living room and kitchen.

As fast as possible, she removed the pins holding her *kapp* and hair in place, then rapidly towel-dried the long, wet strands. Memories of her own *datt's* final days came to mind. Bishop Nafziger had come to him also, to anoint him with oil and pray—not to save his soul but to ease his passing from one world into the next. He had gone in peace only a few hours later. Of course, she'd known many folks who lived days and weeks after the family called for last rites. Was Saul's time close? Only *Gott* knew, of course.

The medicine cabinet contained a comb, which looked clean, practically new. Comb in hand, she attacked the tangled web of black strands from bottom to top, gritting her teeth with each hasty tug. As soon as her thick hair was manageable enough to twist into a bun, she swirled it around at the back of her head and replaced the prayer covering, then straightened her apron. Peeking around the bathroom door, she saw Noah waiting for her.

They entered Saul's room together. Trudy, her husband, and all the children were gathered around the bed. Solemn. Silent.

The warmth of Noah's hand pressed into the small of her back, drawing her closer to the foot of the bed to stand beside him. His hand dropped then, and he stood with both his hands together behind his own back.

She looked up to see Joel watching, but he showed no emotion aside from reverence for the moment. Bishop Nafziger entered the room last and made his way to the right side of the bed. With great tenderness, he raised Saul's head and propped another pillow under him.

"Saul, you know why we have come at the request of your daughter and permission of your son?"

Saul nodded in understanding.

"And you wish for this blessing."

"I do."

After reading the twenty-third Psalm of David, the bishop lay a hand on Saul's shoulder and asked, "And have you any last words to make peace with those from whom you are to be separated until the Lord sees fit to bring you together again in His presence?"

Saul opened his eyes and looked at Trudy first, then settled on his son.

"Forgive me. Go with *Gott*."

Trudy stifled a sob.

Noah reached for his father's hand. "I forgive you, *Datt*."

Saul closed his eyes, and an agonizing silence followed before the bishop continued, "Saul Detweiler, in so much as you have received the forgiveness of the Father *Gott* in Heaven upon the confession of your sins and faith in the blood-bought redemption of His Son in your place, you may leave this world in the peaceful assurance that His angels will guide your soul to His presence forevermore."

The bishop tipped a small bottle into a clean cloth and pressed the oiled linen onto Saul's forehead, then bowed his head in prayer.

CHAPTER TWELVE

The distant drone of an ambulance stirred Rachel from her sleep. Her pillow failed to drown out the noise, which grew louder and closer by the second. The clock registered twenty past five, later than her usual wake-up time, and her bladder was protesting louder than the nearing emergency vehicle outside her window.

The siren quit before passing the house. She stumbled down the hall to look through a window facing the hilltop but couldn't see through the fog. A second emergency siren roared by the house from the opposite direction and soon went silent as well, right about time to reach the Detweiler farm.

Saul.

She'd never dressed so fast in all her life. She grabbed her shoes and stockings and ran barefooted across the hayfield. Halfway there, the hem of her dress, wet from the morning dew, tangled around her legs. She couldn't slow down. If the paramedics left with Saul before she got there, she'd never get a ride to the hospital this time of morning.

Her feet hit the gravel drive, making her feet ache, but she reached the door while the emergency personnel were all still inside. Panting, she dropped to the steps to brush off her feet and put on her socks and shoes.

Behind her, the screen door squeaked. She jumped and quickly moved to the side of the steps in case they were bringing Saul out on a gurney. When she raised her head, there were no paramedics coming through the door. Noah stood alone in the doorway. He stepped forward and let the door go with a light bang as his hand dropped to his side, and he stared ahead unseeing.

Her heart plummeted to her stomach at the sight of his agony. Was Saul gone already? A chill ran up her spine.

Noah had begun to descend the stairs when he saw her. His eyes were glassy with despair, then wide with shock. Or something else?

In a long stride, he was right in front of her. His eyes searched her face for a brief second before the warmth of his touch rested on her shoulder, drawing her closer to him. Only then, she noticed his hand in her hair—ever so gentle—his touch tickling all the way to her scalp.

Her hair! She'd run without donning her prayer *kapp*—a ritual she'd followed for so long, she needn't even think about it. But in those frantic minutes as she'd dressed, she hadn't considered anything other than reaching Noah.

The panic rising within her was undone by the comfort which settled on Noah's face. He ran his fingers through the long strands and brushed them behind her ear to fall behind her shoulders.

"*Datt* is with Jesus."

She nodded; then he buried his head in her neck and wept.

The late afternoon sun shone straight through the giant picture window of the living room, where Noah finally took a seat for the first time the whole day. If there were any dust in this house, it was still waiting for a chance to settle.

Joel had come right away and remained still with Bishop Nafziger dressing Saul's body in the white grave clothes Trudy had sewn for him. Joel, the minister, made the day easier, Noah had to admit. He'd taken care of arrangements for the undertaker to embalm the body and return it to the home for visitation and viewing, which would last for the next two days. Joel assigned three couples from the church to oversee all the work to be done throughout the days of visitation and organized a rotation of men to dig the grave, only asking for Noah's permission on the location at the edge of the farm bordering the Erbs'.

Rachel had only left long enough to make herself presentable, as she put it. The memory of those thick, dark waves cascading across her shoulders and the silky feel of them through his fingers had been a refuge for his thoughts in many a difficult moment this day. He should marry her. He wanted to marry her. He needed to marry her—this very minute if he could. He couldn't bear this night alone.

"Do you want me to stay?" Trudy's voice sliced through his thoughts as she plopped on the sofa. Her weariness made evident the day had taken its toll on his sister as well. Would he be selfish to answer yes?

"I don't look forward to being alone, but you look like you could use a good rest. Tomorrow will be a long day. I'll be all right."

"Can I stay?" The young voice wasn't directed toward him, so he turned and saw Samy looking up at Joel for a response.

Joel looked from his daughter to Noah. "I'll spend the night here, if you wish."

The offer stunned him, but all he saw in his sister's reaction was relief, so he accepted.

"Please, can I stay, too? I can do Saul's chores." Samy tugged her father's attention back to her.

Joel didn't answer but looked to Noah.

He wasn't going to be the one to deny her. Her tender plea touched recesses of his heart he'd not known existed. "She's more than welcome here. *Datt* loved her." And Noah was learning why.

Joel nodded his assent to Samy. Behind them, Noah glimpsed Rachel watching. She stood in the entrance between the living room and kitchen holding a dishtowel over her heart and wiping a tear from her cheek with the other hand.

"*Kumm*," Joel called to him, forcing his attention away from Rachel. "I must go home and tend to things but will be back. I'd like to speak to you outside before I go."

Samy remained in the house with Rachel and Trudy, as Joel and Noah made their way outdoors. Funeral arrangements needed to be discussed and likely a host of various and sundry other details; but alone with Joel in the driveway, the man broached a different subject. Not to Noah's surprise, really.

"So, you never married. Any reason why?"

Noah had been asked the question a hundred, if not a thousand, times before. The standard reply that he'd never met the right woman was almost true. And the man before him knew exactly the reason it was not the full truth. Noah had known the right woman all along—all his life.

"I spent several years alone on the prairie, herding cattle—just me, my horse, and a dog. When the Lord pulled me back into civilization, folks tried to set me up. Never took."

Joel's mouth had turned up in a half-grin. His eyes sparked with a hint of laughter. "The Lord pulled you back, you say. He does have a way of setting our paths straight."

"Can't say I knew He was the One doing the ironing out of my ways. Not at the time. But looking back, I see His hand all over the circumstances, which led me to Stedman and the Second Chance Ranch. The Lord was finishing the work He began in my life as a child. He kept after me until the day I finally turned my heart over to Him, once and for all."

Suddenly, Noah understood the path that led him home—led him straight back to Rachel. "I promised to follow Him wherever He leads me."

Joel's jovial expression had turned serious. "And you believed yourself to be following His guidance when you came here?"

"It was a step of faith to come." And faith was slowly turning to sight.

"So, those other women didn't take." Joel emphasized Noah's earlier words. "Any idea why not?"

Women sounded a little too plural for just three. The first two he hadn't gotten to know beyond a first date. The last one became a good friend, although he'd suspected she wished for more. "There was only one I considered. I couldn't be the man she needed. I didn't belong in her world."

"And which world do you expect Rachel to fit?"

The question stunned him. "I don't . . . " What? He hadn't even gotten to that question himself yet. How was Joel so far ahead already?

Joel raised a hand, as if to let the question pass. "You need not answer me, Noah. I have interfered too much in both of your lives in the past. And I am sorry for it. Only you must consider the question for yourself. For her. You cannot claim ignorance of what you would be asking of her were she to join you in your life outside the church. Your assurance to me that you would be leaving soon isn't much comfort anymore. What happens to Rachel then? As her friend and as a shepherd under the Lord, I am only asking you to use caution."

Shunning. Some would consider the excommunication akin to a life sentence if she married outside the faith, for there was no turning back from marriage.

"The *Meidung*, you mean. She'd be starting all over with no one but me . . . and God. He's enough, you know. But I've no intention to force her away from the support and the bonds of church and family she's always known."

If Joel felt any relief, Noah was hard-pressed to see it, and he didn't understand Joel's meaning about interfering in the past.

"I can't say as I really know what you meant about having done too much already."

"I had a lot of influence over Rachel growing up. She was—still is—like a little sister to me, so I felt the need to protect her." Joel paused as the uncomfortable truth settled between them—Joel had believed Noah wasn't good enough for her. "I did so by making sure there was a healthy distance between the two of you when you both got up to courting age. I regret playing *Gott* when I had no right." Joel looked away and hesitated before adding, "Maybe we wouldn't all be here in this predicament if I'd not been so quick to judge."

The way Noah remembered things, Rachel had been infatuated with Joel during their school days. Joel was older, taller, more handsome—all the things pre-teen girls dreamed about. Saul used to needle Noah that Rachel was only his friend because she cared about injured, helpless things. And while Noah had done his best not to show his jealousy over her crush on Joel, he couldn't say he was always successful.

But as they got older, things started to change. He'd had a real chance of winning Rachel's heart. And he blew it.

"I may have been jealous, and I reckon I was resentful. I'd say I'm one who owes you the apology, in this case. I sure don't hold anything against you now. I can even say with confidence you were right to be protective of Rachel."

"All is forgiven and forgotten, then, as best we can. Although I'm thinking, it's best to remember enough, so as not to make the same mistakes again. When *Gott* sees fit to give us a second chance at relationships, we ought to take heed to not make the same mistakes over again."

A memory flashed. He'd pushed it away through the years, only to recall in moments when he needed reminding of why he'd left.

Before Noah ran off, he'd figured on toughing life out with his *datt* for a couple more years, then marrying and moving into a home of his own. He'd only have to be around his *datt* to work with the horses. In fact, they'd been in a position to make enough money to support two households more than comfortably. But on that particular night—his seventeenth birthday—he'd seen clearly that he had no future in the place he'd been born.

"Fact is, Joel, you did us both a favor. I wasn't good for her. Maybe we were meant for each other, but I had to get right with God first."

The lines furrowed across Joel's brow lessened. He placed a firm hand on Noah's shoulder. "I am relieved to know you have made peace with *Gott*. My regret is that you felt forced to walk that road alone. The community ought to have been there to help you with the burdens you carried. *I* should have helped you."

Joel's heartfelt sincerity penetrated to long-forgotten broken places, like a bone being set to fuse back together as a whole. "I don't hold you at fault. Still, it means a great deal to me for you to say so."

He'd been alone most all of his life but not with a dead man lying in another room awaiting burial. The house would be cold—the way Saul liked it.

Noah shivered. "I know this—all the pitching in to take care of every detail—is simply the way things are done to you, but I appreciate it all more than I can say."

"We've both learned some lessons the hard way, *ja*? I pray mine make me more fit to serve as a shepherd of the Lord's flock here at New Hope. And may His ways in your life make you the man *Gott* has called you to be, as well."

Without forethought, Noah found himself responding with an outstretched hand. Joel accepted with a firm handshake, then headed to his home to care for his own animals and family before returning so Noah needn't spend the night alone.

Whatever Noah had expected when he'd left Alberta to come here, making peace with the Amish wasn't part of it. He'd no notion of a perfect reconciliation with his father—only the chance to apologize for his part of the rift. A gracious and good God had granted him that much, plus some.

Take up the cross. Go with Gott. Saul's parting phrases meant something. His *datt* expected more from Noah than to simply make peace with his past. Noah felt as if Saul planned a puzzle and set-up the pieces for Noah to put together. And Rachel was in the final picture his father had in mind. No doubt about it. For once in a long, long time, he and Saul saw eye-to-eye on something. If only there'd been more time. If only so many years hadn't been wasted. Like Joel said, all Noah could do was go forward now and try to avoid the mistakes he'd made in the past.

He entered the barn, where someone had already done all his chores. Although his hands longed for something to do, he knew the work was done for him in kindness. He climbed the ladder to the loft and looked around the area where he'd slept and been awakened by Samy his first morning at his *datt's* house.

Throwing the loft shutters wide open, he viewed the expanse of the farm. Three men walking away from the house in a straight line. Each wore a blue shirt with black pants held by suspenders and carried a shovel slung over his shoulder. They crossed the hayfield and disappeared from sight on their way to the edge of the farm, where they'd dig the first grave for a member of the New Hope Amish church district.

Noah figured this funeral was uncomfortable for some, since neither of Saul's close kin belonged to the church. Neither he nor Trudy ever joined the church and weren't under the *Meidung,* so their help wasn't forbidden; only, the interactions were strained at times. Noah knew much was being done out of commitment to Saul, who was a member of their district. But he'd been aware as folks came and went through the day that their concern genuinely overflowed to Noah and Trudy. A sense of pride to have come from these people rushed through his veins. Something he hadn't felt in a long time.

Before descending the ladder to return to the house, Noah closed the upper window and found a nail to hold his cowboy hat. In three days, when the funeral was over and the church folk were no longer doing his chores, he'd come get the hat. For now, he could blend in a little more to make things easier for those whose kindness was ministering all the way down to fissures left thirteen years ago on his young soul.

The rental car keys met his fingers as he jammed them into his pocket. He may as well move the vehicle out of sight for the coming days as well and park it behind the barn—out of sight. *Datt* would've appreciated the gesture of respect to the visitors who'd be arriving to say their goodbyes.

Walking from the barn back to the house, the sensation of being watched drew his eyes up to the kitchen window, where Rachel's face and shoulders were framed pretty as a picture. Her hand came into view with a quick wave, and a smile spread across her face.

He waved back in a motion to join him outside and watched as she faded from view. He couldn't fathom how he'd lived without her for so long. And whatever it took, he didn't plan to do so again.

CHAPTER THIRTEEN

From where Rachel stood washing dishes, she had a clear view of Noah at the hayloft door. Minutes later, he emerged from the barn without his cowboy hat and drove his car out of sight. The kindness and respect behind the gesture made her heart swell.

Noah was a *goot* man, humble and considerate. Why must he be off-limits to her? If her desires had ever been pulled so forcefully against the ways of the church, Rachel couldn't recall it. Maybe if Noah had asked her to leave with him on the eve of her baptism, she'd have known a similar tug-of-war between church and self. Only, he hadn't. Nor was he doing so now.

She'd asked how soon he'd leave after the funeral. He didn't know, he said. What was she thinking to allow love to awaken when there was no way to satisfy it? Yet all it took was a wave to draw her out the door and to his side.

She hesitated when he held out a hand for her to take, all too aware Reuben and Laura might soon come outside ready to leave until morning. They would be helping, along with David and Kathryn Detweiler, Noah's distant cousins, and Menno and Linda Wagler. Even Albert was somewhere nearby, having come to help dig Saul's grave.

"May I take you home?" Noah asked.

About to respond that Reuben and Laura would soon be ready to go and she could ride with them, she noticed Saul's horse hitched behind him.

A courting buggy. Could it really be the same buggy he'd purchased on his sixteenth birthday?

"*Datt* kept it all these years." Noah sounded a little sheepish. "Of course, it required some repairs last week to make it roadworthy and sellable." The mention of a sale was like a twist on the dagger of his forthcoming departure. He stepped closer, studying her reaction. "I don't know what I'm going to do, Raye but right now, I'd like to take you home. You've worked hard all day. It's the least I can do."

The buggy held a fountain of memories. Their first kiss, chaste enough to feel unfinished—until the beach. Laughter, loads of laughter. Long conversations of their hopes and dreams. Revisiting those old days didn't seem wise at the moment, not when the talk of the two of them was already scandalous. Indecision held her at bay.

A dark shadow crossed Noah's features before he turned his head to the side, and his shoulders slumped. He needed her now on this most awful day. He had no one here. And now she'd made him wonder if he even had her.

His face turned slowly to meet her watchful, silent plea for understanding. She hadn't meant to be hurtful. He reached for her hand in the barest hold by the tips of their fingers.

"Raye, I don't want to make it harder for you." The blue of his eyes dulled. "It's too late with *Datt*, but maybe the Lord still has a plan for us. I was a coward before. I don't want to be one this time."

"You're turning my argument upside down on me."

"Is it working?"

"*Ja*." She walked toward the buggy, then looked over her shoulder at him. "But only because I'm too tired to argue."

When she heard his faint chuckle behind her, her own escaped, along with a smile. How did he manage to sink her resolve so easily? Because he needed her, simple as that.

She climbed into the buggy and sighed with the relief for her achy feet.

Noah climbed in the other side. "Raye, why don't you rest those fears tumbling around in your head, too? Just let it be for a few days. Let God speak to our hearts through prayer and Bible-reading without jumping ahead of Him in the planning out of our lives."

"Give Him the reins, you mean."

"Exactly."

The short ride home was long enough to rock her almost asleep with the sway of the buggy and the rhythm of the horse's trot against the pavement. The day had been long—so long, she was half convinced two had gone by since her early morning dash through the hayfield after the ambulance woke her.

Drifting into a dream-like state, the last time she'd seen Noah became more life-like than the new island home surrounding them now. Still, the details were fuzzy with things she'd never been able to decipher.

"What happened that night, Noah? I've never understood—not fully understood. Why did you leave?"

For the second time of the evening, the memories of Noah's seventeenth birthday resurfaced.

"I didn't know God then." He knew she deserved more of an answer. His mind drifted back to find the explanation she needed.

Drill after drill with the bishop, he'd learned all about God, faith, his heritage, the Amish confession, the Bible, and even salvation. But on that eve of their baptismal vows, Noah's faith ebbed low. He'd tried. Hard. Even for Rachel, he couldn't pretend a belief in God he didn't possess.

"At the time, I had no idea how much of my decision-making boiled down to that fact—my lack of trust in God. You know how hindsight is?"

She looked at him. Patient, silently pleading for more.

Perhaps it was wrong to speak ill of the dead, but Saul's secrets couldn't hurt him where he was now. "I don't know what *Datt* has confessed before the church. I do know he made his peace with God after I left, so I have no right to bring up his failures. But you deserve to know the whole of it. My failures, too. Maybe those are the ones you deserve—need—to judge what is best for your own future."

She looked ready to contradict him but then pressed her lips shut.

"All right then, I'll tell you everything the way I remember, and it's not a pretty tale."

On the end of a long breath, he began to relive the memory aloud.

His datt was already drunk in the early afternoon of Noah's seventeenth birthday—a day he always began his binge early—and the anniversary of his mother's death. This time, Saul had been drinking since the night before.

Saul had followed Noah into the barn to take care of the horse after a ride with Rachel, and Noah braced himself mentally for the verbal assault sure to come.

"You think you're the only one courting that girl? Well, you ain't. You may be the only boy, but she's interested in a man."

The jabs were none he hadn't parried a million times. "Datt, you're drunk and have no idea what you're talking about."

"What do you think you've got to beat out Joel Yoder?"

The blow was calculated to hit Noah's deepest insecurities about his looks and his family. The bishop's stepson was better-looking and had a family anyone would love to join. He had a living, loving mother and a respected father. Two things Noah would give anything to have.

"Joel and Rachel are not courting, if that's what you're implying."

"Are you blind? Everyone knows she's followed after him since she was a little one. And I've seen the way he watches you, ready to pounce on you if you even look at her cross-eyed. Once she takes her vows, he'll move in."

That was the thing about the Amish. Once they got a story in the making, they retold it until fact and legend blurred. The Erbs and the Nafzigers were close, more like family than neighbors. At church gatherings, people found little Rachel Erb's infatuation with the minister's older stepson cute. Maybe it was when she was seven or eight. Now, she was turning into a woman. Still, they had her trapped by an idea they'd giggled and gossiped over before she knew her own mind.

"I don't know what Joel thinks, but I know Rachel's mind. And that's all that matters."

"There's no such thing as knowing what a woman thinks. Your own mamm thought she'd get better. That was a lie. And let me tell you, Son, kisses don't mean a hill of beans."

In the space of one rage-beating thump of his heart, Noah's fist landed square on his father's jaw, plowing the drunken man straight to the floor. And for one long beat of Noah's heart, he didn't care if the man ever got back up.

Blaming his mamm *for dying. Spying on Noah and Rachel. Belittling the two people Noah held most dear.*

The moment remained frozen in time in Noah's memory. Even now, with Rachel at his side, his father gone from this world, and years of healing behind him, the memory hurt.

"I've never struck a man since, Raye. But that day, I realized the hate within me was strong enough to kill. I ran. I ran to save us all."

If he expected judgment in her eyes, he found none, nor pity. Her touch was full of compassion through the softness of her fingers skimming across his forehead and brushing aside the hair over his eyes

"Oh, Noah," she whispered, then rested her hand for a brief second on his cheek. "I wish you hadn't suffered so."

"Somewhere in the between times, we both changed and made peace with God. I believe he's with *Mamm* in Heaven now. But it's hard, Raye—hard to believe he's gone, and every chance to make things right with each other has passed."

She remained thoughtful beside him before speaking again. "The Lord can restore what is lost, can He not? Surely, He hasn't brought you back here to send you away empty."

Out of words, Noah nodded and held onto her hand like the lifeline he so desperately needed. God could do anything—if He chose, of course.

CHAPTER FOURTEEN

Some mornings, Rachel could do her job on autopilot, which she would have liked to have been the case today. However, debriding an abscessed horn on a goat kid wasn't a great time for her thoughts to be wandering.

Was Noah all right? Of course, he and Trudy would receive all the help they needed with meals and such. But who would talk to him, comfort him?

Eww! The smell brought her back to task as putrid pus squirted from the area where the baby goat had been disbudded.

"You could be famous, you know." Tony walked across the room to inspect the infected area. "The veterinary version of that doctor on viral videos who pops enormous pimples."

"You're just trying to get my goat. You know I don't watch those things."

"Nice pun." He moved closer, and she stepped back and adjusted the light. "Good work, too. They'll have to do this twice a day. Show them how to dress it." He pulled off his gloves and sanitized his hands before reaching into his pocket for his prescription pad. "Here's the antiseptic I recommend they use, and we'll follow up in a week, unless there's no improvement."

"I'll take care of it."

"What do you need, Rachel?"

"Nothing. I can actually read this one."

"Funny, but I'm not talking about my prescription. I think your heart is somewhere else today." He slipped his notepad back into his lab coat. "I'm very sorry about Saul Detweiler." She believed him. Tony helped Saul find homes for his miniature horses and admired the way the man cared for his animals. "If you need time off in addition to the funeral, we can arrange it. I know the Amish band together in a time like this."

"Everyone has a role to play, especially in a small district like ours. My oldest brother and his wife are one of the three couples assigned to make sure Trudy and Noah have no work to do other than grieve and visit with those who come to the house."

"I see." He picked up the kid. Cradled in the crook of Tony's arm, the little goat bleated a protest. "I think I'll give him a bit of pain reliever before he goes."

There was something in the way he stayed in place—or maybe it was in his voice—but she knew he wasn't satisfied. She'd tried all morning not to think about the gossip he'd likely heard. Now the stories hovered between them, neither of them wanting to address the truths or falsehoods directly.

Her cheeks grew hot with embarrassment, but some things had to be faced. "I suppose you've heard what some folks are whispering about me and Noah."

His eyes flashed with an emotion she'd never seen before—not in Tony—a spark of the righteous anger she'd witnessed in Reuben the other night.

"I know you better than to believe any gossip, Rachel. You don't need to worry about that for one second. What I most regret is how my helping you onto that horse only added fuel to the fire. It's ridiculous really. And I'd laugh it off if it weren't hurtful to you."

She hadn't heard that part of the rumors. Either her *mamm* hadn't either, or she'd omitted it. Besides, the smallest of imagination was all she needed to figure out the gist of what had been said. "Some folk like to make something out of nothing. Most times, an Amish woman wouldn't be . . . handled like that by a man not her husband or close relative. But you meant no harm. I know that."

"I'll be more careful in the future; I can tell you that." Tony pulled up an office chair and sat beside her. "Sometimes, though, there's a sliver of truth behind rumors, and I'm gathering in this case there's some history between you and Noah Detweiler."

"There is, but . . . "

He held up a hand. "You don't need to defend yourself to me, Rachel. I know your character. When I first met Noah that night in the parking lot, I had no idea who he was. To me, he was just some out-of-towner ogling a pretty Amish woman. I didn't find out who he was until the wedding. I put two and two together after Saul told me his son had brought him. And I didn't need any tittle-tattle going around Amish town to figure out you two had something powerful between you.

"I told you I would always be a friend to you. I'm not going to be made a liar by some gossip. Sometimes, Rachel, a friend just has to be there when he is needed. Even if he can't do much. Right now, what I can do for you is let you go be where you belong today."

Tony was a friend of the best sort. "*Danki*, Tony. Thank you for understanding . . . for believing in me."

He looked down at the baby goat now resting in his hold. "When my dad died . . . " When he looked back up, his expression had changed to as serious as she'd ever seen Tony. "When my dad died, I'd have given anything to have someone like you just to be there."

He reached a hand toward the slip of paper in hers. "Let me take care of this. You're needed more somewhere else."

The paper slid from her fingers into his grasp. "I . . . "

"No need to thank me for being the greatest boss in the world, eh? I'll see you next week."

Unsure how the man could switch emotions so fast, Rachel was at a momentary loss. Especially as she knew he spoke the truth from her experience in her own *datt's* passing. What she wouldn't have given to have had Noah by her side.

"*Ja*, well, I'll take care of this mess first."

But Tony had already slipped to the waiting room with his patient; she was talking to herself.

Poor little kid. The amount of infection she'd drawn out of his sweet little head was remarkable.

Ugh! She covered her nose as she leaned down to gather up the waterproof pad where the infected matter had collected.

Too bad she didn't have Noah's cell phone number. She'd rather not make the long trek to the Detweilers' on her scooter. Just as well, really. The day was unusually warm for springtime; and arriving a sweaty, smelly mess in front of heaven-knew-who-all was not her preference. But if she went home first, her *mamm* would have too many questions.

Lydia would understand. She dialed the number from memory.

"Lydia's Amish Shoppe. How may I help you?"

Danki, Lord. Her friend's voice was exactly the one she'd hoped to hear. "It's me. I need a favor."

"Rachel, I'm so glad you called." Lydia's voice toned down to a whisper. "I need to talk to you."

"Are you all right? It's not the baby, is it?"

"*Nay, nay,* nothing like that."

"Well, I was hoping to come by your place to *redd up* before checking on Noah and Trudy." Rachel didn't explain why she didn't want to go home first. As she expected, Lydia put the pieces together on her own.

"I'll call to see if Dan can give you a ride here. Then we can have just a quick chat before you go to see Noah, *ja?*"

Shortly after hanging up with Lydia and settling a few odds and ends before she felt all right about leaving work for the remainder for the week, Rachel walked out of the vet's office to see Dan King's minivan pulling into the parking lot. Lydia sure hadn't wasted a second in calling her neighbor and one of the community's favored drivers.

Rachel climbed into the front seat. "You're quick, Dan. Thank you for coming."

"It's nothing. A couple miles round trip but seemed important to Lydia."

True. Lydia definitely had something more on her mind than Rachel not getting hot and stinky. As Dan pulled to the front of Lydia's shop, Rachel pulled out her bag to pay.

"No need for that now; I'll just put it on Joel's tab." He winked. Joel wouldn't keep in debt to the man, but the neighbors exchanged favors all the time. Since Dan's heart attack, she knew Joel often plowed Dan and Cait's garden and other more difficult chores.

She didn't want to take advantage, though. Dan was always such a good friend to the Amish in New Hope. "I can pay."

"Now, then, don't look a gift horse in the mouth. Lydia says you're going to help your neighbor. I can surely do my part. I'll miss Saul, too."

"Thank you, Dan." She pushed the door open. In an effort to stay strong for Noah, she hadn't cried yet. Dan's neighborly kindness shook her bottled mourning over the loss of Saul. She couldn't open the lid, not now.

As if understanding, he let her go without more talk.

Dan was the kind of man she imagined Noah to be in his non-Amish world. Considerate of others, a good neighbor, God-loving—but not Amish. If she ever left the Amish, she'd want to be that kind of person, too. Would she really have to change so much?

The best parts of her heritage would always be a part of her. God never changed. So long as her faith remained in Him, then she wouldn't either, at least not at the core of who she was. Not even in a non-Amish world.

She stopped and released the knob on the door to Lydia's shop before entering and leaned back against the outside wall. How had she never thought of that before? The answer was easy enough. She'd never had a reason to leave before. And now, she had a powerful-strong one.

One socked foot after another, Noah paced the length of the hall, stopping every few lengths to glance around the corner through the picture window and check for visitors. So far, only a few church members had dropped by, but he knew more would come later in the day.

They were doing things he ought to be, like cutting hay on such a hot day or finishing repairs to the barn. His feet itched for his boots.

"Go on, then." His sister moved into the doorway of the spare bedroom. "I know a man can't abide in the house all day. If you must work, there's sure to be something you can do out of sight where none will try to do the job for you."

'You got the baby to sleep, then?" She'd brought a portable crib and taken Isaac to another room for his morning nap.

"I did. Now, go on and work out some of that tension before you wear a hole in your floor."

His floor? "Your floor, I think you mean."

She shook her head.

He motioned her to come into the living room. Rachel's sister-in-law Laura was in the kitchen preparing lunch, and this was as good a time as any to have a somewhat private discussion.

He sat and patted the spot beside him on the sofa. *"Kumm."*

He swallowed. Hard. Where had that come from?

If Trudy was startled by his use of Amish dialect, she kept it hidden as she sat beside him. He gave his head a rough scratch and started over.

"I'll have to return to the ranch in Alberta before too much longer but not before I finish the repairs to the property. I should have asked you first before starting. Guess I wasn't thinking straight, but anything I've done should increase the value for you. Whatever you need to be done, I'll help you. I can stay until everything is in order."

Her eyebrows squeezed together, and her mouth hung open before she snapped it shut. "I don't understand. *Datt* left everything to you. He . . . " Her delicate fingers wrapped around her knees until her knuckles turned white.

"Trudy." He placed a hand over one of hers, cold to his touch. "I only ever assumed everything would go to you. You've been here—all along."

"I've done my best, Noah, but he only ever wanted you."

The pain in her voice held back his scoff. *Datt* wanted him? Hardly. But Trudy was scarcely able to hold back the pain she'd concealed from him so well up to now. He took both of her hands, hoping to impart some warmth back to them.

"Believe me, Trudy. When *Datt* sent you away to live with Constance, he was protecting you from himself."

"It was difficult to understand as a child, but I accepted that explanation. Now, as a mother, I cannot." She looked up at him her eyes filled with both sadness and fire. "I love my children. I cannot fathom abandoning them—being unwilling to change for them. I pushed it from my mind, trying to forgive. But now . . . maybe I never really forgave him after all. All I feel is the rejection."

He had no answer, except to wrap an arm around her stiff shoulders.

"I'm sorry, Sister. I left you, too. *'S shpeit mich.*" It grieved him—more than he could say.

Her shoulders slumped, and she leaned into him a bit. He pulled her closer, allowing them to grieve together in silence until the squeaky hinge of the back screen door alerted them to the arrival of more company.

She pulled away to stand. He rose beside her and leaned closer before they were interrupted, then dropped his voice low for her hearing alone. "We will discuss the farm later. I won't allow you to go without an inheritance."

"Speak of the devil," she whispered back to him and nodded toward the kitchen. Shoulders straight again, she wiped her hands on her apron, then rounded the sofa to enter the other room. "Hello, Constance. *Vi bisht du?*"

Their father's sister was strict Old Order. In fact, Noah was a bit surprised she'd made the trip from Ontario. She couldn't have possibly approved of Trudy's choice of husband because his Mennonite church allowed electricity and cars. Nor would she be accepting of Bishop Nafziger and Joel Yoder's more relaxed interpretations of the verbal traditions governing the Amish way of life.

Trudy needn't face the woman alone. In fact, all he was required to do in order to close the woman's mouth and judgmental perusal of her surroundings was set foot in the same room. He entered the kitchen and cleared his throat.

Constance froze mid-sentence, even as a false innocence swept across his sister's face. So, Trudy hadn't warned their aunt of his presence. From his vantage, he was pretty sure his little sister was enjoying the shock factor. Then he realized, even if Constance didn't recognize her brother's son and spitting image, a man in English clothes was abomination enough.

"Noah." His aunt stated his name as if she were a school teacher taking attendance and quite in control, only to dismiss him entirely with a curt turn of her head.

No wonder Trudy had felt abandoned.

Lording his authority over others wasn't Noah's habit. Still, for Trudy's sake, his aunt might require an occasional reminder of the boundaries. If anyone was to be in charge, it would be his sister—and with his blessing. He could don the patriarchal hat, if only for his aunt to clearly understand how this would be.

"Welcome to *our* home." He held his gaze steady as her sharp glare swerved back to him, as the realization dawned on her. He was the head of this house now. And with the choice of the word *our*, he was including Trudy.

"I would like to see my brother." Her manner was humbled, if only a bit.

"*Kumm.*" Trudy held out a hand. "I will take you to him. You were a *goot* sister to him, and he loved you." His sister's compassion toward their aunt outweighed her own pain and resentment.

As the two women walked away down the hall, Noah had to wonder at how God's love worked in a heart. He recalled all too well the trap of bitterness and unforgiveness he'd endured before he'd allowed God's love to penetrate his own pain. God's work on him was far from finished. Noah knew that much. But what end did the Lord have in mind?

Noah's attention was drawn to the window through which he saw a lone figure walking up the lane toward the house.

Rachel.

Did she know her hips swayed? Not a cat-like sashay that made a man feel like a woman's next prey. Rachel moved like a melody, as if her whole being were in tune with the song of life. And he found himself more mesmerized by her than by any supermodel or actress on a stage.

Gravitating closer to the glass, he lingered. Done wandering through the past like a ghost in his memories, his thoughts soared to what the future might be with Rachel in it. She slowed and caught him staring at her.

Last night he'd found comfort from Rachel's reminder that God could redeem the time Noah had lost. He'd even flirted with the idea of

God's plan being to restore Noah to his previous life. His heart raised in a rebellious thump. God wouldn't really ask so much, would He?

Rachel was still watching him from the other side of the glass. She pressed a hand against her heart. He returned the gesture. Even at a distance, he saw her blush, and a heat of his own flooded his veins. He'd never ask her to change and never take her away from here. He just couldn't figure how he could ever stay.

Rachel stopped when Noah held up a finger for her to wait and then disappeared from view at the window. Craning her neck to see around the corner of the house, Rachel watched him hop down the steps on one booted foot while tugging its mate onto the other. At the bottom, he stomped the second boot firmly into place and caught her watching.

"Come with me?" His head tilted to the barn. "I have some work to finish, if you don't mind keeping me company." He stuck his hands in his pockets. "Unless, you have other things to do."

"*Nay*, nothing but to be with you."

The slow smile that spread across his face heated her cheeks for the second time already. This time, she'd not be so stupid. This time, she knew the precious rarity of a soul made happy simply by being with another. This time, she wouldn't let him slip away, not without her.

Joel had been right to believe Noah wouldn't leave without her this time. The sudden decisiveness to follow him hit her hard enough to knock the wind from her lungs.

"Raye?"

She inhaled deeply. "*Ja*, I'm coming."

Before long, she was rolling paint with a long pole extension to reach way above her head, where Noah used a hand brush to detail the new trim from a ladder. Up and down the wooden planks, the fresh, red paint brightened the old.

Now was probably as good a time as any to broach the topic Lydia had shared with her; plus, she'd meant to tell him about Stedman right away.

"Lydia got a phone call this morning. Seems you've let your voice-mail get full and aren't answering your cellphone."

"The battery died. I use the rental car to recharge it—just haven't had the chance. Odd, though. I shouldn't have that many messages. I talked to Stedman before it died. Not sure who else would need to call."

"He's been calling. He called the shop early this morning to let you know he'd be here with his wife tomorrow for the funeral."

Noah's methodical brushing stopped. "I should have known he'd come."

"I thought you'd be pleased."

"I am. More than I'd imagined, actually. It's just I know how busy he is already without me at the ranch. I didn't want to be a burden."

"Being with someone you love in their time of need is not a burden, Noah. You know so. It's a two-sided blessing."

"Is it, Raye?" He looked down at her through his raised arm. The sun hit her in the eyes as she looked upward to him. The ladder rungs moaned in their turn to carry his weight as he descended until he was on the ground beside her. "Because there's nothing I'd want more than to be a blessing to you. I am blessed beyond anything I deserve. With Stedman and Marilyn and Second Chance Ranch.

With you." He stepped nearer. He smelled like honey and salt, and his eyes were as stormy as the ocean. "But am I the man you deserve to share yourself with?"

She opened her mouth with a ready response, but his fingers pressed lightly against her lips.

"Don't be too quick, Raye. I wasn't that man thirteen years ago. I've changed. God has made me a new man, but that doesn't automatically make me the right one for you. I want to be, but I'm still waiting for His answer."

Her surety evolved to frustration. He wanted her to think about it. Really?

"What do you suppose I've been doing all these years?" She pivoted back to rolling paint and pressed a little harder than necessary. Paint oozed from the thick and saturated lambswool cover and dripped in heavy rivulets down the wall. "I'm glad you have made peace with *Gott*, Noah. Maybe I should have known you were struggling with faith. I'm sorry to have been so blind back then. But I'm not the same either. I didn't understand about love or what I wanted at that age. Maybe I was starting to figure it out, but I know my own mind now. And I know I want you."

"You weren't blind. I was good at hiding things. And I've always wanted you." Noah came behind her with a brush and smoothed over her mess. "But we don't always get what we want."

The journal he'd written the year before he left that began on his sixteenth birthday and ended on his seventeenth was a fine example. "Your journal was mostly about . . . "

"You." He laughed, an odd thing at such a moment, and it irritated her. "I'm well aware. All I ever thought about was you, Rachel."

"I was going to say *us*. You wrote about me and you together, Noah."

His innermost thoughts and feelings displayed in ways he'd never shared with her in person. If he had—if she had known—how different their lives might have been. But he still couldn't believe the best for the two of them together.

"In your journal, I never found any of your reasons to leave. If anything, I only found reasons to stay. But then . . . then it just ended."

I'm sorry, Raye. The last entry haunted every happy memory.

"If Saul hadn't given me that journal, I'd be married to the wrong man now. Whether you realize it or not, the right man is you. And I have been waiting, Noah, longer than any woman ought to wait." She was beginning to feel a little crazed—one minute ready to follow him to the ends of the earth, the next ready to wallop some sense into his hard head with the extension pole in her hand. "How many second chances do you think *Gott* will see fit to give us? Maybe you're hiding the truth from yourself."

"Aren't you even a little afraid, Raye? I'm not saying God can't be in this. I'm just saying I have to consider the consequences."

"And I suppose you think it's all your decision to be made? As if I'm too ignorant of the world out there to know what I'd be getting into or naïve about the loss of community and family I would suffer."

His mouth fell open and remained unhinged. She'd shocked him and could feel the rise and fall of her chest from being angry as she waited for him to respond.

"That's not what I said, Raye. Not even what I thought." The agony in his voice, the apology, made her regret arguing with a man who needed a friend in his time of grief.

She softened her words but had to know. "What did you mean, Noah?"

He might have explained, but Laura appeared from around the other side of the barn with two glasses of lemonade. She handed them each a drink, then spoke to Noah.

"Reuben has gone to fetch Drew and some others to do this work. He is sorry he didn't think of it sooner. You ought not be forced to carry the burden of making things tidy for the funeral in your own time of grief."

"There's no reason to feel bad on my account. The work helps me."

"Even so . . ." her sister-in-law said as though the matter was settled, then shifted from Noah to Rachel. "And we'd be grateful for your help with preparation for the funeral meal."

Her brother and his wife had been chosen to oversee the funeral arrangements in the custom of relieving the burden from the family. They were doing their duty as they knew best. Still, Rachel knew this was a deliberate interference to separate her from Noah.

She also knew why—to protect her from the nasty gossip. Rachel didn't give two twigs about that anymore.

Only when Noah reached for the pole in her hand did she realize her fingers were squeezed as tight as a vise. He gave a gentle tug as if to remind her to let go. She couldn't.

"Thanks for your help, Rachel." His formal tone pierced her heart. One argument wouldn't ruin their friendship, surely. The problem was she wanted more, and everyone was getting in the way. But Noah's eyes begged in silence for understanding. He didn't want to make trouble.

For the first time in her life, she thought she might. She'd been the peacemaker ever since she could remember, smoothing the ruffled feathers Sarah and Albert left behind at every turn. Since her father died, she'd even had to cover the bitter words of her *mamm* for the sake of peace.

Her heart pounded a fury against the injustice of it all.

"Please, Rachel," Laura's soft voice pleaded. She moved near Rachel's ear, opposite of where Noah waited for her to release her grip. "Of all times, today, we must rely on our traditions to see us through."

Of all the things the Amish did well, Rachel knew their ways helped through grief the best.

For Noah, she surrendered the pole. Would she have to let him go as well? Again? Unable to bear watching as he walked away, she dropped her gaze to the ground. Why did it have to be this way?

Her own faith was slipping off that Solid Rock she'd sung about the other night. She didn't know how to stop the fall or whether she wanted to. There was only one thing she knew she wanted, and he wasn't cooperating either.

CHAPTER FIFTEEN

Coffee mug in hand, Noah rocked on the front porch as a new wave of buggies trotted up the lane. In the side yard, others loaded up to leave. This was the second day of visitation. He'd greeted face after face until his mind was numb from the repetition of condolences and nice replies.

Inside the house was somber, but outside, folks who'd not seen each other in many months chose to visit while their children played. Noah chose a sitting spot half-out of sight of those around the corner. He'd listen to the happy sounds from the children and enjoy his hot drink while he waited for the taxi bringing Stedman and Marilyn from the airport.

"Can I join you?" He hadn't heard anyone follow him, but Rachel had found him.

"Please do." He slid over to give her room, and she settled into the glider beside him.

They hadn't discussed their past or argued about the future since yesterday morning. He only hoped she hadn't given another second worth of consideration of leaving the Amish for his sake.

Yesterday, they'd practically tip-toed around each other. He had his reasons. She had hers. But today, she'd remained quietly by his side, a comforter he knew he didn't deserve but relished all the same.

"*Danki*, Raye, for sticking this out with me."

"*Danki*, is it?" Her eyes glittered with a tease. "Sounds *goot* coming from you again."

She couldn't know how nice it felt to simply be himself. He'd spent years undoing the natural inclination to speak his first language. In his efforts to fit into the current culture, he'd almost lost who he was.

With Rachel, Noah never needed to put on any kind of act. He'd always appreciated that about her. He'd tell her so, but the last thing he wanted to do was give her more evidence for why they belonged together. He couldn't until he'd found a way to make it possible—and for her to leave the Amish was not one.

She had no idea how miserable she'd be in a non-Amish life. She'd wither away from loneliness. He'd been all-confident with Joel about God being enough. God had been enough for Noah, but then God began to move his heart back to building relationships with other people.

God didn't make man to be alone, and Noah was more than sure he didn't make Rachel for that either. Rachel had always fit into the Amish community. She thrived here, and he wasn't about to steal that from her.

She bumped him with her shoulder.

"I hate to interrupt whatever is going on up there." Her eyebrows lifted as she looked over the rim of her cup toward the top of his head. "But I was wondering if your friends might rather stay with me and *Mamm*. We're about the only family left with room for out-of-town guests." She lowered her voice. "And with Constance, Saul's house would be sort of . . . " She shrugged, but he understood what she wouldn't say.

"That's kind of you. I think they may have gotten a room at the bed and breakfast."

"Well, just remember in case, *ja?*" She peered down at the contents of her cup, then back to him. "The truth of it is that I'd like to take care of your friends, Noah. After all you say they've done for you, it only seems right to give them a home-like welcome."

Having no idea she'd all but strengthened his resolve to never take her from her home, Rachel smiled at him. "Only if it's to their liking, of course."

"Oh, I have no doubt they'll take you up on it, Raye. It will mean a lot to them. To me, too. Thank you." Then over her shoulder, Noah saw the vets blue truck turning the bend. "Looks like your *Englisch* friend has come."

"*Englisch*, listen to you." She poked a finger into his bicep and twisted her head to see. "Don't sound so surprised. Tony had a great amount of respect for Saul. They bonded over your *datt's* miniature horses."

"You know, I never got to ask him why he switched to the minis. I can only guess he couldn't live without horses altogether."

"Probably. I can tell you he loved those miniature horses, maybe more than his breeders. His heart was as broken as Samy's when he had to sell them."

"Just the telling of it makes me sad. Why couldn't he keep them?"

"He claimed not to have the energy, which was true enough, but Samy couldn't accept his reason. She believed she could have taken care of them for him."

"I believe she might have been right." He thought on it for a bit. "A man might also feel like he had to have everything in order, too. Maybe it was part of his way of settling his affairs before his time to go."

Noah certainly hadn't intended to allude to anything painful for Rachel, but she stiffened beside him, then stood abruptly and returned to the house.

Time to go had done it. He didn't like thinking about leaving again either. He could follow her, but they couldn't talk among all the women inside the house. And what purpose was more talk serve over an impossible impasse? Sometimes, a body just needed space, and he figured Rachel had a right for whatever she was feeling to remain private.

He headed toward the vet, parking right in line with the buggies, and reached the truck at the same time the tall man unfolded himself from the cabin.

"Hello, Tony. Nice of you to come." Noah offered a hand, hoping for a new start.

In return, the vet's handshake was firm and warm. "I am truly sorry for your loss. Saul taught me more than a few things about horses. He was, by far, the expert in that department, and I'll miss him."

"He knew horses, for sure." Noah was surprised at the lack of sarcasm in his reply. He could allow his father to be good at something without dragging his faults into play. Had he learned, finally, to forgive? "There's food aplenty inside. You'd be doing us a favor to share a plate. My sister is here . . . and Rachel."

"Yeah, it's been a tough week without her help at work." The man looked Noah square in the eye. "But I know *this* is where she belongs."

As if Noah needed a reminder.

"It's good of you to come today. I'm waiting for someone, but please, go on in."

"Just one thing, while we have a private moment. Saul kept his business rather close to the vest, so to speak."

"True enough."

"Well, I made several calls for him that he always asked me to keep confidential." His head turned slightly in the direction of the house, which Noah understood to mean even Rachel didn't know. "Now he's gone, someone needs to know he still owns two brood mares and a valuable stud. When they got to be too much for him, he boarded them at a horse farm on the other side of Montague, where I've been seeing to their care. In fact, I was required to make a call out there early this week. I'm not worried about the compensation; don't misunderstand. But obviously, some decisions are going to have to be made, and you seem the logical choice to be making them."

"I, um . . . that makes sense." So much for leaving things in order. What had his *datt* been up to? Noah needed to read the will. There must be one from the way Trudy spoke about the house. But the vet was waiting for a response. "Thank you for letting me know. Maybe I can catch up with you later."

"No rush, all right? Stop by the office anytime, after all of this. I just didn't want you to get blindsided or leave town without knowing."

Noah gave his first impression of Tony another look. So what if the vet was over-protective of Rachel? Noah supposed he could forgive him for that. He was actually a really decent fellow. "I appreciate it."

"No problem." Tony's attention moved to something behind Noah. "You appear to have a work crew headed this way."

The young men who were preparing Saul's barn for his funeral tomorrow, no doubt. The Amish never shied away from hard work, and the lessons he'd learned in doing the same for others in his youth had served him well as a man. What he hadn't been able to comprehend in its fullness at their age was how much comfort the shared labor brought to a grieving soul.

"I'd never be able to submit to the Amish faith, but still, I admire them. The longer they are here on the island, the more I understand the value of their ways. I'm not one to judge anyone's reasons for leaving, you understand, but I do wonder if you are still a man of faith?"

The question was straightforward but not meddlesome in the way Noah had perceived Tony before. Sure, he was concerned for Rachel, no doubt. But Noah took no offense; if anything, his estimation of the man crept up a notch.

"I didn't have a relationship with God when I left the Amish, at least not like I do now. Back then, it was more one-sided—God pursuing me, protecting me, loving me, until I woke up to the truth." *We love him, because he first loved us.*[4] "God's love for me is what brought me back here to try to make peace with my *datt*. I suppose it's no secret we were estranged. And I reckon if I didn't love God, then I wouldn't have come. Love works both ways, doesn't it?"

"Who am I to judge, right? But not everyone is what they seem. It's no different in my own church or with the Amish, I'm sure. Being a member of a certain denomination doesn't necessarily mean a person's heart is right with God." The formality Tony had used with Noah before changed to an easier cadence, as if he spoke to a friend. "Saul wasn't a man to preach at others. He was too humble for that. He had his way of bringing God into the everyday that encouraged me to do the same." Tony rubbed the back of his neck, and Noah realized the man bore his own grief in the loss of Saul Detweiler.

---

4 1 John 4:19, King James Version. Public Domain.

"Thank you for telling me." Noah felt his heart cling to this new image of his father. And this man had been his father's friend. "I'll walk in with you."

Noah could at least do that much for a friend of his father. And as they walked to the house talking of horses, Noah realized his actions were also his own way of honoring his *datt*—the one he'd known long before alcohol and grief had taken the man away from him. A man who welcomed Amish and non-Amish alike in a friendly manner.

Memories swirled through his thoughts like images flipping through the pages of a book from the back to the front. Before Second Chance Ranch, before the long years alone on the prairie, before falling in love as a teenager, before tragedy took his mother—all the way back at the beginning resided treasured pictures of a healthy family living on a beautiful horse farm, where bad things only happened to outsiders.

"Your old man is the best around these parts, little buddy." The clean-shaven man in fancy boots and a collared shirt who smelled of a strong, spicy lotion patted Noah on the head.

Noah wasn't learning anything he didn't already know. And try as he might not to be over-proud, the Englischer's *praise puffed him up as he passed the reins of the black thoroughbred into the man's outstretched hand.*

"When I was a boy, I'd have given my right arm to learn from a man like him. He's what we call a horse-whisperer. You're a lucky lad. And with a little more luck, you can be just a good when you grow up."

If Gott *wills—the answer he was trained to give—stalled at the end of Noah's tongue. He only nodded at the gentleman, who took his recovered racehorse to the waiting trailer and left.*

Noah, the boy, wanted nothing more than to be just like his datt. *There were no* ifs *about it. And why wouldn't he? One day, he would be married to a* wunderbar fraw *and live on a money-making farm, overrun with the best horses in Ontario—just like Saul Detweiler.*

As Noah and Tony made their way through the house, he felt the stares and questions following them down the hall. But the only eyes he cared about were Rachel's caramel browns making his pulse race with their tender concern.

He'd been wise, that boy Noah. A *wunderbar fraw* she'd make, for sure.

CHAPTER SIXTEEN

The day of the funeral required an extra early start. And despite the time difference between the ranch and the island, Rachel's guests were up as early as she was. In the space of an evening and a rushed breakfast, she'd already recognized how easy it must have been for Noah to love Ray and Marilyn Stedman.

"I'm happy to do the dishes, Beulah." Marilyn rose from the table in sync with Rachel's *mamm*. "I know you must have a lot to do."

Rachel held her breath. She could read the battle in her *mamm's* thoughts as she stared pensively at Marilyn, who must be a similar age, dressed in long sleeves and a blue jean skirt, no doubt a departure from pants in an effort to show respect.

"Well, then, Rachel could get to helping Laura sooner. We'll, do it together. Many hands make light work. Ain't so?" Her *mamm* smiled at Marilyn.

At least, Rachel believed she'd seen a smile pass between the two women. How odd—on her mother's part, anyway. "I'll be back to take you to the funeral."

"*Ach*, no need for all that backwards and forwards. I'm sure a rancher can drive an Amish horse and buggy, *ja*? A horse is a horse."

The rumble of Stedman's laugh came before his answer. "I believe I can handle it."

"*Goot*, then. It's all settled." As if nothing unusual was happening, Beulah Erb turned to walk to the sink.

Wondering what had come over her *mamm*, Rachel gathered the tote filled with homemade bread they'd baked for the funeral meal. She said goodbye and headed out the door.

"Here, let me." Stedman held the door for her, then followed. "How about I give you a ride?"

He did have a car, which was likely her *mamm's* reason for roping him into driving the buggy—one less *Englisch* vehicle at the funeral. The thought was a relief, in a way, being better than some more nefarious sort of meddling afoot.

"Oh, I don't mind walking, really. It's not far."

He nodded understanding, then reached for the tote. "Well, then, at least let me carry this for you. Gives me an excuse to go along and see Noah. I'll come back for the ladies."

Stedman was assertive, yet kind, in a good, fatherly sort of way—once again reminding her of the fact Noah had a home far away from here—and from her. She gave him the container. "Noah will be thankful to see you before the service this morning, for sure."

"How is he doing?" Stedman's voice was low and deep, his brows pinched together in concern. And he asked her as if she'd have a better idea than he might.

"Well, you know him better than I do." As much as she hated to admit it. But she knew the old Noah and was only just learning to understand the new one. "I think he is still struggling for peace. But he will get there. I think . . . I feel certain he will." *This time.*

Because this time had to be different.

She turned her head to see Stedman studying her reaction. His eyes glimmered with concern—maybe as much for her as for Noah—but he only moved his mouth in an assuring smile before turning his attention back to their path. The one Noah had mown through the hay for her the day before.

"I don't believe I do," Stedman continued while maintaining his stride. "Know him better, that is. Time does change a person. And for the child of God, He uses it all to make us more like Christ. But you were the kind of friend to him that only come once or twice in a lifetime for most of us. The kind of friend who knows who we are underneath, the way God created us to be."

Rachel didn't know what to say to all of that. Tears stung the back of her eyelids. "How could you know all of that?"

"If you mean, did he tell me? The answer is no. You were a piece of the puzzle he kept hidden all these years. But that night when we pulled into the vet's office with a flat and he laid eyes on you, that's when I saw it."

"I don't see how . . ."

"Without a doubt, you were the reason he came back. I've been working with stray souls long enough to fit it all together on my own from there."

Stray *souls*? Not stray cows or horses, like a regular rancher, but souls. "What exactly is it that you do at Second Chance Ranch?"

"A little bit of everything you expect on a ranch. We have some cattle but mostly horses. Marilyn, though, had a heart for something more. She's a child psychologist and wanted to utilize our resources in ways to help children. One thing led to another. Then, almost fifteen years ago now, we began a charity focused on equine therapy. Second Chance Ranch was the name that fit everything together."

A compelling connection drew her heart to the idea of such a place. A simple *how nice* wasn't sufficient to express her feelings and yet was all she could manage to say. Her imagination was lit, and she wanted to know more. Why hadn't Noah shared all of this with her?

"You're welcome to visit anytime," Stedman offered as if he saw the eagerness she hadn't expressed aloud.

"*Danki*, I'd like that." She smiled and let the matter drop. For whatever reason, Noah was keeping his other life closed to her. And now was not the time to dwell on his reasons or how she felt about it.

"So, I get the feeling our presence makes things a little awkward. Is there something we can do to make it easier for the Amish?"

"I think you're already doing all you can. This is how it is. We have our ways, but we understand others are unfamiliar with our traditions. You are not expected to act Amish. We appreciate the honor you pay Saul by being here for his son. More often than not, families nowadays are a blend of those who still practice the Amish way and those who have not joined the church. Still, they are family. Even the shunned, well . . . "

What was she doing speaking of such a sensitive and personal topic? She needed to quit talking. "Well, we find ways to make it work as best we can." *Most of us, anyway.*

She let the last thought remain unspoken. And so far in New Hope, there had been no one who had crossed that line. A chill ran up her spine. Would she be the first? Because she was dangerously close in her mind to taking that chance to be with Noah. And the Second Chance Ranch made the idea seem even more possible.

"What does Noah do at the ranch?"

"Maybe you and Noah need to be having this conversation." His eyebrows rose with the words, and her face flamed at the rebuke. He was right, of course; she and Noah still had much to talk about. But then, Stedman's demeanor softened as he began to answer her question. "He pretty near runs the place. I'll tell you that. And he's a wonder with those kids on the horses."

She and Noah really did need to talk. He'd never said anything about working with kids. Not that she was surprised after the way he and Samy understood each other right from the start.

She thought of his journal. How poetic he'd been on the page with his feelings. He wasn't a man who didn't know how to express himself. He just didn't like to talk about himself much. At one time, he hadn't needed to, since she knew everything about him.

Had she misunderstood the way things were between them? Maybe a kiss was just a kiss to Noah. Had he actually promised anything other than not to leave without saying goodbye? He hadn't. And he'd given more reason to think he didn't want her in his new world than that he would. Suddenly, she couldn't remember how she'd come to think she might go with him. He'd never asked. In fact, he'd never even hinted.

As they neared the house, she stopped at the barn. She'd hoped to find Noah there and have a word alone before everything began. But she thought better of it now.

"I expect you'll find him in there." She directed Stedman to the barn. "He's not been too good at letting others do his chores for him."

Stedman chuckled under his breath. "No, I expect he hasn't."

Bracing herself for a hard day in which she may not get another chance to speak with Noah alone and no longer knowing if she wanted one, Rachel reached Saul's back door, just as his pallbearers crossed the threshold with his casket.

Noah followed behind them, his focus fixed on the pine box in front of him as he passed by her. Rachel stared at the back of him as they carried Saul away to the funeral cart. She entered the house without Noah ever knowing she was there.

Joel inhaled deeply as the last of the mourners filed away from Saul's newly covered grave. He'd expected his first funeral as a minister to be difficult, but Saul's brought some more unusual challenges than most.

Perhaps another minister might recuse himself of shepherding Saul's children as they were not living inside the Amish faith. But Joel found no Christ-likeness in an attitude that turned away from this family in their time of need. If anything, now was the time they needed the church of their childhood the most.

Walking away from him at the end of the line of mourners, he could see the backs of Trudy with her husband and children, then Noah off to the side with the older *Englisch* couple from Alberta.

His gut soured with every recollection of how things may have been different for Trudy and Noah. He knew the discomfort was his own personal guilt but also a communal guilt. When Saul failed his children, they all bore some of that failure.

Joel wanted—they all wanted—New Hope to be different. Running away to another province hadn't solved every problem. And clearly, this issue had followed them. So, how was he to right the wrong? Could he?

"*Kumm*, Joel." Lydia's voice beside him beckoned him to leave. Their two children had waited long enough.

He bent down and picked up Owen. "Won't be long before you're too big to carry." Then looking down at Samy, he took her hand. "And you have been very *goot* to remain still so long. Don't you think so, *Mamm*?" He winked at Lydia.

She smiled, but his *fraw* looked pale. The pregnancy was hard on her, but he didn't want to worry her with his thoughts. He only wished she would have gone with his mother and the bishop at the front of the line, along with those who'd ridden down the hill in buggies instead of walking.

As they fell in step to climb through the field, he let Owen down and reached for Lydia's hand. "*Danki*, for remaining by my side."

An extra spark of life flashed in her face as she looked up to him and squeezed his fingers. "Always, my love."

They remained quiet then, out of reverence for the occasion. When the others crested the hill, Lydia held him back and took the children's hands to keep them from running ahead.

"What are we to do about Rachel? The talk has only been in whispers, but now Saul is buried . . . " She leaned closer to his ear, no doubt an attempt to keep the children out of the conversation. "Albert and Vonda are stirring the pot. Her own brother." The final words raised, despite her best intentions.

Albert had been unhappy since the bishop had refused to discipline Rachel for getting the education she needed to be a technician at the vet's office. He was sure the bishop's leniency would result in a mass exodus of their youth from the church. And if Rachel chose to go with Noah, her brother would use that decision against both Joel and *Datt* Nafziger anytime they chose the way of grace versus the law in guiding the church.

Datt had been confident Rachel's commitment to the church was firm. Joel hadn't drawn the lot to be minister at the time, but he had supported the decision his stepfather had made as bishop. He still would, in spite of Albert—in spite of the current dilemma.

But to marry outside the faith . . .

"*Ja,* I know. I warned her, but I cannot make Rachel's decisions for her."

"Oh, Joel," Lydia was looking down at her feet, then far off to some distant place he couldn't see. "There must be a way for them. Couldn't you talk to him? Maybe . . . maybe, he would come back."

Not likely. In fact, he couldn't recall many who'd returned to the Amish after they left. None of their own generation. He had more of a sense that Rachel was considering jumping the fence.

"Has Rachel mentioned this as a possibility to you?"

"*Nay,* she hasn't. And I wouldn't want to get her hopes up. But . . . "

"You think he is considering such a move?"

"I think he loves Rachel and that he is a man who seeks after *Gott.* He has to have at least thought about it."

"And you want me to give him a push in this direction?"

Lydia gave him a little nudge with her shoulder. "*Nay,* I want you to get to know him and see. Befriend him. Because there are others who will run him off the first opportunity they get."

And Rachel would likely follow right behind him. Lydia didn't have to finish what he already knew. And he owed the man at least as much as Lydia suggested. He tugged on Lydia's hand to stall before they reached the others.

"This is a testing, Lydia. A testing of us all, but it will be the greatest for me. These decisions will go far beyond what happens with

Noah and Rachel. And there's Mark's situation to consider also. You understand how I act will set a course for our church for years to come."

"*Ja*, I know the burden you bear is heavy. What can I do?"

"Pray. Without *Gott*, I . . . "

"We will pray together. And also, *Mamm* and *Datt* Nafziger, they will pray, too. *Gott* will not forsake you, Joel. He has called you to shepherd His people through this time for a reason."

Their small community had only just begun. He had no desire to lead them into a schism of faith, pitting family member against family member. Yet he had promised to walk uprightly in the sight of *Gott*. And he would do what was right as best he knew how. Though not everyone would see it that way.

CHAPTER SEVENTEEN

Don't go.

Noah's silent plea to Rachel, who stood surrounded by her family inching closer and closer to the door, was useless. He was trapped in an unending conversation. The man, a distant relative, meant well—Noah supposed, at least. And he didn't want to be rude. But the one-sided monologue was keeping him from Rachel.

Right as Noah cleared his throat to interrupt, he felt a tug on his shirt sleeve. Samy looked up at him, her hazel-green eyes wide and half-covered with loose strands of long, red curls. "Noah, when can I show you something?"

Noah gave the man who'd stopped for a breath an apologetic shrug. Not truly sorry for the interruption in the least, he knelt down to eye-level with Samy. "Where is this something?"

"Outside."

Bless her. Noah straightened and excused himself from the conversation. "All right, Squirt, show the way."

Halfway across the room, Noah stopped Samy's determined stride and spoke quietly for only her to hear. "Can Rachel come see, too?"

She nodded.

"Well, then, how about you go get her, and both of you meet me outside. In the barn?"

Her head bobbed up and down with more enthusiasm. "The place where you were sleeping."

A smile ticked Noah's lips up. She must be referring to his first night here and the following morning when they'd first met. "The hay loft?"

"Uh-huh." She smiled and skipped off through the crowd of people to pull on Rachel's sleeve this time. As Rachel's head bent toward Samy's, Noah made a quick exit the other way.

He hadn't counted on interrupting Drew and Emma around the back of the house. From what Noah saw, Rachel's nephew and his sweetheart had done nothing more than lean in for a quick kiss. Still, the young woman's blush, along with the annoyance on Drew's face, told him all he needed to know. Drew had worked hard for that moment, and now it was ruined.

Pretending he hadn't seen them at all, Noah maintained his stride toward the barn before allowing himself a chuckle over the pair of love birds. To be seventeen again—the things he'd tell himself. He'd start with not taking himself so seriously. Maybe someone should tell Drew that he'd get another chance if it was meant to be—no need to rush—and definitely not to quit too soon. He scratched an itch behind his ear. Maybe he should listen to his own advice, even now.

In the barn, everything appeared in order. As did the loft when Noah climbed up there. Samy was a little mystery, but he didn't mind how unimportant this thing of hers might be. It was significant to her, plus she'd rescued him. He sat on a hay bale to wait for her and Rachel, thankful for a quiet moment.

When Samy appeared with Rachel close behind her, Noah leaned over the ladder to help each of them into the loft. He didn't miss the amusement dancing in the golden flecks of Rachel's brown eyes. Apparently, she didn't mind being rescued either. Someone really should tell Drew about second chances.

Noah grasped her hand and gave her a boost. He didn't want to release hand right away, and she didn't seem anxious to let go either. But then her eyes flashed, and she jerked away as if she'd gripped a hot skillet handle instead of his hand. He couldn't make sense of her mood change. What had he done?

"Nine, ten, eleven . . . " Samy was already on the far end of the loft, counting boards. She spun around with her mouth wide-open in a panic. "I don't remember what to count. I forget the number!"

With a single and long stride, Noah was in front of the child. He recognized the signs of an impending meltdown and knelt in front of her. "I'll help you, okay?"

Still panicked, she wasn't making eye contact.

"Samy." He said her name slowly and continued in a slow and quiet tone. "It will be okay; I promise." Her frantic movements slowed as well, so he continued, "Sometimes when I forget something, I can remember if I think about something else for a little bit."

Noah knew if he asked her too many questions right now, she'd panic more with the effort of trying to answer. They needed a distraction until she was fully calm. "Can you tell me about the miniature horses?"

She stilled but seemed unsure how to answer. Maybe the subject change stunned her.

He kept up the diversion. "I never got to see Saul's little horses. When I was your age, we had all thoroughbreds on our farm." Noah kept his voice calm and watched her reaction, which indicated an interest just as he'd hoped. "You love horses, don't you?"

Samy nodded. "Will you bring them back?"

She caught him off-guard. And if he wasn't careful, he'd upset her. Still, he couldn't lie to appease her. "What do you mean?"

"Saul said the paper would let you bring them back." She turned frantically back to the wall where she'd been counting the boards, then looked back to him. A giant tear slid down her cheek. Her lower lip trembled.

"Hush, now. It will be all right." He rubbed her arm. "We will find it."

Noah began to press on the boards, expecting to find a loose one. He counted aloud to reassure Samy and gave a hard nudge to each plank. The seventh creaked as the nails gave under the pressure. "Is this the one?"

A few more tears had joined the first in a trickle down her sweet face, but her eyes beamed back at him. She shook her head up and down with excitement. Close behind them, Noah caught a glimpse of Rachel watching intently.

"Go ahead, then." Noah nudged Samy.

She pressed hard with both hands against the old wood until the bottom wedged open with a space large enough for her hand to pass beneath.

"Careful," Rachel warned. "Who knows what might be behind there? Maybe you should let Noah . . . "

But Samy was already pulling a leather satchel out of the opening. She pushed it toward Noah. "He told me to."

"My *datt*, Saul, told you to . . . to give it to me?"

"*Ja*, after he was under the ground." She gave it another push, as if he ought to take it. "He said you would come, and you needed it. So, I had to put it somewhere safe to find it for you."

∞

Rachel wasn't sure why she'd been invited on this expedition with Noah and Samy. Nevertheless, she watched, captivated. Stedman's mention of Noah's work with special needs children came to mind. Noah certainly had a gift of understanding when it came to Samy.

Noah still hadn't touched the leather package. Instead, he spoke to Samy. "Is that why you tried to come here after the wedding?"

She hung her head, still embarrassed, poor child. "I don't know."

"It's okay if you can't explain. Some of the things we do are just too hard to explain." His voice was warm and comforting. "Saul trusted you very much. And you have done a very good job helping him. And me. *Danki*, Samy."

Just then, Samy's head came up. She flung herself toward Noah, her arms wrapped around his neck and her face pressed into his chest. Noah appeared stunned for a moment; then his arms squeezed tight around the girl. He cast Rachel a sidelong glance full of love and kindness. And maybe a tear.

Her own vision blurred. With a clean corner of her apron, she wiped at her eyes to see again. Samy was already done with both task and hug, apparently. She pulled back from Noah's embrace and walked to the ladder, shaking bits of hay from her dress.

Rachel looked to Noah, who shot an amused grin in the girl's direction. He called after her, "See you later, Samy."

"Okay." Her voice drifted up to the loft from at least half-way down the ladder. In no time, she'd scampered out of the barn to go on about her own business.

"Well." Noah's voice drew Rachel attention back to the loft and the pouch still on the floor in front of him. He motioned her to come closer and sit beside him. "Guess we should open it."

We? She wasn't so sure. The contents were clearly for Noah alone. Saul had gone to great lengths on that account. But Noah was already unwinding the thin, leather band holding the package shut.

"Seems like a risky way to deal with anything important, you know?" Noah's fingers tapped the opening. "Kind of a heavy burden to put on a little girl, making her act like his banker to keep a safe deposit box for him. Of course, he'd have his reasons."

"You won't know until you open it." Rachel heard the impatience in her voice, even though none of this was her business.

The pouch was the size of an envelope. There were no bulges to indicate any contents other than paper documents. She had guessed from the start that Saul had hidden his last will and testament in the thing.

Noah's chest heaved with a sigh. "*Datt* always had his own way of doing things. Even this. And somehow, I dread it. From the little I've gathered from Trudy and Tony, I have a lot more decisions ahead than I thought."

"I don't understand. What about Tony?"

"He told me *Datt* still has a thoroughbred stud and a couple mares on a farm somewhere around here." He blew out a breath. "You didn't know either?"

She shook her head. "Neither of them ever told me." She left off how odd it seemed for Tony to hide that kind of information. She supposed Saul requested he keep it a secret. But why?

Noah pulled out the papers and unfolded them. "'Last Will and Testament of Saul Detweiler.'" He paused, folded the will, and put it back. "This should wait for Trudy . . . and a lawyer. And I have a feeling I'm going to be around for longer than I thought."

His blue eyes sought hers, but she couldn't hold his gaze. Not while she felt such a sharp disappointment at the reminder—sooner or later, he would leave. She should be glad he'd mentioned longer, but longer would make the coming separation more impossible to bear.

"Raye?" His fingertips tenderly sought her hand, but she was afraid to entwine her own with his. He pulled back. "What is it?"

Her courage faltered. He hadn't shared anything about his life at the ranch with her. Sharing the idea that had begun to take hold in her heart may be too presumptuous. She'd probably sound foolish. But the way he looked at her now, so tender, so concerned. Oh, how she wanted to be with him forever.

"I don't want you to leave without me again. I'm not asking you to stay. I'm wondering whether I should go . . . with you."

Noah eased away from her, slowly, as if she were a wild animal about to strike. "You don't mean to the ranch, do you?" His eyes pleaded as if asking for her to back down, so he didn't have to shoot.

She hadn't thought he'd reject her. Again.

"So, it's to be the same. I have no choice. One day, I will simply find that you are gone." She refused to allow a single tear to flow. Instead, she allowed them to fuel her anger. She was on her feet in an instant, while somehow managing a rein on her tongue.

Noah's fingers tugged at her sleeve as she raced to the ladder. "Wait, Raye . . . please."

Wait. That horrible, hateful word. *Nay*, she was tired of waiting. She descended the ladder without giving Noah another glance. She'd been a fool indeed.

A heavy thud behind her startled her to a halt.

"Don't go." Noah's voice was pained. Had he hurt himself? She turned to see him rising from a squat. How far had he jumped? "Don't go."

"I can't wait again, Noah. I can't. Either you want me, or you don't. You should know by now."

"I do." He stepped closer, a tad wobbly on his right ankle. "I have always known you're the one for me. But robbing you of everything you've ever known has never been an option. I won't do it. Not then. Not now. Not ever, Raye."

She pinched the bridge of her nose and closed her eyes, willing herself to show patience. "Noah, why does being together have to be impossible? You're not making sense."

He remained at arm's length. "I understand you are familiar with life outside of the Amish. But they have their families, Raye. You'd lose everything, and believe me, I know how that is."

"Then how am I the one for you? That's what doesn't make sense. You can't waltz back in and take up where you left off, then desert me for the same reason all over again."

"It's not the same as back then."

"It sure feels the same to me, Noah. Only, maybe worse because now I know it's coming." *And how much she was losing.*

"But I'm not the same, Raye. Please don't give up. I just need some time."

"Time is precious." The new grave over the hillside was proof enough. A shadow crossed Noah's face, and she knew he'd thought of the same. Her own fight drained out of her. This wasn't the day for ultimatums to a man who had only just buried his father. Still, he needed to understand.

"So is my heart, Noah. You cannot do with it any which way you please." The words came out on a thin string of breath. No longer angry, she was simply begging to be understood.

His demeanor crumpled. She'd hurt him. More than anything, she wanted to rush to him and smooth over the effect of her words. She couldn't stand to be at odds with anyone, especially Noah. But allowing her heart to be trampled brought no peace, either. She couldn't endure a continued longing for what may never be.

"I understand" was all he said before she turned to go home.

CHAPTER EIGHTEEN

Noah had risen early the morning after the funeral. Stedman had come over from the Erbs' house a short time later. And they'd been working in tandem all morning, repairing a rundown loafing shelter on one of the farm's more remote pastures.

"I'd say you're strung about as tight as your friend Rachel was this morning." Stedman pointed at Noah with the hammer in his hand. "Want to talk about what's going on?"

Noah didn't. "I think I'd be better off pounding some nails right now."

"Fair enough." Stedman resumed a steady beat with his hammer. "Let's move on to a different subject, then, 'cause the way you're going after those innocent spikes of metal is giving me a headache."

Noah drove an extra nail into the final board for good measure. And maybe to pause Stedman's clear determination to talk. But from experience, he knew the man would only be deterred for a short while once he'd made up his mind to address an issue.

Stedman was as head-on with confrontation as he was with hitting a nail on the head or breaking a new horse. Neither nail nor horse stood a chance. Noah knew he didn't either.

Still, Stedman was going easier on Noah than usual this morning. He had that fatherly way about him—at least, what Noah had come to appreciate as the way of an adult father-and-son relationship.

Noah gave the new boards a push. Satisfied they were solid, he leaned his back against the wall and looked Stedman square in the eye. If Stedman wanted to know what was on his mind, other than Rachel, he'd tell. He could use some help unraveling the mystery of it.

"Time, Stedman. That's all I'm thinking about this morning. Why is it always against me? There's either too much or too little. If I could bottle up all those listless hours spent on the prairie watching cows chew their cud, I sure could use a hefty dose of them right now.

"I wasn't stupid enough to think coming here was going to be easy, but I never anticipated the pull to . . . to stay. I can't make a decision like that in a hurry." And he couldn't tell Rachel he was considering a move like that until he was sure. He'd be giving her hope for something more than he may actually be able to offer. And by not telling her, he'd pushed her away. "And maybe it doesn't matter at all. Maybe I'm too late." Too late for *Datt*, and now too late for Rachel.

Stedman raised an eyebrow, giving Noah his best listen-here stare—a caution to ease up on the doom and gloom. Stedman had little patience for negativity. "I also have *Datt's* will on my mind and could use your advice."

"That's more like it. Let's talk solutions. This place has a lot of potential. Whether you choose to use it for yourself or sell it, you stand to profit."

Those were the basic terms of the will. Everything went to Noah. His *datt* had taken great care to maintain enough assets for Noah to go back into the horse business and left Noah with far more than he'd lost by leaving. However, if Noah sold, then he and Trudy split the money fifty-fifty. He didn't care if Trudy got it all, and he sure didn't want her to end up with nothing. Would it be enough to share his profits if he stayed? Only his heart leaned to a non-profit, like the ranch.

"I'm trying to find solutions, Stedman. Only my mind can't get wrapped around all these choices and unknowns yet."

Noah felt the warm, steady grip of his mentor's hand on his shoulder.

"I'm not gonna hide the fact, I don't want you to leave behind your work at the ranch. But work is work, Noah. And when it comes to ministry, you can do good for others wherever God sees fit. Sure, you need time to make a big decision. But be careful. Remaining double-minded and indecisive will tear you apart. At a time like this, when the choice isn't strictly right or wrong but two possible right ways to go, there comes a point where you've gotta make a choice and let God bless the outcome. Your job is to remain faithful to Him whichever way you go and allow Him to do His part."

The advice left him strangely more off-kilter than Rachel's plea in the barn the day before.

"No pressure in that." The sarcastic comment slipped. "Either way, my decision affects the two people most important to me. I really wish God would just tell me what to do."

Stedman looked up to the sky, then back to Noah. "He's dependable, Noah, whatever you decide. He's the only constant, unchanging One for any of us."

Noah should have guessed Stedman's response to his consideration of leaving the ranch would be one of faith in God to work out the details. He admired the man's dependance on God to take care of him in everything. Could he do the same?

"You'd make a good Amish man, Stedman. Undoubtedly, a better one than me when it comes to surrendering to the Lord."

Stedman's throaty laugh echoed through the shelter. "I've struggled to come to terms with this possibility, even had a few heart-to-hearts with the Lord trying to keep you to myself. So, don't be christening me as some sort of saintly cowboy. You know better."

The one thing Noah knew for sure was that he wasn't ready to part with this man who'd fathered him so well into adulthood. Especially not right after losing all hope for more with his real *datt*. Stedman might see the good in both of Noah's options, but Noah saw the inevitable losses, too. And his heart wasn't ready.

Stedman bent down to pack up their tools, probably as hungry as Noah was. With no way to tell the exact time, he hoped they hadn't worked too long. He'd rather not upset Rachel's *mamm* by showing up late for lunch. Beulah including Noah in an invitation to lunch was a strange turn of events.

Noah gathered his share of the load. Without a truck, Noah had hitched up Saul's only remaining horse to a small cart to haul the needed timbers and few tools. Stella made a docile buggy horse, but Noah was hesitant to make her work too hard. Likely, Saul hadn't found a buyer for such an old horse. But with only the tools to carry, she'd have a light load.

Noah untied the reins and led Stella along the worn dirt path with Stedman beside them.

"It doesn't have to be like last time, you know." Stedman's tone was thoughtful as they marched through the field together. "Either way you decide, you don't have to leave everyone and everything behind again. You're not a terrified teenage boy this time, Noah. You are a responsible, God-fearing adult, who can make good decisions. Whatever you do, walk in the confidence of who you are in Christ. That's something you didn't have years ago. And it should make all the difference."

Stedman and Marilyn would be leaving the next day. Their return flight was early Sunday, so they planned to spend Saturday night in Charlottetown to avoid any inconvenience to their hosts. Noah hated to see them go. He'd be in need of Stedman's advice again.

He had to figure out the phone situation, among a million other things. Was he kidding himself that he could go back to the Amish way of life? Cowboying was primitive at times, so he hadn't thought on the challenge in that aspect so much. But some comforts of technology and the modern world had become assets. He missed his truck the most. He'd miss Rachel more.

As they approached the border between the farm and the Erbs' place, Noah paused. "How has it been over there for you and Marilyn?" He didn't want to say he had some misgivings about putting them under Beulah's roof, though he expected she'd be hospitable, despite their connection to Noah.

"You know Marilyn. She can get along in any situation. But I think Beulah is enjoying her company as much as Marilyn is thrilled to be learning more about the Amish." He laughed then. "By the expression on your face, you're as surprised as Rachel seems to be. I'm guessing Marilyn adjusting to the situation isn't what's shocked you. Am I right?"

"Let's just say Beulah never cared for me much. And the fact that *Datt* portioned off that section of the property for her came as a surprise, too. There wasn't any love lost between the two of them either. The only reason I can figure is that he didn't need two houses—just one and the land."

"Maybe he was doing right by helping take care of a widow. She was a part of his church, right? Even if they'd had their differences."

Stedman pointed out the obvious, and Noah wasn't sure why he'd overlooked it.

Still, he couldn't totally remove his suspicion that Saul's motive had been to keep Rachel close for when Noah returned. Because Saul somehow never gave up on that hope or his chance to make things right. And that part comforted Noah—gave him a renewed respect for his *datt* on this day after his burial—that for all his mistakes, Saul had tried to the very end to make up for them. Sure, *Datt* had some crazy ideas of how to go about restoration, but he hadn't given up.

Beulah Erb fretted her rheumatic fingers against the side hem of her apron. She'd asked to visit with Noah out on the front porch after lunch. A visit was another peculiar request coming from Rachel's *mamm*, but he wasn't about to refuse—not if he stood any chance of marrying her daughter.

Rachel was at work, and Stedman and Marilyn went for a drive to see the Prince Edward Island shore. Being alone with Beulah for an afternoon chat didn't bode too well.

Noah sat in a rocking chair next to Beulah's, though no actual rocking was taking place. He wasn't relaxed enough, and Beulah sure wasn't either. Having no inkling what she wanted to say, Noah found himself worrying the rim of his hat while he waited out the silence.

"Harold would know what to do. But he's not here, is he?" She finally began by bringing up her late husband. "He knew, though, some kind of way, this day might come. He never explained, but now I see his reasons." She began to rock then, slow and steady, with her head leaned back.

Noah was still at a loss. "He was a wise man, Harold."

"*Ja*," she snapped as if he'd offended her by telling her what she already knew. Or perhaps he'd interrupted her in the middle of a journey back in time. Either way, she continued pumping her feet back and forth with a touch more force than before.

"No matter how I pleaded, Harold refused to talk Rachel out of breaking things off with Joel. And as much as I hate to bring up those past times, it bears saying to you—and only you, mind—that he forbade me and Sarah to bother her on the subject any more than we already had done."

Beulah's chair came to an abrupt stop. "'She has good enough reason,' he said. Made no sense at the time. But Harold put his foot down so rare, I didn't argue.

"Now, I'm no perfect woman, Noah Detweiler, but I love my daughter. Your *datt* and I had some harsh words back when . . . "

His *mamm* passed. Noah knew it. And he knew how difficult it was for a woman raised as Beulah had been to speak openly about the past, about loved ones and friends gone on to Jesus. He also knew Beulah didn't want her daughter in a marriage like his *mamm's*. When the going got tough, Saul fell to pieces. When they all needed his strength, he'd hidden from them in a bottle. Oh yes, Noah was very aware, but still, the reminder stung.

"It's not our way to speak of the deceased, and I mean no disrespect. But for my Rachel, you understand, I need to know."

"Beulah, I can tell you in all truth I've never tasted a drop of alcohol. Never. And by God's grace, I never will."

"That's *goot,* and I'm glad to hear it." The pace of the rocking beside him slowed to a more relaxed pace. Beulah reached for a basket of yarn beside her, and soon the click of knitting needles kept pace with her rocking.

Noah rested his elbows on the arms of his chair and cupped his chin in his hands. Once again, he relived the vision of hurt he'd seen on Rachel's face at his refusal to take her with him to Alberta. He could have been gentler about it.

He slouched against the back of the rocker. Why had he been such a . . . such a Detweiler? So cocksure, so unwavering. Good traits for herding cattle or breaking horses. Not always so positive for dealing with people.

So, I don't get a choice? Her question replayed in his thoughts. She'd chosen him. The realization sucked the breath out of his lungs. How had he not comprehended what she was saying? He was as big a fool as he'd been thirteen years ago when he assumed that she'd choose Joel.

"Noah, are you listening?" Beulah huffed. Whatever she'd been saying, he missed it.

"Sorry, what was that?"

"What I need to know is what you're going to do about this gossip. I may be smarter than to believe all the clothesline chatter, but what's being said is ruining my Rachel. So, if you've grown into the man my Harold believed you'd become, then why aren't you doing anything to stop it?"

"What gossip, Beulah?" His chair thudded against the wall from the force of his standing. "Not one word has come my way." He jammed his hat on his head and faced the woman as directly as he knew how. "You'd best tell me everything because nobody else will."

CHAPTER NINETEEN

Staying busy at work provided a helpful distraction. Rachel needed a normal day, and she'd had one. Mostly.

And she'd mostly kept Noah out of mind, until he showed up to go on some business about a horse with Tony. She hadn't been able to think about much else since they left.

The office was empty. She'd cleaned all there was to clean and ought to go home. She filled the bottoms of all the trash receptacles with extra can liners—not because she was stalling. It just never hurt to be prepared with extra trash bags.

The back door squeaked open, and she jumped.

"You still here?" Tony called out. He found her sliding a small bin back under his office desk. His nose lifted up in the air, and he sniffed. "Smells surgically sterile in here. Did I miss a memo about spring cleaning?"

"You must have." She held her chin up, refusing to acknowledge she'd dallied around until he returned.

"I've got a few things to wrap up here before I go. But if you're done, you can probably catch a lift from Noah." His amusement showed through his mock-serious expression.

She stared. Her usual supply of witty returns completely dried up. And she wasn't even sure she was ready to face Noah yet, not after the way they'd parted yesterday.

"Go on, then. I've got work to do." Tony winked and shooed her out the door.

After a deep breath, she pushed her shoulder against the heavy back door and almost plowed into Noah on the other side of the exit.

"Oh. Mercy, Noah. I didn't know you were there." She made the terrible mistake of looking into his face and watched his smile bloom. Her heart stuttered. He wasn't angry, for sure. He looked pleased as his eyes took her measure—pleased to see her.

"No harm done." He stepped back to give her room.

She felt herself smile against all her good judgement. She'd warned him not to toy with her heart. How was she supposed to remain unmoved by this rogue cowboy who'd stolen her heart so many years ago?

"Were you waiting?" *Ach*, but she was sure he hadn't been, not for her after all they'd said. "I don't mean for me. I mean, did you need something?"

Unlike the silly awkwardness causing her heart to race, Noah was all collected when he wrapped his warm fingers around her hand. "I was waiting for you."

Relieved, she dared look at him directly. His eyes searched hers, hopeful yet cautious. She wanted to blurt out how tortured she'd been, wondering how things would be between them. Wondering if he understood her feelings or if he was offended.

He held her gaze and whispered, "I've missed you."

She wanted to tease him. It had only been a day, but she felt exactly the same. "I waited for you to get back," she confessed instead.

"How about a ride home?"

They walked to the far side of the lot, where he'd parked Saul's wagon and tethered the horse—a gray roan standardbred with dark socks—that was definitely not Saul's Stella.

"Who's this?" Rachel knew Stella was beyond her prime, but surely, Noah wouldn't go buy a new horse.

"What do you think of him, Raye? He's only eight years old."

She thought this gorgeous gelding was bred to pull a cart, so unless Noah meant to take up horseracing, the only reason to own him would be to pull a buggy. And standardbreds lived a long time. Rachel didn't know what to think about Noah purchasing a buggy horse fine enough for to last another fifteen to twenty years.

"What's his name?"

"Romeo." Noah's eyebrows bobbed up. "Suits him, don't you think?"

"*Ja*, it does." At least she knew what she thought this time. "He looks like a horse Saul would've loved. He knew a good horse, for sure. Oh, this must be one of the horses you told me stabled on a farm out near Montague. What are you going to do with him?"

"Not sell him, if that's what you're thinking. Tony is going to help me bring the others to the farm as soon as I have the place ready." He squeezed her fingers. "C'mon. I'll tell you everything on the way."

Sometimes, everything you thought you knew changed in a moment. As she climbed into the seat and Noah came around to the other side, Rachel sensed this was one of those times.

Noah was quiet as he drove Romeo through the busy crossway and turned up the two-lane road toward home. Amish farms stretched along the next two miles, and the man beside her suddenly fit right into the view.

Ja, an important change had occurred since yesterday; only, she couldn't pin it down.

"Noah, can I ask you a question?"

He took his eyes off the road for a moment to look at her. "Of course."

"What did you mean yesterday when you said you're different now?"

His attention was back to the road, but his response was quick. "I take it you're not referring to the fact that I'm taller and much more handsome."

Without a second thought, she swatted his arm.

He laughed before taking in a deep breath and turning more serious. "I suppose I had some excuses for running away like I did. Back then, I believed I was leaving behind a hopeless cause. I'd given up on *Datt* long before I left. You kept me going, Raye, but then I gave up any hope for us." He sounded pained as he spoke, and Rachel felt a stab to her heart with his confession. But he wasn't finished. "When it came time to join the church, I just couldn't do it . . . because I'd given up on God, too."

Saul had been nothing short of terrible. And she had been naïve about her feelings for Noah, not realizing fully how much he meant to her until it was too late. "Noah, you weren't all to blame—"

"Perhaps," he interrupted, "but I still haven't answered your question." He pulled the wagon over in a field just beyond the Bellers' dairy and scooted around on the bench seat to face her. "I needed God, but I pushed Him away along with everything else. And I lived like that for almost seven years. Alone. Just me, the cattle, my horse, and a dog on the prairie. For a while, I was all right. I guess bitterness and anger provide fuel for a body longer than you'd expect. But there came a point where I saw I was turning into the man I'd run from. I was a miserable wretch when I met Stedman, and he helped me find my way to Jesus. Growing up, I'd gone through the motions to please everyone else. But my new faith in Christ changed me, Raye. I felt as if God took a firehose and flooded out all the sludge of built-up wrongs and regrets, all the while pouring in new life from an unspoiled, clear spring. I still needed help to deal with the past and move forward, but God gave me a beginning and hung with me all the way."

"I love Jesus, Raye, more than anything in this world. And if He wants me here and sees fit to give us a life together, I'll make whatever sacrifice He asks of me. After all He's done for me, I can give up a little bit of independence to follow Amish rules—even my pick-up truck." His eyes twinkled at his last words were spoken, as though he understood just how heavy the weight of his confession was on her own heart. He leaned forward and wiped away a tear from the corner of her eye with his thumb.

"You wouldn't be happy outside the Amish. You know that, deep down. You have to know because you would never have considered leaving the Amish but for my sake. I can't ask that of you. Here, at New Hope, we can both honor God's will for our lives. I don't believe I could have joined the old congregation. But with Bishop Nafziger and Joel, I am confident their teaching on salvation is sound.

"Raye." He held both of her hands close to his chest. She could feel his heartbeat and feared her own had stood still. "Give me time to prove myself to the people here. And when the time comes, I will be asking you to marry me. Can you wait for me, just a little longer?"

He'd stunned her, for sure, but when he put it like that, well . . . "I can wait for you, Noah." She pulled his hands to her lips and kissed his fingers. "But not very long."

"Rachel, darling." His voice was rough and his blue eyes a tempest. "I promise waiting is not any easier on me than you."

For one blissful minute, she relished Noah's adoration, feeling as if all good things truly might come to those who wait. So then, why did she have to recall Albert's vitriol toward them both and to ruin it all? If Albert had his way, joining the Amish was no sure thing for Noah.

Noah must know so. She watched him closely as he released her hands and quietly returned his light-footed gelding onto the road. His jaw flexed as he stared straight ahead.

Ja, he knew obstacles loomed ahead, but he'd made up his mind. And when Noah Detweiler made up his mind, he didn't mean to do it halfway. He'd taken so long to believe in them. She didn't want to ruin this moment any further by discussing her brother's contribution to the difficult road ahead of them.

Rachel hummed lightly until the tension eased from Noah's shoulders, if only the slightest. The faith Noah talked about—they both needed it now as much as ever.

Midday sun glistened on tender, green grass wet from a passing shower. The small corral Noah had repaired with Stedman the previous evening remained grassy from lack of use. Not for long. Romeo pranced along the fence line and whinnied.

Noah rested a foot on the bottom fence rail and tossed the remnants of a lukewarm cup of coffee. Stedman poured himself more from the thermos he'd brought up from Beulah's kitchen.

"I could make you some fresh," Noah offered.

"Can't go around wasting good coffee."

Good was debatable, but Noah just shook his head and changed the subject. "What do you make of this fella? He's lonely, I think. But I'll get his friends here soon enough."

Stedman leaned into the gate with his elbows spread wide and arms flat against the top rail. "He's a beauty all right. So, was it love at first sight with Romeo here that made up your mind so fast?" Stedman chuckled. "Or did you come to your senses about the rare treasure of a woman waiting all these years for you? Can't say as I blame her for reaching the end of her rope."

"Rachel is a treasure. And she's patient, but it's not like she was sitting around twiddling her thumbs and pining over me. If God hadn't kept her for me . . . " *For him*—the magnitude of God doing such a thing for him was overwhelming. If God really meant for the two of them to become one, Noah was well aware of the priceless gift he'd been given. And how much more she was worth than he ever deserved.

Stedman clasped a hand on the back of Noah's shoulder. "Looks like you've got company."

Noah turned his head to see Samy riding her velvety bay mare, Amazon, through the edge of the pine woods. Joel walked up beside her with Samuel Nafziger, the bishop, too.

Noah didn't much care for the anxious tension that knotted up in his gut. There was no reason for it, not anymore. Good memories never wear out—or so the saying went—and the last week had stored up plenty on these kind folks' behalf. He'd worn out his old memories of Joel and the bishop long ago. The time had come for change.

Still, these two men, more than any others, would make decisions to affect the course for his future with Rachel. So, maybe his nerves had some cause for stirring his insides.

Joel helped Samy down from Amazon's back. She walked directly to the opposite side of the fence from where Romeo stood sizing up

Amazon. Most children would go right to the spot closest to the horse unless they were afraid of the animal, which was not the case with Samy.

Samy clicked her tongue, gaining Romeo's attention, then waited patiently as he sauntered in her direction. Both child and horse were curious about each other. Before long, Romeo allowed Samy to stroke his neck and forehead.

"Looks like he's found the friend he's been calling for this morning." Stedman nodded at the two fast friends on the other side of the corral. "How about I watch over these two? I suspect you men have some talking to do."

That was Stedman, never one to beat around the bush. Noah had planned to talk to the minister and bishop, anyway. He may as well get straight to business, as well. "Samuel. Joel. Would you like to visit a spell in the house?"

The plan suited everyone fine, especially his offer for coffee. Noah figured they needed a post-lunch perk as much as he did before any heavy discussion.

They sat around the kitchen table, while Noah filled them in on the pertinent details of Saul's will. He noticed the bishop's expression held no surprise, while Joel appeared to be concentrating on every aspect Noah shared.

Behind them, the percolator gurgled on the stove, and the aroma of the fresh brew signaled their coffee was ready. Noah poured a cup for each of them.

"*Danki.*" The bishop spoke first as Noah sat back down. "Saul came with us to this new community because he believed God could make all things new. He was grateful for the forgiveness he'd received from the Lord and by his church, but he still struggled to be at peace."

Because his datt wanted Noah's forgiveness.

"I admit, the road to forgiveness has taken me a long time. And self-forgiveness has been even harder. The problems between *Datt* and me weren't all of his making. I struggled with my own guilt for years. I'm grateful God pulled me back here in time to find some peace for us both before the end."

Joel looked up at Noah then with compassion and a surety about what he was about to say. "We aren't truly able to forgive others or accept forgiveness for ourselves before we understand how much God has forgiven us and the great pain He suffered to offer us that peace."

True. Noah wished he could have expressed the words so well himself.

Samuel stroked his beard. "Noah, your *datt* wanted forgiveness, true, but he also wanted to restore what he felt he had taken from you. You see this in his last will and testament, do you not?"

Of course, he had. Though when Samuel put his father's purpose into words, the impact struck him with more force. The land, the horses, the finances all added up to prove the bishop correct. And Rachel—*Datt* did his best to reunite them as well.

Noah wanted to respond, but his emotions choked out anything he might say.

With a nod of understanding, the bishop continued. "Joel believes from your conversations lately that you have come to this place of salvation through faith in what Jesus has done for you. Is that right?" Samuel's voice relayed both comfort and hope. He'd always been a caring man.

"I have, Samuel. I wouldn't be here today if God had not changed my heart and set me free from guilt—along with a load of shame and doubt."

"This is why we are here." Joel leaned forward, eager to get to the point, apparently. "We hope you will consider joining our congregation here at New Hope."

Was this going be so easy? Nothing was ever easy for Noah. He'd accepted the fact years ago that in his life he'd have to work hard for the things that mattered most to him. Noah turned to Samuel to make sure he was in full support of all Joel had said.

Samuel nodded, "Most of all, Saul settled here to give you a second chance at Amish life away from all the old memories. And if *Gott* is willing and you desire the same, I would welcome you with open arms."

Noah pushed back in his chair and walked over to the stove. He fumbled around a bit, checking on the coffee for no good reason. He needed a minute to collect himself. When he finally found his voice strong enough to continue, he leaned against the counter and faced the two men.

"I would have come to you first, only you beat me to it. I want to marry Rachel." Neither man at the table appeared shocked. In fact, Samuel hid a smile. "But I want to join the church first."

"I am glad to hear it." Samuel rose from his seat, followed by Joel. The three of them stood together in the middle of the kitchen. Samuel continued, "But we have to warn you, as you consider, there may be some trouble to face. But if *Gott* wills for you to join us, then He will make the way plain."

Noah felt his blood rolling to the same boil as the percolator minutes ago. "I've been made aware of some gossip. While I wouldn't pay any attention if I was the only one being slandered, I'm not. And what I can't understand is why anyone would want to bring so much trouble on Rachel."

"If God can shut the mouths of lions, then He most surely can stop a man's idle words." The bishop left the name of the instigator unspoken, but Noah got the message.

"Noah." Joel gave him a direct look. Not so much a warning as a promise. "We will do this the way of the church. We will go to our brother alone first to see if he will repent of the falsehoods and hurt he has caused."

Noah had no desire to know who'd started the rumors, although Joel seemed to think he did. "I'm not out for revenge, only truth. Besides, I wouldn't even know who began it all." From Noah's experience, someone who made up such lies, or maybe even believed them in some twisted frame of mind, wasn't likely to admit to their wrong so easily. "I don't envy you the task."

A silent communication passed between bishop and minister.

"Well, then, I believe it is time to pray." After the bishop offered a prayer for God's will to be done, he made a point to offer an invitation for Noah to worship with the people at Abe Nafziger's house on the Sabbath. Then, they said their goodbyes.

Tomorrow was coming fast, but he had every intention to be there.

CHAPTER TWENTY

After his goodbyes to Stedman and Marilyn late Saturday afternoon, Noah ran through scenarios of how he'd be received when he showed up at Abe and Sarah Nafziger's house for church in the morning. There was only one way to find out, and he planned to.

In the meantime, the evening was coming in like a slow train. Noah drummed his fingers on the armrest of the only comfortable seat in the living room and contemplated an excuse to go see Rachel. Did he need one? Once more, there was one sure way to find out. He set out across the field toward the Erbs'.

As the house and drive came into view, he noticed a few extra buggies in the grass and recalled the Saturday when Rachel had brought him supper from their family get-together. He'd forgotten about the weekly tradition and hadn't intended to crash a family gathering.

Maybe he ought to come by later. The idea reminded him too much of a young fella courting his Amish sweetheart in secret. He laughed out loud. He was too old to play the teenager again. He and Rachel had moved far beyond silly games. And more importantly, he desired everything they did from here on out to be fully transparent and open. Secrets bred gossip. He hoped bringing their relationship to the light of day would root out the talk.

Just then, Drew stepped out of the house and caught sight of him.

"Hello," the young man called as he came nearer and met Noah a few yards away from the house. "I suppose you've come to see Rachel."

"An easy guess," Noah teased. No use denying it.

"Well, then, you may want to know she usually slips out the back door just before dessert. Can't say where she goes, though."

"And you're sneaking off, too, I take it."

Drew nodded, his only answer a mischievous grin.

Before Rachel's nephew got too far, Noah called after him, "How long until dessert?"

"You don't think I'd leave before dessert, do you?" Drew laughed and jogged in the other direction toward his courting buggy.

Noah checked around back near the old cellar where Rachel had him wait once before, but he didn't see her anywhere. Where would she go?

A sense of being watched drew his attention to the house. There at an upstairs window, Rachel waved down at him. She stepped back, and a curtain fell to block any further view of her.

Noah pushed himself up to a standing position, brushed off the seat of his pants, and headed straight to the back door, hoping Rachel would meet him there. He hadn't really counted on revealing his plans to the whole Erb clan yet.

All afternoon, he'd mulled over how to go about this whole process. Things were moving a little fast. He'd prefer to go about this big of a change in a more methodical way. And a quiet visit to Sunday services tomorrow seemed like the next logical step. Just enough to give everyone the hint that he might stay. He still preferred that plan.

After a few minutes of waiting for Rachel at the back door and still no sign of her, he knocked. Thankfully, Reuben's wife, Laura, was the one to answer his knock and let him inside the mudroom which led to the kitchen. In fact, she'd opened the door wide with a smile.

She hadn't shown any of the shock now registering on the face of her husband and brother-in-law, Albert.

Quickly aware he was an unwanted guest, Noah planted boots squarely in the center of the room. Whether Rachel's brothers liked him or not, he was here to stay. He also knew he had the understood Amish rule of hospitality at his advantage.

Reuben took less than a second to adjust to a neutral expression. But Albert's face reddened hotter than a blazing forge.

"What are you doing here?" Albert's question sounded more like an accusation. His hands fisted at his sides, as though he meant to throw Noah out of the house. So much for Amish hospitality.

"Brother." Reuben's warning to his younger sibling was even and low and earned him a glare before Albert clamped his mouth shut.

Albert's wife, Vonda, stepped out of a side room with Beulah just behind her.

"Beulah." Noah nodded in greeting to Rachel's mother out of respect, but she remained frozen, except for the slightest turn of her eyes to her oldest son.

Only Reuben wasn't looking at his mother or Noah. His attention was beyond Noah's head. And before Noah turned, he knew who he'd see. Rachel was there behind him, paused on the stairway, pale and unsmiling.

Rachel's stockings may as well have been glued to the stair where she'd stopped at the sound of Noah's voice. She looked over his head to the tense room, where he stood in a face-off with her family. At least they couldn't keep talking about Noah behind his back.

Noah held onto his hat, as he'd likely removed it when entering the house. He hadn't yet taken his blue eyes off her. He did that thing where his fingers moved to tip an imaginary hat, making her heart flutter. Could he see the love for him stirring within her?

His brows pressed together in serious determination. He turned back to the room filled with her family and cleared his throat. No one was staring at Rachel now. Noah had their full attention.

He aimed at Reuben and Albert but spoke loud enough for anyone present to hear him clearly. "I've come to speak privately with Rachel, but first, you may as well all be aware that I have also spoken with Joel and Bishop Nafziger about joining the congregation at New Hope."

Rachel's hand flew over her heart as a ringing of audible gasps came from the direction of her *mamm* and Vonda. Her *mamm* signaled for Rachel to come with an outstretched hand, and Vonda practically hissed as Rachel slipped passed her.

"This is not the way." Albert's angry retort captured her attention. "You cannot simply join the church just so you may marry an Amish woman." Albert raised his arms, close to flying into a rage before Reuben laid a hand on his brother's shoulder and pulled him away from the center of the room.

Surely, Noah wasn't doing this for her. A vow to the church was a commitment to *Gott*, too serious to be made to please a person. And yet she'd been ready to break her own vow for Noah. Was that why he'd refused? Noah wouldn't be a part of her breaking a vow she'd made not only to her church but foremost to *Gott*.

She'd been silent all through dinner, refusing to defend herself. But now, this was different. She pushed to the center of the room.

"You are mistaken Albert. If anyone has proven he understands the seriousness of joining the Amish, Noah has. I offered to go away with him, but he refused."

If anything, Albert grew angrier. "All that proves is your own wickedness and his evil influence over you. You bewitch every man into doing your bidding. Why else would the bishop allow you to bend the rules so far?" A bulging blood vessel zagged down his forehead. Albert had said as much before, although this time his venom struck harder. "It would be better for us all if you did leave."

"Albert!" Reuben's temperate calm turned to a roar.

"I'll not be silenced in my own family, Reuben." Albert reared his head back, and Rachel braced for the venom she knew was coming her way. "First, you lead Joel; then, who knows? I've seen how familiar the vet is with you. How many men have you been with to have your way?"

In one long stride, Noah was nose-to-nose with Albert. "Do not disrespect Rachel in such a way again. Ever."

Mamm whimpered, already distraught from discovering Albert was the source of the lies about Rachel and Noah. If only Sarah was there to comfort their mother, but Rachel moved back to wrap an arm around her mother's shoulders.

Reuben stepped between Albert and Noah.

Not a single muscle in Noah's stance twitched. Albert backed away like most bullies when confronted head-on.

Reuben's face was harder than Rachel had ever seen as he spoke to Noah. "You need to go. I must handle this." His voice dropped a notch when he added, "Watch over my sister. I will come for her at your house when this is settled between us."

With a gentle push from her *mamm*, Rachel latched onto Noah's elbow and encouraged him away from the men in the room. As she hastened toward the back door, Laura stopped her.

"Here." Laura wrapped a shawl around Rachel's shoulders, then ran her hands up and down Rachel's arms. The kindness did as much to warm Rachel as the motion. "Everything will work out. I will see you in a little while when we come for you, *ja?*"

Rachel nodded and forced a smile, even though she felt none of Laura's optimism.

"Thank you," Noah responded to Laura, then took a firm hold of Rachel's hand as they set out toward his farm.

"Are you all right to walk?" he asked as they neared the fence between the two properties. He appeared cross, she noted by the deep lines furrowing his brow, but his tone was all concern.

"It's not far." Perhaps his anger at her brother would ease by the time they'd crossed the way. They walked a fair distance before she broke the silence. "Only my *datt* ever defended me like you did. It has been hard at times, since he died."

"The only thing that kept my fist out of Albert's face was the regrets I've lived with from trying that method before. And knowing I'd never be welcomed into the church."

"It would be a sin."

"Would it?" Noah sighed. "I don't mean that. But he does need to fear some sort of consequences for his hatefulness and cruelty."

"I don't know why he is so angry or what I ever did to make him hate me."

"There's always the possibility it has nothing to do with anything you've done. You're just a convenient target to attack for his own insecurities."

Noah's assessment fit her brother and his actions, though she'd never considered him from such an angle. "If that's true, I think I may be able to bear him a little easier."

"It's not a justification for the man, Raye, only an explanation. He is still in the wrong. He cannot continue to treat you so harshly." Noah was still cross. His rigid shoulders and terse voice belied the storm still brewing beneath the surface.

They hiked the rest of the way in silence. As Noah worked out his anger, each pounding step became less forceful along the way. And by the time they neared his house, she no longer sensed the same urgency and tension in him.

He held the door open for her. Inside, the kitchen was darker than the dusk-lit evening outside. He reached behind her, his arm brushing her shoulders, and turned on the lights. The gas lights hummed and set a soft glow in the room.

"Would you like a hot drink or something cold?"

She turned to reply and found herself much closer to him than she'd anticipated. His eyes were searching her face. If she'd been about to say something, she'd forgotten what.

"You're precious to me, Raye. I never should have left you. If I'd known . . . " He shook his head. "That's just it. I may have stayed for you, if I thought I had a real chance. But then, I may never have come to a true faith in God. I'd still be as bitter and angry as Albert—pretending to have faith but only following a set of rules to cover up my own failures."

"*Gott* has taken care of me. I don't know why Albert cannot accept it is the Lord Who has provided for me, not . . . well, not as he supposes." Her heart twisted in shame, though she'd done nothing to deserve her brother's accusations.

Noah's hand cupped her face, his thumb rested at the tip of her chin. "God has been faithful to us, hasn't He? We can trust Him with what lies ahead . . . *ja?*" His mouth crooked up at the corners with the slip of the Amish word, and his eyes sparked again with his good nature. "And Rachel, I don't need to have been here to know the truth about you—about your character. Satan is the father of lies. We shouldn't give him one more second of thought to the gossip. We live by the truth and walk in the Light."

She nodded in agreement. Of course, he was right. They could trust the One Who'd brought them this far. She only wished her heart would agree a little faster.

He dropped his hand and stepped back. "I'll make us some coffee if you'd like a cup? I think I remember seeing some decaf in the cabinet."

She'd been in his kitchen enough over the past week during the funeral preparations to know where everything was. She reached over his head and pulled down a canister of ground decaf. Noah lit the stove and set the percolator to heat.

"I'm still wrapping my mind around you coming back to the Amish—not just for a visit—but home for good," she blurted as she sat down at the table to wait for their coffee.

He slipped into the chair in front of her. "If you'd told me so when I first received your letter about Saul, I'd never have believed it either." His blue eyes danced, then settled into a more somber mood. He stretched out the pause and held her in his gaze for a long minute. "I also expected you would be married. I don't know any words to describe how I felt to find out I was wrong. I knew I couldn't walk away from you again, so I made up my mind to avoid you. I thought I could make some sort of amends with *Datt* over a day or two, then go back to life as usual on the ranch. I must have known, though, deep down."

The pot on the stove sputtered loudly, and Noah left the table to retrieve the hot coffee. He tipped the dark liquid into two mugs on the counter. Steam rose from both, as he stirred cream into hers then carried it along with his straight black coffee to the table.

All the while, she was contemplating exactly what he might have known.

"What was it?"

"Hmm?" He took a sip of the drink far too hot for her liking yet.

"You said you must have known something."

"The truth." His eyebrows raised as he lifted the mug back to his mouth and watched her from above the rim. His smile—a sure sign he knew he was being impossible. "So, do I get to ask you a question now?"

He was changing the subject, and she let it go.

"All right."

"I didn't mention joining the church because I hadn't decided and didn't want to give you false hope. I didn't mean to hurt you. I'm sorry for that."

He hadn't exactly posed a question but paused so long, she felt compelled to answer. "I forgive you."

"Thank you." He stood up and ran his fingers through his hair. "I want to marry you, Raye. The sooner, the better. I think you know that."

"You said so before, *ja*." Rachel's heart pounded. Knowing a thing was far different than the experience of hearing so in his own words. "But you can keep on telling me. It gets a little sweeter each time."

"Can I say how much I want to kiss you right now? I would, too, if your brother weren't coming any minute to fetch you."

She stood and made her way in front of him. "I don't think that will get old either."

"Don't tempt me, Woman." His eyes darkened, and he pulled her closer. "You're not the only one who has waited a long time."

"I'd marry you tomorrow, Noah. No matter what happens with the church, I still want to marry you."

He ran a finger along her cheek and stopped at her lips. He paused so long, her lungs burned from holding her breath. He exhaled into the stillness and stepped away.

"One step at a time, Raye. Let's see if God opens up this door for us."

Church membership required more than a recommendation by the bishop and elders. The full membership would vote. New Hope members didn't agree on everything, of course. Still, they usually managed a way to get along. But everyone who'd grown up in the church knew voting could be unpredictable.

"Is it right, though, Noah, to hang our future on what the church decides? This is too personal."

He rubbed the back of his neck. "I'd like to believe it's the Lord we're trusting with our future, Raye."

When she'd taken her vows of church membership, she'd believed the best way to live a godly life was in submission to the Lord and to the church. This was the reason so few followed the Amish way. And never in her life had she desired to rebel against the submission she'd entered into of her own free will. Until now. Noah joining the Amish was a selfless surrender of himself for her sake.

"It doesn't feel right. You give up everything, while I do nothing."

"Raye, that's not how it is."

A knock sounded from the back door.

"I guess that will be your brother." He didn't move to open it. "I'd rather not end the evening this way."

She did her best to smile and ease his worry. "You'll be at church then."

"Raye." He hovered over her, then raised his arm to wipe her cheeks with the cuff of his shirtsleeve. Ignoring a second knock, he pulled her head against his chest and held her there. "Please don't cry, darling."

Until he wiped her face, she didn't realize her tears were flowing so freely.

"I didn't mean to." She glanced up at him just as a third knock almost banged down the door.

"It's not locked," he whispered through a chuckle. He stepped back and held the door knob. "I'd like to see you tomorrow. Not only at church. Just you and me. Would you come with me for a ride?"

"I'd like that," she agreed before he opened the door for Reuben.

As she climbed into the buggy with her brother's family, Rachel wondered what Reuben had stayed to tell Noah. She looked over to Laura, who only gave a small shake of her head and motioned to the children. Rachel would have to wait to find out what had transpired in her absence.

Reuben climbed into the buggy and urged the horse into motion. Rachel looked back to see Noah framed by the door posts watching them. She waved, and he raised a hand back to her.

"Don't set your hopes too high." Reuben's voice was low, so the children couldn't hear over the trot of the horses. "Noah may have *goot* intentions, but Albert is dead-set on making trouble for him. I think most of the people will see Noah's intentions are pure, but there's no guarantee. Joel and the bishop will do right, but with your own brother against you . . . Well, nothing is a sure thing where people's emotions are concerned."

Ach. Rachel pressed her fingers to the bridge of her nose and closed her eyes. All she ever wanted was peace. Maybe that was why she'd become more comfortable with the idea of leaving with Noah—to avoid this conflict. Sure, she'd be removed from membership. Many in her own family would never speak with her again. Right now, that didn't seem so bad. And at least, she'd be too far away to feel this tension.

I'd like to believe it's the Lord I'm trusting with our future.

How had she ever called Noah a coward? He was facing this spiritual battle by faith. He'd taken on the pain of his past, and now he was pressing forward. Her previous admonition of Noah rose up to accuse her this time. When had her faith shrunk so small?

One step at a time, that was all she could do and pray it was enough.

CHAPTER TWENTY-ONE

Noah awakened—if possible, considering he'd hardly slept—to the chatter of pre-dawn birdsong. An emptiness had settled over the place after Rachel left. He hadn't liked the solitude, not at first. But he'd had time to think—and pray.

The previous day had been a whirlwind of emotional events. And only two days after he'd buried his father, he'd need some quiet to find perspective. He couldn't rush such life-changing decisions.

He'd meant what he said to Rachel about trusting God with their future, but maybe he'd been a bit hasty in dismissing her concern about joining the church. He'd missed the signals that joining wasn't just about him. It was a decision on her future, too.

Albert had never been the brotherly sort. He only ever paid attention to Sarah because she riled him. Rachel was the baby sister; and when Albert hadn't ignored her altogether, he'd seemed jealous. Noah had never known Rachel to pay him any mind. Thinking back, though, his lack of affection must have hurt. Now that Noah had a better idea of what she'd suffered since her *datt* was no longer alive to fill her need for love and protection, he had a clue as to why she'd offered to go with him to Alberta.

He and Rachel had a lot of heart-to-heart talks ahead of them. He'd never expected her to be willing to jump the fence for him or anyone else either. She was right. They needed to be sure this was the right choice for their future.

As much as he wanted to marry Rachel right away, the fact this process of joining the Amish would take weeks or months was really for the best. Just another instance of Amish tradition based on the wisdom of generations of experience.

They wouldn't rush to accept him as a full member, even though some had readily shown kindness and friendship. The membership process was bound to take time. Time he needed. They both needed. But waiting was the one thing sure to set Rachel to running like a spooked horse.

He tackled the outdoor chores before full light and scraped together a breakfast washed down with three cups of hot coffee. Only after showering did he realize he'd nothing appropriate to wear to an Amish church meeting. Not that he'd blend in, anyway. He'd be attending as an outsider, allowed because of his heritage. A direct invitation from the bishop helped, too.

His clothes were all store bought, but at least he had the black slacks and an ordinary, white, dress shirt Stedman had brought to him for the funeral. He could leave off the belt and wear a pair of his *datt's* suspenders instead. He hadn't been able to do so for the funeral. Rummaging through the old man's things while his body lay in wait—he shuddered. The task wasn't much more pleasant even now. He'd be quick about it.

At the end of the hall. he came to a stop in front of the closed door to Saul's room. For two days, he'd ushered visitors through the same door to pay their respects. Then, he'd closed the door when the Amish pallbearers carried Saul's lifeless body in a plain, wooden box to be buried. Now, his hand tremored above the knob.

He couldn't do it. Not yet. Dressing Amish would have to wait, he decided firmly as he walked past Saul's Sunday best hat on the peg by the back door.

The morning services were being hosted by Abe and Sarah Nafziger, whose farm he'd already become familiar with when searching for Samy. He debated walking the short distance versus hitching Romeo to his *datt's* buggy. The sky was clear blue with the barest breeze, the calmest he'd experienced on the island so far, and a walk to church suited his mood best.

How often had he walked hand-in-hand with his *mamm* to church on a beautiful Sunday? Too many to count. A vision of Rachel and their own *kinner* dressed in Sunday best and traipsing together along this island drive was an easy picture to imagine. One to warm a man down to his soul.

At the end of the drive, he counted three buggies pass along the road in quick succession. He made his way in the same direction and caught sight of Rachel at the dip between the two hills. He lengthened his downhill stride and shortened the distance between them by half.

"Raye."

He couldn't tell if she heard him and was about to call again when he noticed her attention headed in a different direction. By the time he reached the spot where he first spotted her, Rachel had already walked into her sister's house.

Abe's gravel drive split the distance between his traditional farmhouse on one side and large barn on the other. The way families divided on arrival, women to the house and men to the barnyard, mirrored the aisle that split them down the center of the wooden church benches for worship. He couldn't very well follow her without making a spectacle of himself.

Only women would be in the house, getting in order from the eldest to the youngest for entering the nine o'clock service in the barn. Noah drifted among the men visiting outside and loosely lining up in a similar order for meeting time.

He'd have to wait to see Rachel. Even after church, the men and women wouldn't mingle very much. Rachel had been right; waiting wasn't so great. Especially not when surrounded by so many memories.

If he could get through an Amish church service once, then surely, he could repeat the process until he could put the past to rest. He prayed worship among these brethren wouldn't always bring this overwhelming sadness.

Being on the island and far away from the place of his memories in Ontario ought to help. And not all, but enough of the folks milling about until service time had been present years ago for his *datt's* confessions. They were the same folks who'd offered Saul forgiveness time and again.

Grief—fresh and merciless—struck at his heart, then blurred with memories long past.

"In the name of the Lord and of the church, I offer my hand. Arise." Samuel Nafziger's words of restoration lit a candle of hope in Noah's chest as the minister gave Saul Detweiler a holy kiss.

For six weeks leading up to the service of restoration, young Noah had witnessed his father sit on the front row with his head in his hands, contrite and humbled. He'd promised the entire congregation before Gott to abstain from drunkenness. He'd do better. He'd ask the Lord to help him. And for the past six weeks, he had. Watching his datt's *shame was almost unbearable. No matter how bad things were at home, Noah didn't like to see his* datt *broken in front of everyone.*

So, when the minister declared Saul's sin was to be forgiven and re-membered no more, Noah felt the disgrace of the past weeks would be worth it if his datt *was finally at peace. Alcohol had stolen his father as surely as cancer had killed his mother. But now—now, things could go back to normal.*

Only the healing didn't last.

Noah bit the inside of his cheek to halt the memories. He'd lost count over the next several years of the number of times his *datt* confessed the same sin, received forgiveness, then broke his promise again. The people showed Saul grace upon grace, but he returned to his bottle with no mercy. Finally, the humiliation had become more than Noah's heart could bear.

What—Noah had to wonder—had happened after Noah left to give Saul the strength to overcome his addiction?

Years ago, at Stedman's persistent urging, Noah sought counsel-ing to come to terms with his anger toward both Saul and God. He might never have been able to make this trip if not for the healing he'd experienced after some wise counsel. And he found it difficult to believe Saul had given up his habit simply from a shock when Noah left. There had to be more to the story.

Herschel Beller engaged him in friendly conversation, and a few other men greeted him warmly. The only scowl he'd noticed was

Albert's. If there were others, he wasn't going to seek them. He'd mind his own business and let the Lord do His. Joining the church shouldn't be a popularity contest—not to Noah's way of thinking, which he realized was his Amish upbringing showing through.

Samuel Nafziger, who would begin the procession into the service, had been in a conversation with his two sons, Joel and Abe, since Noah arrived. But now, Noah noticed the bishop was headed his way.

"Glad to see you this fine Lord's Day, Noah."

"*Danki*, Samuel."

"We will be going in for service in a minute. You may sit in the front row to show you're interest in joining the church. Or if you prefer to sit in the back as a guest today, that will be all right."

Noah hesitated. He hadn't known he'd have a choice.

"Take a minute to decide. It's up to you. But we may have some church business to take care of at the end. If so, you may just excuse yourself at the end of the regular meeting."

Noah had seen that look on Samuel's face before. Only now, the lines on his forehead had multiplied and grown deeper. He was a kind man and a burdened one. As a non-member, whatever was to be discussed was not Noah's business, but he wouldn't be surprised if Albert was at the heart of it. "I understand. Maybe I'll sit at the back today to cause less disruption."

"Maybe that's for the best. But we have no desire to make a secret of your plans. We are committed at New Hope to live transparent before *Gott* and each other."

"I'm glad to hear it." But for Samuel's sake, Noah would cause as little stir as possible today. "Your openness and welcome mean a great deal, Samuel."

"*Gott* bless you." The bishop smiled and excused himself. If service was to be prompt, he needed to lead the congregation into the place of worship.

Noah fell into the back of the line of men as they entered the barn to be seated. The women filed in through a side door to the other side, and Noah caught a glimpse of Rachel crossing the gap between the house and the barn.

He felt a light poke in the ribs. "Hard not to watch, ain't so, when you got your heart set on one?"

Noah smiled at Drew. "For sure and certain, you're right about that."

Once inside, Noah slipped onto the end of the last row. He was seated among good people. Not perfect but unselfish men and women willing to sacrifice their own personal freedom for the benefit of the whole. A mighty lofty ideal in today's world.

The Amish had persevered through trials for generations by bearing one another's burdens and standing together in unity. He appreciated the value of community in a way he couldn't as a young man. He'd thought the grass might be greener on the other side, so to speak. People were just people everywhere, he'd discovered, and trouble came to all. Only God, in His time, could make all things right. And life was too short to fight doing things His way. Not that Noah thought the Amish tradition was the only choice for a Christian to live a Christ-honoring life. In fact, he didn't recall too many Amish who would be so prideful as to think so. But was Amish the way that God ordained for him? Only time would tell.

CHAPTER TWENTY-TWO

A sudden gust of wind twisted Rachel's skirt around her legs and threatened to loosen the pins of her prayer *kapp*. Outside her brother-in-law's barn, the bluster sure had increased since Sabbath service began earlier in the morning. With a hand raised to hold her *kapp*, Rachel hurried across the yard to help her sister with the church lunch. At least there was no rain—only the salty smell of the sea in the air.

An old memory flashed of a harsher gale, a pounding rain, and another mad dash across the same path from the barn to her sister's kitchen—the night she broke her engagement to Joel Yoder. Goose pimples shivered across her forearms.

Right when life seemed to be coming around full-circle for her, Albert had to go raise a stink. She crossed her arms and brushed away the raised bumps.

From the side porch, she looked around, hoping to catch sight of Noah before the rest of the congregation flooded out of the barn. He'd left, of course, right before the mess with her brother began, but he'd still be around somewhere. Wherever he was, she couldn't see him, so she stepped into the kitchen.

Lydia looked up from the bowl she was filling with peanut butter sandwich spread. Rachel noticed a tell-tale sign of relief in the way Lydia's shoulders relaxed. Rachel's sister, Sarah, always managed to put Lydia on edge, and the two had been in here more than a few minutes getting lunch ready to serve.

"I see the wind picked up." Lydia smiled and nodded toward the mess of hair falling around Rachel's face.

Rachel swiped the loose strands behind her ears. "*Ja.* I wonder if we should have the men set up another table and take the food to the barn to serve. The food might blow right off folks' plates if they try carrying them from here to eat at the tables in the barn."

A grunt from the other side of the kitchen turned Rachel's head to see her sister standing with a fist propped firmly against her hip.

"Don't be changing things around now. It's all ready. If a person can't manage to carry a plate across the way, then they've got no business eating it." Sarah glared at Rachel, then shot an equally hard stare at Lydia.

How did that make any sense? Rachel held her peace; she'd been teasing anyway. And no wonder Sarah wasn't in the mood. It was going to be a long and awkward afternoon. Albert made sure of that.

Lydia turned back to uncovering the sandwich meats, but not before Rachel caught her eyes raised heavenward. "*I know.*" Rachel mouthed the words, and a half-smile tickled the corners of Lydia's mouth. Might as well laugh. There was no use in crying.

Rachel turned around to find Sarah standing with her hands on her hips and open-mouthed, but she closed it without saying another word. Rachel saw the hurt before her sister bustled back over to the icebox.

Her heart squeezed. Sarah was her unflappable sister. Rachel hadn't meant to cause her offense. The three of them always carried on like this. What was happening to her family today? Their world was turning upside-down, that's what.

Voices echoed into the kitchen from the mud room as more helpers arrived for serving the meal. Lydia gave Rachel's hand a squeeze and motioned her into the next room.

"Sarah has been upset all morning, even before the meeting. Several times, she mentioned missing the family meal at your place because she had to be here to get ready for hosting church today."

"I see." Sarah didn't like being left out of such an eventful evening, no doubt, but Rachel knew it was more than that. In truth, her sister's reaction was probably more normal than Rachel trying to pretend nothing had happened. They were both embarrassed and upset.

"Vonda and Albert were here early. And when I arrived, I'm positive Sarah had been crying. I've never seen her cry. But you know, the last person she would want to comfort her is me. If I'd had any idea what was coming . . ."

Rachel couldn't remember ever seeing her sister cry either. Sarah had a temper, but when it came to tears, her sister possessed an unnatural self-control for holding her emotions back.

"*Danki*, Lydia, for telling me. I'll see what I can do."

But Sarah had gone outside with their *mamm*, and Rachel didn't get the chance to talk to her before the routine order of a Sunday gathering took precedent. Only, it wasn't a usual gathering at all. As the men and children filed through to get their food, there was a peculiar solemnness. Everyone was going through the motions in an attempt at normalcy, but the friction in the air might set a tinder to flame.

Noah never did come through the line, and that set Rachel's heart to worrying far more than any of the unspoken questions on the people's faces as they'd passed by her. She didn't blame Noah if he'd gone on home early. She didn't feel much like socializing or eating either.

Once everyone had been through the line, Rachel grabbed a peanut butter sandwich but lingered outside rather than joining the other women at the tables set up in the barn.

Children's laughter carried on the wind across the yard drawing her attention to the row of buggy's parked along the fence line. A game of hide-and-seek appeared well underway and the *kinner* as innocent as they ought to be.

"I'm sorry, Rachel." Sarah's voice startled her.

She turned to face her sister on the side opposite of the children at play. "For what?"

"I should have been there last night."

"*Ach*, Sarah, there's nothing you could have done or said to make any difference. Albert and Vonda have chosen their way. He made that very clear. You know he's as unmovable as a mountain when he's set his mind. He believes he's right, and anyone who doesn't agree is bound for the devil. What good is anything any of us might have said to him?"

"Maybe. Though it doesn't feel right to give up on him."

"That's because you're almost as stubborn." She tried to smile, but the effort came out flat. "Sarah, we don't have to give up on him. But we can't very well stop him from choosing his own way."

"I didn't know anything about the gossip. I hope you know I'd have shut those traps before those busy-bodies had a chance to set them. I've been working all week to prepare for having the church service here today. With Saul's passing, I didn't want to ask you or Laura for help. And even Lydia and Joel were busy. I was trying so hard to . . ."

"Do it all yourself." Sarah should have been named Martha. Though for all her faults, she was a hard worker and never complained, no matter how heavy a load she carried.

"Folks were spread thin enough as it was. I was only trying to do my part, and . . . give you time with Noah."

"Really?"

"Sister, you don't think I never figured it out, do you?"

Along with a half a dozen or so others, apparently.

"I know I behaved badly when it all happened. It was so lonely here when Abe and I first moved without anyone else. And if you didn't come with Joel, I was afraid we'd be apart forever. But you have to believe, I only wanted you to be happy. When you were so accepting of Lydia and Joel's marriage, I finally began to put it all together that there was someone else for you. And I know Albert blames you, but I'm the one who put the idea in Saul's mind to sell to *Mamm*, so you could be close to us—to Noah if he ever came back."

"Sarah, you didn't!" Rachel watched her sister's smile bloom. "*Ach,* but you did."

"I've been holding my breath ever since Noah showed up. He always loved you. You deserve to be loved like that. That's all I ever really wanted for you. And now, Albert has ruined—"

"He hasn't ruined anything because that's not in his power. The truth will always come out in the end. We cannot help what other people choose to believe, but enough will see the truth."

"I do hope you are right." Her sister didn't sound persuaded, and Rachel likely sounded more convinced than she actually was herself. "Do you think Noah will even still want to join the church after all this?"

Wasn't that the million-dollar question?

"Sarah, where is *Mamm*? I haven't seen her since before lunch."

"Oh, I almost forgot. She asked Noah to take her home before Reuben could offer, which was a little odd. She didn't feel well. Can you blame her? Albert really didn't show a care for anyone today, did he?" Sarah didn't pause long enough for a response. None was needed.

"Noah said he'd come back to get you, since he'd walked to church and had to take *mamm's* buggy."

"That was nice."

"*Ja*, Rachel, he's always been real nice—like our *datt* and my Abe. Don't let him go this time."

"I'll try not . . . " Rachel's voice cracked. She decided to head in the direction of home before anyone caught her crying. "*Danki*, Sarah. I love you."

"Go on, now. I bet you'll meet up with him on the road." Her sister waved at her like she was shooing a fly, but Rachel saw the shimmer in her eyes. Life sure was full of surprises lately.

CHAPTER TWENTY-THREE

At the end of Abe and Sarah's lane, Rachel saw Noah coming—not with her *mamm's* buggy, but on foot. He always walked in long strides. He wasn't especially tall but could cross a distance in a hurry. And it seemed as though he was faster than ever today. He was dressed the same as he'd been for the funeral. He hadn't appeared any more comfortable that day than he had when she'd spotted him taking a seat at the back of the service this morning.

As she walked uphill in shorter spans to meet his downhill jaunt, she tried to picture him in Amish clothes. The only hard part was the hat. Somehow, the cowboy hat fit him so well. Oh, but she'd enjoy sewing a nice Sunday suit for him.

Her breath hitched—and not from the climb. Such ideas as sweet as they felt, also scared her. A what-if always lingered in the corner of her thoughts whispering that her hope was premature.

"Hello," Noah called from a few feet away. When they met, his hand slid to hers as his fingers wove between her own, joining them together—the way they were meant to be—what-ifs aside.

"You haven't been crying, have you, sweetheart?"

"*Nay.*" Not since she'd spotted him, anyway. "I was thinking on much happier things."

"Oh, yeah? Like what?"

She refused to allow the blush rising in her chest to fan a flame to her cheeks. Well, she tried. By the self-satisfied grin on Noah's face, she supposed she hadn't succeeded all the way.

She squeezed his fingers. "Just dreams."

He slipped his arm around her back and pulled her to his side as they walked. "Dreams are good. Even better when two people share the same one."

She lay her head against his shoulder for the next few steps, then pulled away to look up at him. His expression was so gentle and warm, she could drown in that sea of blue. Her foot missed a step.

"Careful." Noah caught her shoulder.

For sure, the smooth, paved road under her feet was a real tripping hazard.

They veered off the road into the yard at her house. "Would you like to come in?"

"I'd like to talk—somewhere private. Beulah said she was going to rest, so maybe outside."

Rachel knew just the spot. She led him around the house to the old dugout cellar—far enough to avoid any family who might stop in but close enough to help her *mamm* if needed.

While she propped herself on the side of the wall facing the house, Noah stretched out his legs from the opposite facing her.

"You have the best view." She referred to the scene behind her across his farm all the way to the Yoders'.

He wiggled his eyebrows. "I could enjoy this pretty picture all day."

She kicked the toe of his outstretched boot and changed the subject from his teasing. "You're doing a good job of holding back your curiosity. Unless *Mamm* filled you in."

"She didn't. And Raye, I don't want you feeling like you have to share things from the meeting that are meant to remain in confidence. I know the rules."

Of course, he did. When a member confessed and asked forgiveness, the people were to follow God's example and remember it no more. No talk produced no gossip. They were to move forward united in forgiveness and unity.

Oh how she wished today's meeting had been one of confession, forgiveness, and a return to unity. "If you're thinking Albert repented of his lies, then you have it wrong. He claims all he's said is true . . . Don't burst a blood vessel, now. More than a few stood to back my innocence."

"As they should." The pulse in Noah's temple was still visible, but his white-knuckled grip on the stonewall had eased.

She may as well get the rest told. This part was no secret. "But Albert . . . well, he and Vonda are leaving the church. They've decided New Hope is too progressive for them. They plan to sell their farm and move to a stricter fellowship in another church district."

"Because running away is easier than facing up to your own mistakes." There was no judgment in his statement. Only sadness and a faraway stare.

"Noah." She watched his focus slowly return to the present—to her. "Let it go. I've forgiven you. Saul did. *Gott* has. I only want us to go forward through life together."

"*Kumm.*" Noah held out a hand and pulled her to sit on the sunbathed stone beside him. He tucked her loose hair behind her ear, making a shiver of delight run the length of her spine. His kiss on her lips was tender and light, just enough for her to sigh before he pulled back. "Me too, Raye."

He stood then, still holding her hand. "I'll be back later. Maybe it's not such a good Sunday for a buggy ride. But I'll come check on you and Beulah. All right?"

She didn't want him to leave, but they both needed time to reflect on all that had happened this morning.

"As long as you come, *ja*." She hadn't meant anything about the past, but the crease of his brow worried her. "I only mean I'm not ready to say goodbye for today yet."

"I can't forget the past altogether, Raye. Still, I knew what you meant."

"What is it then?"

He rubbed the back of his neck, the way he'd always done when searching for the right words to express himself.

"Raye, I was wrong to think I could decide our future on my own. I did that thirteen years ago, and I've been falling in the same trap again. This time, we decide together. I'm not going anywhere. Not without God's blessing and not without you."

He'd definitely picked the right words.

With a full heart, Rachel watched as Noah crossed through the field to the home she dared to dream may be her own someday soon.

"I think I'll be going on to bed early tonight." Beulah announced less than ten minutes after Noah arrived back at the Erbs' for an evening visit. "You two go chat out on the porch where you won't disturb my rest."

From her seat next to him, Rachel glanced at Noah from the corner of her eye with a brow raised in question. It wasn't even six o'clock. The sun wouldn't set for more than two hours. "Don't you want to wait for your tea, *Mamm?* The kettle's on."

"Oh, that. I can see to my own tea. Go on, now. I'm likely to fall asleep any minute. And if anyone else shows up, you just keep them out there with you young folk."

Noah followed Rachel out the front door, holding back a chuckle since Rachel appeared concerned. As they sat in the two west-facing rockers, Rachel pinched the bridge of her nose.

"What mystery are you trying to solve now?"

She glanced over to him with wide eyes for a second, and then she laughed.

"Does it work—that nose thing—because you're still doing it after all these years?"

"Not really." She sighed. "No one has been here to see *Mamm*. I can't tell if she's relieved or upset. Seems as if Reuben would have checked on her."

"Don't worry, Raye. She told Reuben not to bother coming today when she had me bring her home from church. Some folks just prefer to be alone for a while when they've gone through a shock. I can tell you she didn't know Albert was the one spreading those tales. Between yesterday and today, she's taken a couple hard blows."

"And how am I not supposed to worry?" She raised that eyebrow at him again.

"Tell you what, I'll come see her tomorrow while you're at work. All right? I think she felt like I was somewhat neutral for her this morning.

So, maybe that will work again. And if she sends me off, then at least we tried." And he hoped Rachel wouldn't fret all day.

"*Danki*. That's a good idea." She began to rock the chair, then held a hand over her eyes to block the direct light from the lowering evening sun. "*Mamm* has a sixth sense if she didn't want to be bothered. Here comes Joel."

"I have an idea. There's something I'd like both of your opinions on." Noah stood. "Would you like to come for a walk around the farm? We'll see if Joel will come with us. Two birds with one stone."

"Sounds a lot better than sitting here talking our way around the craziness of my family."

"Hush now; the minister will hear." Noah grinned and held out a hand to help her up. She swatted at him and threw a pretend glower over her shoulder on her way down the front steps.

He loved her. Every little thing that made her Rachel Erb. If they didn't marry soon, he was going to bust. As they met Joel and changed direction with him to the farm, Noah tried not to think too hard on how much depended on what Rachel thought of the dream he was about to share.

He felt so very close to having two dreams come true. If God was willing.

CHAPTER TWENTY-FOUR

Joel listened to the excitement in Noah's voice as he led the three of them around the property Saul had purchased with his son in mind. And the glow about Rachel might rival an electric light. He tried not to chuckle.

"What?" Rachel noticed him for the first time in the past hour.

"You appear pleased with Noah's ideas—and no wonder. Noah, you've got me excited, too. We've never had a business such as you describe." More a ministry than a business, and Joel's heart was latching onto the concept. "Because of Samy's disability, I have a better understanding of how important your kind of work is for families like ours."

They'd come back around to the barn, where Noah explained the new stable he planned to build for therapy horses, creating a place similar to Second Chance Ranch for helping special needs children.

Rachel had grown quiet. Joel could so easily see how well suited she was for the kind of life Noah described. For certain, Rachel must know as well, yet she remained a little on the outside of the conversation. These two apparently didn't have a full understanding between them yet.

Noah pulled three straw bales into a semi-circle for seats. "I don't want to get my plow in front of the horse. There are legal issues to consider. Any type of therapy is regulated, and government rules may vary from province to province. And for all I know, there may be another similar type organization on the island." Noah turned to Rachel. "And we haven't even had a chance to discuss this yet."

Rachel plopped down on the bale right in the middle. "*Ach*, Noah, even if there are other equine therapy places, none of them have your heart or your unique experience. If God is calling you to this work, who am I to disagree?"

Joel was pretty sure he knew exactly who Noah wanted Rachel to be. And as Noah's wife, she'd have more say than most Amish men liked to let on about the way things really worked in their marriages.

"Stop laughing like that, Joel." Rachel scolded like a sister. He hadn't meant to, but it did his heart good to glimpse such a happy future for her.

"All right. You two don't need me hanging around when you've obviously got some things to clear up on your own." Joel didn't miss Noah's sideways wink at Rachel. She blushed, which only served to broaden Noah's grin at her.

Ja, Joel needed to get on out of here. "But I did come for a reason, other than to make sure Rachel was all right after this morning's affairs." He scooted to the edge of the rectangular bale underneath him. "And I doubt there will be any time better than this to tell you both."

Noah and Rachel looked at each other for a brief moment before Noah spoke. "All right then, may as well be now."

"Neither of you knew my father, Abram Yoder. By the time you were born, he'd passed and my *mamm* had married Samuel. Before my *datt* died, they were best friends and came up during the sixties and seventies."

Joel paused to make sure they understood what those decades had been like for the Amish. Noah leaned forward with interest. "You mean the days when so many Amish were leaving the Old Order?"

"*Ja*, it was a time of spiritual revival. But that renewed earnestness among some for a clearer teaching of salvation brought a great upheaval, too. The division especially troubled Samuel. He pleaded with my *datt* not to leave the Old Order church. Abram wasn't at odds with the traditions. He was only perplexed at how the teaching of the church had drifted so far from the original truths, a belief so powerful that many of our forefathers accepted imprisonment and death rather than recant."

"I don't understand." Rachel shook her head. "We've heard those stories all our lives, Joel. No one has forgotten their suffering—not in all these four hundred years."

"We've never forgotten their persecution but maybe gotten a little fuzzy on the Bible truths that began it all. The Dordrecht Confession is clear that salvation is by faith alone through Christ alone. The works we do for our Savior are not for admittance to His Kingdom but out of obedience to His commands for this life—to become more like Him.

"But somehow over time, our practice leaned heavier on tradition and our own efforts for salvation. My *datt* and Samuel chose to remain in the Old Order because they believed *Gott* had called them to bear that beacon of truth once again. That the working out of our salvation is not for redemption but rather an expression of the grace we've received."

Noah nodded slowly in agreement, but Rachel's brows drew together in concentration.

"But, Joel, this is what Samuel has taught me—all of us—our entire lives."

Noah placed a hand on her knee for a short second, drawing her attention to him. "And also why I couldn't join so long ago. I knew I didn't believe. Others may be baptized and take their vows simply to follow the Amish way, but Samuel taught us we must be faithful in our hearts. And, Raye, my heart was full of all the wrong things—and stayed that way, until by God's grace, I saw my sin and repented. I could never have undone my own sin, no matter how I might have tried. Only Jesus' blood could wash my heart clean and set me free.

If Samuel had let me slip in the fold just to keep me Amish, I might never have come to a true faith."

"*Nay*, I wouldn't have wanted that, Noah. I'd live the past all over again just to know we will be together in eternity. Thirteen years is nothing compared to forever."

Joel cleared his throat before they forgot he was there.

"I'll try to get to the point."

Rachel sighed. "*Danki*, Joel. I don't think you came out to give us a history lesson."

"Careful, Raye, the next lesson will be on patience." Noah bumped her knee.

Rachel crossed her arms, and Joel didn't care that he laughed out loud.

"I only bring up Abram and Samuel because I think they found themselves in a similar situation as Noah here—and you, as well." He pinned Rachel with his best minister stare.

She uncrossed her arms. "I'm listening, Joel, really."

"The matter comes down to their choice to live by the Old Order to preserve what they believed was our true heritage, so future generations would understand God's gospel of grace and forgiveness through faith alone. We are the next generation. I will not try to coerce either of you into the same choice as Abram and Samuel. Even though I do hope that you will remain here with us at New Hope." Joel paused at the longing he saw in Noah's expression when the two glanced at each other. They needed to marry and soon.

"Rachel." She startled at her name. "Albert has done us a favor today."

Now, he had her attention.

"How so?" Noah leaned forward, his elbows braced on his knees and hands folded together.

"Albert is leaving to avoid accountability for his gossip and lies. By joining a stricter fellowship, he's also avoided the *Bann*. He will no longer be a member, but he will not suffer any other consequence. At least not from us. God is his Judge. So then, how can I be justified to enact church discipline on Rachel if she chooses to go with her husband to a less strict fellowship when she has done no wrong?"

Rachel blushed a deep crimson, most likely at the referral to her yet-to-be husband, but Noah never dropped eye contact.

Joel pressed on. "Rachel's in good-standing among the brethren here, and I will not recommend the *Bann* if you both choose to join the fellowship of one our Mennonite or New Order cousins."

"But others will not agree."

"True, Rachel, some will not. But our way is for the *Meidung* to be a discipline recommended by the bishop and the minister. And in this circumstance, we have good cause not to enact such a measure. I must be able to face *Gott* on Judgment Day and give an account. I cannot say to Him, 'I did such and so because I was afraid of what people would think.' And you are responsible to obey the Lord's direction where He is calling you to do salvation's work with your lives." He looked at Noah first and then Rachel again. They seemed to understand.

Joel knew he'd unloaded a mouthful, and his time to leave had come. He'd done all he could do. The rest was out of his hands.

They sat in the barn a long while after Joel left. Noah kindly answered all her questions about Second Chance Ranch and his ideas for his own non-profit here. Now the extended shadows of evening had faded into the darkening dusk. Rachel stood, and her knees popped from so long in a seated position.

"Joel's not made an easy decision. Even though he'd hear nothing of what this may cost him, you know he will face criticism for it." And her heart ached at the thought of Joel's willingness to go so far on a limb for them. Or, as he explained, for what he believed was right.

Noah stood and stretched. "That would depend on what we decide to do. I don't expect he'll be shouting his decision from the rooftops. Unless we take him up on the offer, there's no reason for him to tell another soul yet."

Did Noah mean he was still considering joining the Amish church? "But why not take him up on it? He's made a perfect way of compromise for you." *For us.*

"He's found a middle ground, and I admire him for it. That doesn't mean we have to take it. Is compromise what you want, Rachel?"

She didn't have an answer at the ready.

Noah brushed off his straw hat before returning it to his head, then offered her his arm. "Are you up to walking home, or would you prefer to ride?"

"Horseback? We make a nice team side-by-side on a pair of horses. Though I'd rather not be on a search and rescue mission next time we ride."

He grinned. "I'd like to go on many a horseback ride with you, too. Soon enough, I plan to have a stable full of horses we can ride together. For now, it's just Romeo and Stella. She's too old, and Romeo is used to pulling a cart. But I can hitch him to the courting buggy if you'd prefer not to trek across that field another time."

"I'd rather not leave at all."

"Raye . . ."

"Don't you dare lecture me. And I can walk just fine." She turned away and took but a step when his hand caught her elbow.

He swung her around then, her body pressed up against him and his hand firm against the small of her back.

"I wish I'd asked you before Joel came. Rachel, I'd marry you this minute with or without any compromise. I only want you. And I don't want you making this choice out of your natural tendency to please everybody. I want you to know, clear down to the deepest part of your soul, that I'm the one God meant for you." His hand slid from her back and then raised the palm of her hand to his heart. "Because right here, God created a spot just your size. No one else will do for me, Raye, no one but you. Wherever the Lord leads us, whatever He asks of us in this world, I need you by my side."

His lips brushed her cheeks, warm and gentle, first one and then the other, kissing the tears she had no strength to hold back.

"Noah, I will go with you to the ends of the earth. And I believe in this vision of yours for a ministry here on the island. I have a soft spot in my heart for the church here at New Hope, but I'm willing to go anywhere . . . to . . . "

"Be my wife." His hands cupped her face, and she was lost in those storm cloud blue-grays of his. "Raye, will you marry me?"

She pushed up on her toes and met his mouth, salty from her tears, with a long kiss.

"Noah Detweiler, you couldn't leave me behind now if you tried. You're stuck. 'Til death us do part."

EPILOGUE

"Hello, Squirt." Noah couldn't help but feel loved when Samy ran out to meet him as he opened the cab door for Rachel.

"I did all the chores. Every day. With Drew, too. And Yo-yo said I could wait for you this morning to get back. *Mamm* said you'd be jet . . . What's that word?"

"Jet-lagged?"

"I think so. What is it?"

"Dead-dog tired."

Her eyes widened in horror.

"I'm sorry. It doesn't really have anything to do with dogs. Jetlag happens when a person has traveled from far away and they are really tired because of the time difference from one place to the other."

"Oh." She turned her head to Rachel getting out of the van.

"Hello, Samy. I sure missed you." Rachel bent down to give her a hug.

Samy pulled back quickly. "*Mamm's* not sick anymore. Sharon Rose is out of her belly."

The joy on Rachel's face looked like it might split her in half. She'd been afraid she might miss the event while they were gone, but all that seemed to matter now was that her friend's child had arrived.

"*Ach*, Noah. I have to go. Right away. Do you mind?" As if he would ever stop her. She grabbed Samy's hand. "*Kumm*, I'll go back to your house with you."

"But *Mamm's* in there." Samy pointed toward their house. "All of them are there. Gamma and Beulah, *Aenti* Sarah and Laura. They filled up your refrigerator and the pantry. They are warming up the house." She paused and studied Rachel a moment, then Noah. "Summer just ended. Are you cold already?"

How he loved this child. "Housewarming means they have brought gifts to give a newly married couple a happy start."

"Oh." She reached for Rachel's hand again. "Well, you can come see Sharon Rose. She's sleeping in there, too."

"Wait," Noah called after the two of them while he paid the cab driver and unloaded their luggage from the back.

Samy had run ahead, while Rachel bounced on her toes with pent-up excitement until he reached her. Without warning, he lifted her into his arms and carried her across the threshold.

"Welcome home, Rachel Detweiler." He'd never grow weary of his beautiful bride in his arms. Or that ruby-red blush of hers.

He set his bride down. They were surrounded by on-lookers—all of whom appeared amused and pleased at the sight.

"Ladies." He tipped his hat then hung it on the peg by the door.

"Welcome home, Brother." Trudy stepped up to him.

He was glad to see her among Rachel's family and thankful to have joined a church community that was accepting of his Mennonite sister. Joining New Hope had been the right decision.

"*Kumm*, Trudy." He motioned for his sister to follow him into the living room. Once they were seated, he began to explain the plan he and Rachel had worked out. "While we were gone, Rachel and I did some talking about the future of this farm. We will be starting a ministry using therapy horses for special needs children. But first, we want to pay you half of the worth of the farm."

"*Nay*, Noah. *Datt* left it all to you." She shook her head.

"*Datt's* intentions were good. He wanted to give me a way to come home, and he did. But God has provided a way for me to share this blessing with you. We won't feel right doing this any other way. Please accept our offer."

She wiped at her eyes and smiled at him. "I must talk to my husband, of course."

Noah reached over and pulled his sister into a hug. He hated to see her cry, even if the tears were happy ones. "God has returned so much to me. And being a family with you again is more than I could have ever dreamed possible."

She pulled back from his hug and looked at him with a great sense of peace. "*Ja*, Noah. I'm thankful that God's ways are so much bigger than our ways."

He'd found that peace, too, and he was eternally grateful.

Rachel sat on the attic floor. Noah's Sunday suit lay neatly folded on her lap—pressed and clean. She'd sewn every stitch with love for him to wear to the church meeting to take his membership vows. Two days later, on his thirty-first birthday, he'd worn it for their wedding. Now that they'd returned from their trip, the time had come to put the suit away and treasure the memories.

The spicy scent of cedar filled the attic when she opened the Detweiler heirloom chest. She'd already made Noah a second set of

Sunday clothes to wear. The first would remain tucked away beside her wedding dress, only to be worn again when they were prepared for their final resting place.

Mercy, but she couldn't think on such days as that right now. Not when she was so blissfully happy at last. She jerked on the lid in a rush to close the unwelcome intrusion on her contentment.

"Not so fast." A board behind her squeaked as Noah stepped from the ladder onto the bare attic floor.

"I have one more thing to go in there." He knelt beside her with his cowboy hat in his hand.

"*Ach,* Noah." Her heart pinched at the symbol of all he'd given up.

"Darling, don't fret yourself for my sake."

"*Ja,* well, I like it, too. You make a handsome cowboy."

"Careful now. You'll swell my head too big for an Amish man's hat." He winked, then lay the black felt Stetson on top of the clothes she'd put there. "For a little while, this hat represented my life, but that life was only temporary—meant to bring me home to you. Fourteen years from my seventeenth birthday until our wedding got me to thinking about Jacob in the Bible. He worked fourteen years for his Rachel. I'm sure grateful my Rachel waited fourteen for me."

He knew how to take her breath, this *wunderbar* Amish cowboy of hers.

"Looking back, it doesn't seem so long as it felt through the wait. Do you suppose it compares to how the joy of Heaven will erase all the troubles we ever felt down here?"

"I think Heaven is exactly the right comparison. I've no desire to look back. I'm only headed forward." He squeezed her shoulders toward him.

"You know we won't always be so happy as we are right now. I worry sometimes, staying awake after you've gone to sleep, about what hard times might lie ahead of us."

"Life is short, Raye, even if we live to be a hundred. We'll enjoy God's gifts as He gives them. We'll feast on your good cooking as long as He provides. We'll labor as long as He gives us strength. We'll rest every Sunday to do it all over again. And when hard times come, He's given us each other to face one day at a time together."

She leaned back against him, her husband whom she loved so. His arm wrapped further around her, and she savored the safety of his hold.

"There's something else I thought about putting in here." She pulled Noah's old journal out of her apron pocket and set it under his hat. "There's a whole story in this wooden memory chest now."

Noah looked into the chest then back to her. "I hope it tells of a Father Who always brings His children home." She slowly closed the lid on the keepsakes. The story held in the chest was also a reminder of how short life truly was. Waiting hadn't been so bad, and now she wasn't in such a rush to hurry life along. *Nay*, she wasn't in a hurry at all. She'd cherish the days, weeks, and years. Until God brought them home.

ACKNOWLEDGMENTS

Writing a novel during a global pandemic has been a different experience in many ways. But one thing stays the same. I cannot do it alone.

A special thank you goes out to my critique partner extraordinaire, Laurel Blount. If not for the hundreds of hours we've logged on Zoom to keep my fingers at the keyboard, Noah and Rachel's story would still be unfinished.

A huge thanks to my boys, who have homeschooled like champs, while Mom writes. They are as happy as this author when she types *The End.*

And to David, my husband, who believes in me and reminds me God has a purpose for my craft on those days when serious doubts tempt me to quit. I couldn't do this without you.

Most of all, to the Lord Jesus, Who enables any good that may come from my words, I am eternally grateful.

Dear Reader,

I hope you have enjoyed Noah and Rachel's story. This has been the most difficult of the series to write. Surprisingly, though, I believe it's my favorite so far.

As always, I love hearing from you and your thoughts on the *Amish Dreams on Prince Edward Island* series. Reviews are a tremendous help to any author, whether on GoodReads, Amazon, Barnes and Noble, or any other retail site.

However, I also enjoy when I hear directly from readers. You can email me at amygrocho@gmail.com, find me on Facebook at www.facebook.com/amygrochowski or learn more about the series on my website: www.amygrochowski.com.

And now, I am off to keep writing. May you be blessed with God's grace and love always.

Until we meet again,

Amy Grochowski

For more information about
Amy Grochowski
&

Runaway Home
please visit:

www.amygrochowski.com
www.facebook.com/amygrochowski
www.instagram.com/AmyGrocho
www.goodreads.com/amygrocho
@AmyGrocho

For more information about
AMBASSADOR INTERNATIONAL
please visit:

www.ambassador-international.com
@AmbassadorIntl
www.facebook.com/AmbassadorIntl

*If you enjoyed this book, please consider leaving us a review on
Amazon, Goodreads, or our website.*

More from Ambassador International

Five years ago, Braelyn's daughter died. Her marriage imploded, and Forest Hill became Braelyn's sanctuary. Five years ago, Drake became lost in overwhelming grief, and he lost his heart to divorce. After serving in the army, Drake is looking for a new life, and he stumbles upon Forest Hill.

Can Braelyn find forgiveness or will she allow bitterness to ruin her sanctuary? And can Drake reclaim his heart?"

Kate Sullivan will stop at nothing to find the man she holds responsible for her sister's death, and movie director Chris Johnston has information she needs. To get the answers she seeks, Kate joins his new production company, but when revenge and love collide, both Kate and Chris get more than they bargained for.

Movie star Maggie Malone has a glamorous lifestyle with everything money can buy—except privacy.

When an anonymous benefactor invites Maggie to participate in a secret project, will her hopelessness find a new direction? Or will she become another celebrity travesty? What if she discovers Hollywood is not Home? Her faith, family, love, and future hang in the balance . . .

Made in the USA
Columbia, SC
05 March 2022

57129034R00137